White Noise
Lark Taylor

White Noise by Lark Taylor

www.larktaylorauthor.com

Book cover design: Ashwood Designs – www.cateashwooddesigns.com

Cover photo: Xram Ragde

Edited and proofread by: Abbie Nicole

Formatted by: Breathless Lit

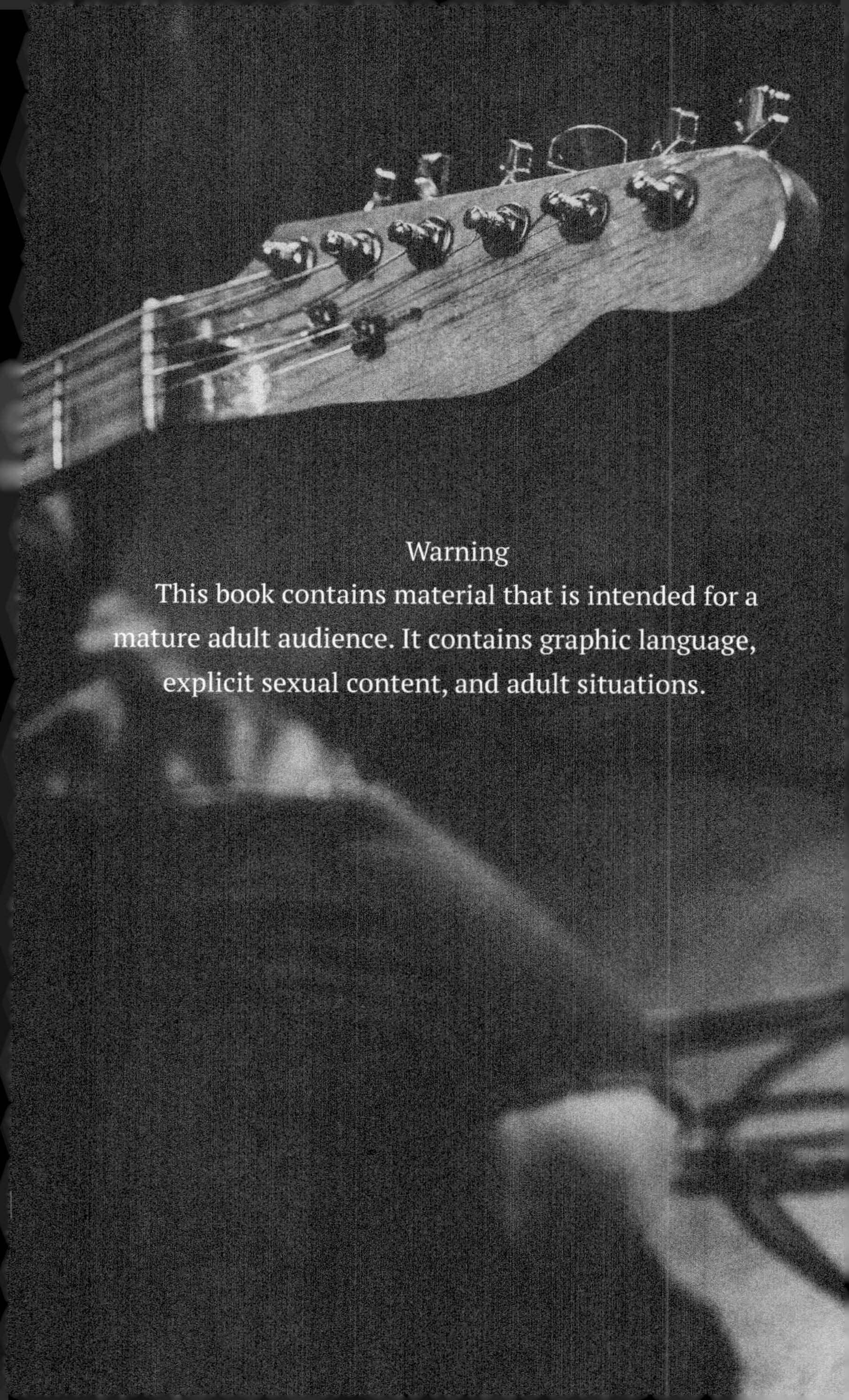

Warning

This book contains material that is intended for a mature adult audience. It contains graphic language, explicit sexual content, and adult situations.

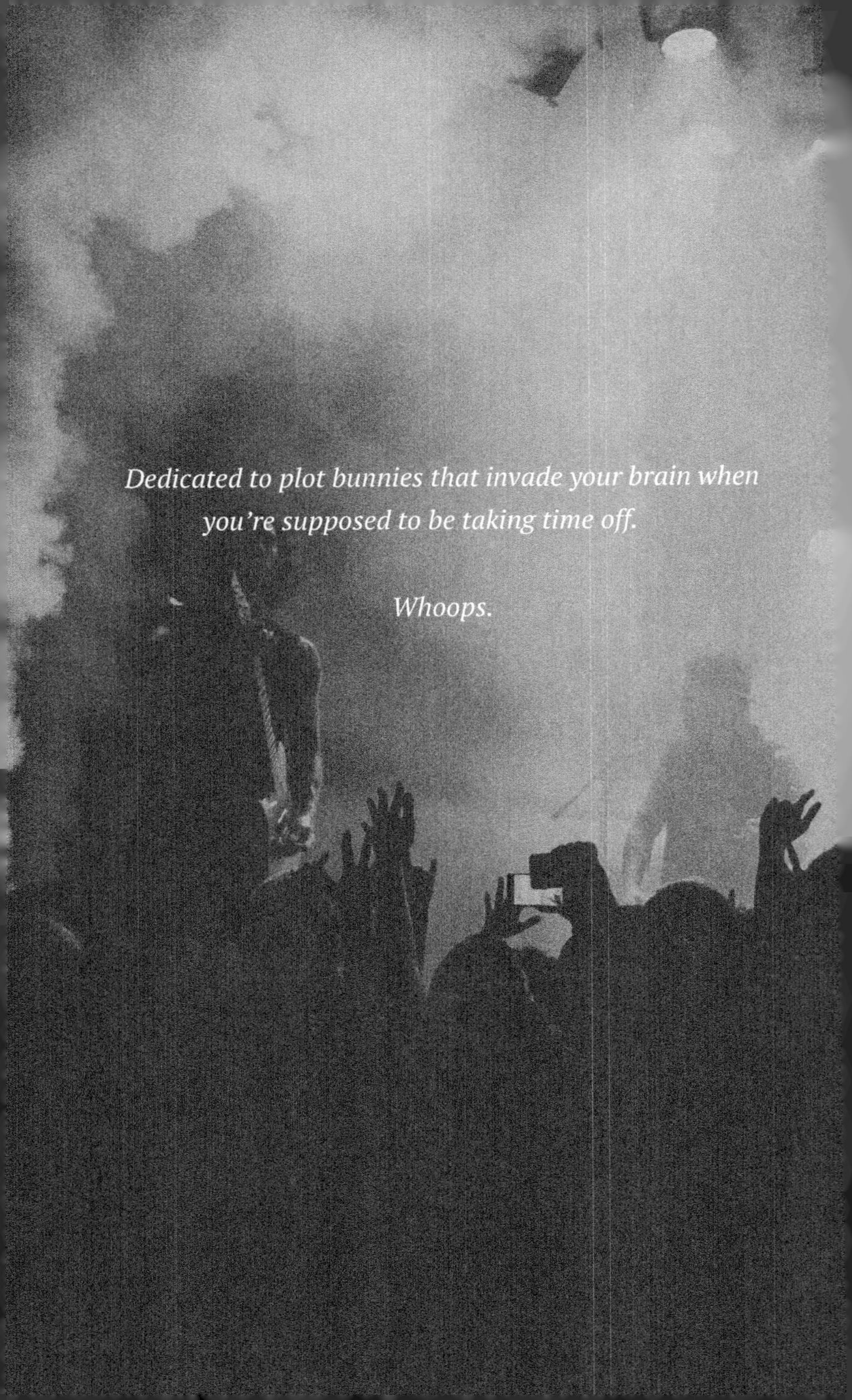

Dedicated to plot bunnies that invade your brain when you're supposed to be taking time off.

Whoops.

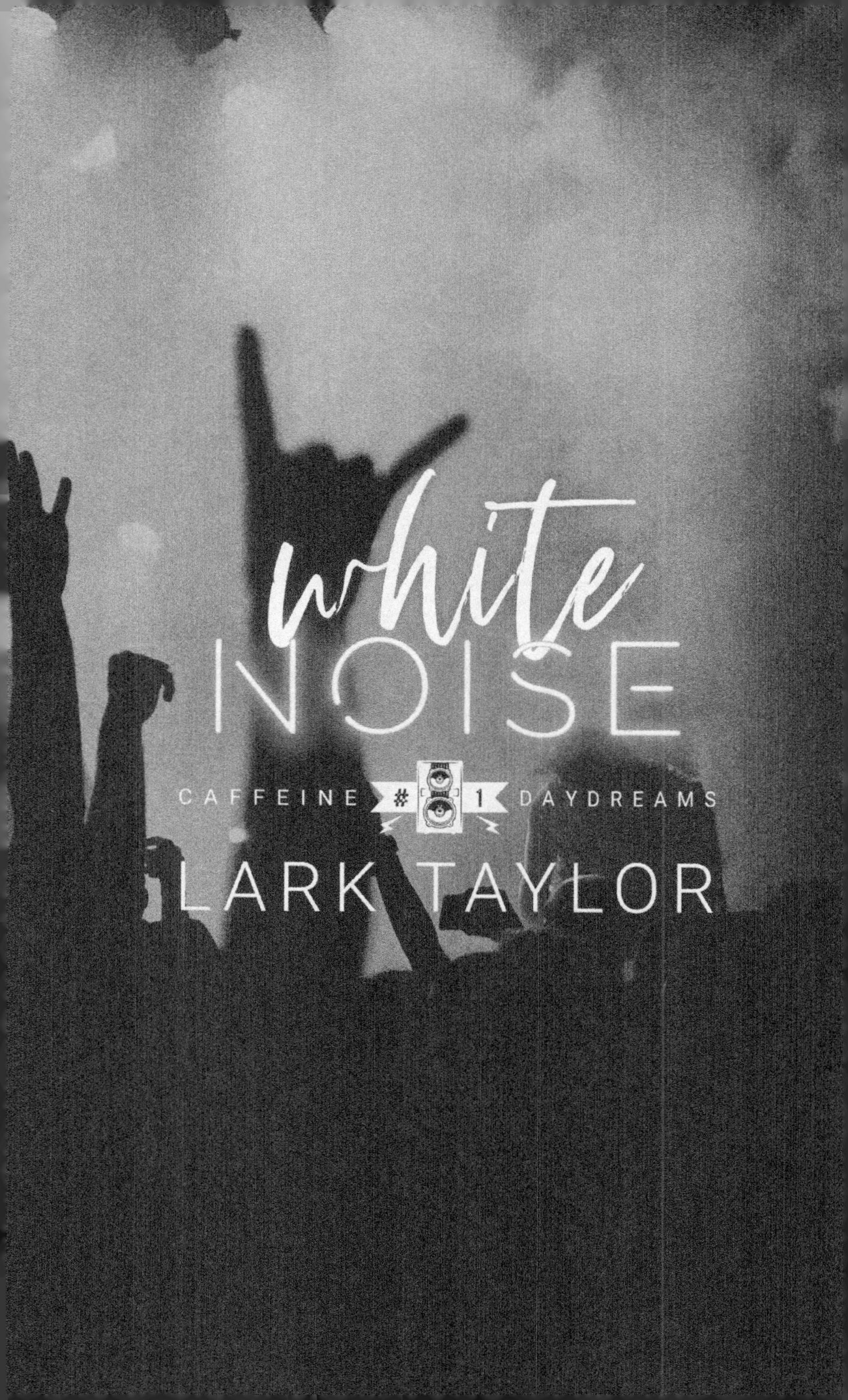
white
NOISE
CAFFEINE #1 DAYDREAMS
LARK TAYLOR

Chapter 1

Ollie

I'd hoped today would change my life, but as I watched my girlfriend of six years get railed by my best friend, this wasn't how I'd thought it would happen.

I shouldn't even *be* here. Right now, I was supposed to be pulling up to the *Identity* offices, ready for the interview of a lifetime.

Instead, I was frozen in the doorway, watching the muscles in Callum's arse flex as he drilled into Suzie.

I didn't remember him looking that ripped. Fucker had clearly been going to the gym without me.

Not what you should be focusing on right now.

My inner voice was probably right. But if I focused on the reality—that the woman I was in a committed relationship with was currently behaving like she was auditioning for a porno—I might spontaneously combust.

I needed to do *something* other than gawp at them while white-knuckling the heavy briefcase in my hand. A younger version of myself would've used it to whack Callum on his way-too-toned backside.

I didn't even know why I'd bothered taking the thing with me in the first place. It'd seemed like a grown-up thing to do for an interview somewhere as prestigious as *Identity*. Fat lot of good it would've done me, given I'd forgotten to put my portfolio in it. You know, the *one thing* they'd asked me to bring along.

How I'd forgotten it was beyond me. It had to be the exhaustion. I'd spent most of the night staring at the ceiling instead of sleeping.

Considering how long I'd waited for an opportunity like this, you'd think I would've been ready for the interview. Confident even. I'd certainly proved my worth at smaller websites, my most recent one landing me an Orwell prize.

Unfortunately, that wasn't how imposter syndrome worked. The more success I garnered, the more my brain told me I didn't deserve it. That it was only a matter of time before someone realised that I didn't know what I was doing and called me out. A large part of me believed I would rock up to this interview only to be laughed out the door.

I'd been so convinced of this fact that my brain had provided me with *several* detailed examples of what could happen. Of how badly I could fuck it up.

Because that was what this situation needed. More pressure.

You couldn't blame me though. Opportunities like this *never* came around...not with a website like *Identity*.

They were the crème de la crème of digital journalism. Hard-hitting interviews, in-depth profiles, cutting satire...*Identity* did it all. After a few years working for them, I could walk into a writing job anywhere.

Normally *Identity* preferred to trial staff on a volunteer basis until they'd proved their worth. That wasn't something I could afford to do. Unlike most graduates, I didn't have rich parents subsidising my rent and bills. Born and raised on a council estate, I'd worked hard for everything I'd achieved. And I might not have a lot, but I was damned proud of what I did have.

A car that only broke down once a year instead of once a month.

A nice small flat in a quiet block instead of a room in a drug-infested houseshare.

Neighbours who wouldn't mug me just because my shoes didn't have holes in them.

It wasn't much...but it was *mine.* Okay, my bank account might hit the red every month, but this life...? It was something I'd barely dared to dream of.

And the fact I got to share it all with a beautiful woman who I'd been with for years?

That had been the icing on the cake.

And now here I was. Watching said icing getting literally licked by my closest friend.

My watch vibrated with a forty-minute warning. Fortunately, I'd built in enough time around my interview for emergencies. Like forgetting something and needing to nip back to grab it...not having my heart ripped out of my chest by the two people I trusted the most.

Since the interview was now the only thing going for me, I needed to get back to *Identity* as fast as possible. Which meant I needed to move.

Why did that feel impossible?

"Callum," Suzie moaned. "Oh god. Yes. Right there. Th—"

"That's the spot?" I interrupted her, my voice finally returning. The pair froze, Suzie's eyes wide with horror as they met mine over Callum's shoulder. "Not very original there, hun. So you mix up your lovers but not the dialogue?"

"Shit," Suzie squawked as Callum scrambled back, dragging the sheet with him.

"Bit late for that, mate," I said heavily. "Seen it all now anyway."

"Ollie, man. It's not what you think." Callum was shoving his legs into his jeans while Suzie shrugged into her dressing gown. Did they think if they got dressed fast enough, they might be able to pretend I'd imagined it all?

"Really? You mean you weren't fucking Suzie? Let me guess, you tripped and *fell* into her vagina?"

Callum flushed with shame, his gaze dropping to the floor. Suzie, however, had a different response. Hands on her hips, she glared up at me. Would've been more effective if her hair wasn't rumpled from where Callum had had his hands buried in it. Bile filled my throat at the bitter look she gave me. It grew even worse when I realised it wasn't the first time I'd seen it on her face.

When had she started looking at me like that?

"Sarcasm, Ollie?" She laughed, a sour hollow sound that pierced my heart. "I don't know why I expected anything more from you. I should've known it'd take more than catching me in bed with your best friend for you to show real emotion."

"What's that supposed to mean?"

She gestured at me in disgust. "Look at you. You're barely even frowning. Most men would lose their shit in this situation. Start yelling. Throwing punches.

Instead, you throw out sarcastic quips like you're mildly disappointed at best."

Images of another man throwing punches flashed through my mind. Screams. Insults. Smashed dishes. Holes in walls.

My breath came faster and I dug my nails into my palms. Counting backwards from twenty, I reminded myself I wasn't him.

I'd never be him.

"Is that what you'd rather I do? Come in here and start smashing the place up?"

"Of course not," Suzie said impatiently. "But Christ, Ollie. I thought you'd give me more than this. Don't you feel *anything*?"

At Suzie's words, I saw Callum shift on his feet from the corner of my eye, one hand rubbing the back of his neck.

Yeah, the fucker better feel guilty. He knew better than anyone why I kept my emotions close to my chest.

I turned my attention back to Suzie, silently saying goodbye to all my hopes for our future. I wished I hadn't felt anything. I'd have given anything for that dead numbness people sometimes talked about.

My trouble was I felt it all. Everything. All the time.

I never got any respite from the rage, the anxiety. The nagging feeling that I'd never be good enough. That I was failing everyone.

But I'd seen what happened when you let your emotions control you. I'd learned the hard way what the consequences would be if I didn't keep them buried under lock and key.

"Is that why you did this?"

Suzie lifted her chin defiantly, but I didn't miss the way her lip wobbled. How she bit it as she always did when she was trying to stop the tears from falling. "No. But I need *more,* Ollie. I need someone passionate, both in bed and out. Someone who will laugh with me. Cry with me. Someone I can stay up all night with, talking about everything and nothing."

"And you think *Callum* is the guy for that?" I shot the guy in question a thumbs-up. "Good luck with that, mate. We both know you only cry when Leeds loses. Which is a lot, to be fair, but I don't think that's what Suzie means."

Callum still wouldn't look at me. The full magnitude of how he was about to lose over twenty years of friendship was probably hitting him…or my carpet was way more interesting than I'd realised.

"At least Callum *feels* things," Suzie threw out hotly. "He fucks me like he means it. Not like it's a chore."

I winced as her barb hit home. Sure, our sex life left a lot to be desired…but that was normal, right? We'd been together a long time. It was natural that things… slowed down.

But they were never very fast, were they? I rubbed a hand over my head like I could make my inner voice fuck off. I couldn't ignore the truth though. I'd been attracted to Suzie from the get-go, but we'd never had that insane passion you saw in movies. We'd never ripped each other's clothes off in a frenzy. Never been so desperate for one another that we'd not made it to the bedroom.

"I wish you'd talked to me," I said quietly. "We could've worked on things."

Suzie took a step closer, her whole body

trembling. "We still could. Just say the word, and it'll be like this never happened."

Callum stiffened at her words, his eyes lifting for the first time since I'd caught them. "What the fuck, Suzie? Are you going to stand here and tell me you're choosing him? What about us?"

Suzie paled, her gaze darting to Callum as if she'd forgotten he was standing there.

Something passed between them. Something raw. Desperate. Honest.

That was the moment. Three hearts on the tripwire, struggling not to fall over the edge and shatter completely.

Even with what they'd done, I couldn't turn off my love for them.

I stepped back, my hands raised in defeat. "No choice needed. We're done here. I suggest you both talk. I've got an interview to get to."

I turned my back on them as I jumped from the wire, leaving them balanced more securely.

That was all I'd do for them though.

It was done. I was done.

With love. With friendship. The whole fucking lot.

I picked up my portfolio from the kitchen table.

Left my flat.

Got in my car.

Drove down the road.

Turned into a side lane.

Put the car in neutral.

Lifted the handbrake.

And with no one else around, no one to see or hear me, I finally let loose.

I screamed until my voice was hoarse. Thumping

my hands on the steering wheel until they began to bruise.

It didn't make me feel any better. Not really. But it expended enough energy for me to pull myself together and get back on the road.

I had fourteen minutes to make my interview.

I couldn't miss it.

It was all I had left.

Chapter 2

Luca

Luca Weston dumped in upscale London restaurant.

Rock star Luca Weston caught on camera arguing with on and off again boyfriend, Calvin Klein model Jorge Rivera.

As another scandal hits, BuzzFeed asks, has Luca Weston lost his way yet again?

"Have you seen the headlines?"

"Yeah, I've seen them," I muttered into the phone. Jack, my bodyguard and driver, shot me a sympathetic look in the rearview mirror.

I'd done little else but scroll through social media since I'd peeled my eyes open and seen the slew of notifications. It was the usual mix of gleeful vultures cawing over my very public humiliation, along with my actual fans expressing sorrow over my apparently broken heart. The fact it was perfectly intact was neither here nor there. My ego was bruised, but nothing more. But I hadn't been able to tear myself away from the vitriol until Jack bribed me into the car with a latte. "It's not great."

"Not great?" I could practically hear our manager, Kevin, boiling over. My eyes met Jack's again. Judging by the tense lines around his eyes, even Jack could hear Kevin's meltdown. "That's the understatement of the fucking year, Luca."

I sighed, my head dropping against the car window, the cool glass soothing the ache. "What did you want me to do, Kevin? I tried to insist we go somewhere more private, but you know what Jorge is like."

No, the second he'd clocked the paparazzi, the quiet mutual discussion we'd been having about ending our arrangement had blown up into an all-out war. He'd ignored my pleas to not act up for the press, instead flinging his drink in my face. No idea what had been in that cocktail, but it had taken two showers to get all the sticky residue off my skin.

Jorge's little display had worked exactly as he'd intended. Within moments, we'd had multiple phone cameras aimed at us, chronicling each second of my humiliation. Jorge revelled in the drama, his voice getting louder and louder as he accused me of everything under the sun. If I hadn't been internally dying of mortification, I might've been impressed. Really, he'd missed his calling with modelling. He was born to be an actor.

Knowing anything I said would be twisted against me, I simply sat in silence until Jack managed to push his way through the crowd to extract me. We might not chat much, but I could count on my bodyguard to know the right moment to step in.

Now I was getting hauled over the coals by our manager. He was still yelling down the phone. As much as I tried to tune him out, phrases like *you should've known better* and *fame-hungry whore* seemed to slip through.

I closed my eyes. I hadn't been in love with Jorge. What we'd had barely constituted a friends-with-benefits situation…for that, we'd have to actually be *friends*. Not just two guys who happened to fuck whenever they were in the same city because it was convenient.

Ultimately that had been the thing that'd made me pull the plug. I hadn't been in love with Jorge, but I was ready to be. Not with him, obviously. He brought an unneeded level of drama to my already chaotic life.

Fucking around with groupies and other celebrities had been fun in my early twenties. But at thirty-four, I was ready to settle down. I was ready for more. I wanted the kind of love that led to Grammy award-winning songs. The kind that left you feeling like you had a hole in your chest when you were apart from them. Like you could finally breathe easy when they were near.

Most importantly, I wanted to be with someone who wanted me. Luca. The guy who loved to cook Italian food and was obsessed with *Air Crash Investigation*. The person who got up in the middle of the night to dash down song lyrics before running on a treadmill until he felt his lungs would burst. The man who could captivate an entire stadium but would choose an audience of one every time.

But that wasn't the Luca other guys wanted. They wanted the frontman of Caffeine Daydreams. The guy who graced covers of magazines and had entire websites dedicated to his daily movements. The one who exuded confidence and sex appeal as easily as breathing.

He wasn't real. That man they all lusted after didn't exist. But that didn't seem to matter to the men and women I took home with me. No one wanted to say they'd spent the evening snuggled in front of the TV when they could say they'd been fucked into the mattress by a rock star.

I wasn't opposed to the fucking side of it. The opposite, in fact. But I was ready for more. Sixteen years in the business had taught me one thing.

It was lonely at the top without someone to share it with.

So fucking lonely.

"...and now I'm having to do damage control with the label. Again."

I rolled my eyes. Kevin was known for being overdramatic. I couldn't see the label getting involved over something as trivial as a lover's spat. This was more Kevin caring about our image. How we were portrayed to the public.

Why he got so hung up on it was beyond me. We were *rock stars*, for fuck's sake. One would assume some bad behaviour was par for the course. The four of us were practically angelic compared to other acts on the label's books.

But we'd had piss-poor management before Kevin. He might be a nag about stuff like this, but there was no denying he was far better than the alternatives on the market. He'd been with us too long now for us to want to upset the ship.

"Two minutes," Jack warned quietly from the front. I nodded to show I'd heard.

I knew from experience that the fastest way to get Kevin off my back and the phone was to agree with him. "Fine. What do you want me to do?"

Kevin's sigh of relief was audible. "You need to lay low until the tour. If we can keep you out of the headlines and off social media, it might be enough to convince the label you aren't a risk. Your contract is up for negotiation next year, don't forget."

I rolled my eyes. As if Kevin would ever let us forget it. He mentioned it any time he even suspected one of us had fucked up. Not that it was even a threat. If the label dropped us, there'd be more lining up to take their place. That wasn't arrogance. It was a fact. With our albums consistently dominating the top of the charts and our tours selling out stadiums, there was no way they'd drop us. But I said what was needed to get Kevin off the phone so I could have some quiet time with my caffeine. "Done."

"There's more..."

My eyes narrowed. I knew that hesitant tone. It was the one Kevin liked to use when he was about to suggest something he knew I wouldn't like. "What?"

"You need to accept the profile offer from *Identity.*"

I rolled my eyes. "I already said I would. I'm literally in the car on my way to the interview right now."

There was a pregnant pause on the line. "Ah, good. This interview is important, but it's actually just the first step in what I'd like to do with them."

"Kevin..." I said warningly.

"Don't panic," he said smoothly. "It won't be as onerous as you think. It'll be a more in-depth profile, looking at the ins and outs of your life on the road."

I gritted my teeth. "On the road? As in, a journalist will be coming on tour with us?"

"That's the idea, yes."

"No."

"Now, Luca, don't be hasty."

"Fuck sake," Jack grumbled from the front seat.

I turned to see what had caught his attention. My heart sank as all visions of sneaking in for a quiet interview went up in smoke.

Hordes of screaming teenagers surged towards my vehicle, the noise deafening even with metal and glass between us. There were elaborate handmade signs, rainbow and bisexual flags waved and thrust in my direction. They were practically salivating in their efforts to get to me.

And I wasn't even out of the car yet.

I loved this side of my life. I did. Let's be honest though. It was anything but normal. And right now, I'd kill for a taste of normal. Something I'd have no chance of if I agreed to Kevin's hare-brained scheme. I needed just five fucking minutes where I didn't have to be *on*. Yes, we had a tour coming up, but once I stepped off that stage, that was my time to relax and be me. I couldn't do that with a nosey journalist hanging around. I wouldn't be able to let my guard down for a second.

"The answer is no, Kevin," I said firmly, sipping my coffee before pasting on my smile. "No journalists on the tour. That's final."

Before he could protest, I hung up, slipping my phone into the inner pocket of my jacket. Raising the hand not holding my coffee, I waved to the crowd through the window. I wasn't sure how much of me they could actually see through the privacy glass, but I didn't for a second want them to think I was ignoring them. At the end of the day, my fans were my lifeblood. Although it would make getting into the building a bit of a nightmare,

I knew what this moment would mean to some of them.

That wasn't my ego talking. It was based on the thousands of daily messages I received online. Being an openly bisexual rock star meant I was a role model for queer youth, and it was a role I took very seriously. Even though I no longer managed my social media, I still did my best to respond to every message from any fan who reached out to tell me I'd given them the confidence to be open about who they really were.

Although the Luca they wanted to see, touch, and speak to wasn't really me, the facade was important.

I didn't want to let them down.

So I waved and refused to let my exhaustion show. Jack slipped from the driver's seat while I waited where I was. I knew better than to get out before he was at my door. My fans were great but...exuberant. One time, a young girl fully wrapped herself around me like a koala. It'd taken two security guards and the promise of a selfie for her to let go.

Personal space and boundaries were foreign concepts so far as my followers were concerned.

The door swung open and the noise was instantly deafening. You'd think I'd be used to it after over a decade in the spotlight, but it was always overwhelming. I got out of the car as gracefully as possible, grinning at the waiting fans.

Jack held out a hand to stop them from rushing me, his face set in a scowl. That was his usual face. Grumpy shit only had two expressions, this one and the one he saved especially for Arlo. That one was a mix of exasperation and confusion.

Couldn't blame him. Arlo was a bundle of

contradictions on the best day. You never knew what version of him you were going to get—the hyped-up party guy who wanted to be the centre of attention or the moody introvert who refused to talk to anyone for days at a time.

Something told me that wasn't the basis for Jack's confusion where Arlo was concerned though. Jack had been a core part of our team since the day our first single hit number one. He'd been assigned to protect Arlo for the first ten years. The two had been as thick as thieves.

Then, out of the blue, management called a meeting with us all.

As usual, I'd been the last to arrive, and everyone else was already there: our agents, our manager, our bodyguards, and all the band members. Arlo had been slumped so far down in his seat that I couldn't see his face. His hood was pulled over his head, and he was so still I almost wanted to poke him to see if he was alive. I couldn't recall a time when he wasn't tapping out some beat or another. Any flat surface, no matter how small, was a good-enough substitute for a drum kit so far as Arlo was concerned.

I exchanged worried looks with Kai and Silas, our guitarist and bassist, respectively. Clearly, they didn't have any more idea what was happening than I did.

Kevin kept it brief as he explained that Arlo and I would be switching security details. Effective immediately.

"Why?" I'd blurted out. Not that I minded the switch. Simon, my bodyguard, was good at his job, but the same could be said about anyone on our team. But there was no way Arlo would be okay with being parted from Jack. He trusted him like no one else.

Kevin glanced between Jack and Arlo so briefly that I

almost missed it. He cleared his throat. "You've been in your current setup for a long time. It's good to shake things up every now and then. Keep things fresh."

Arlo gave a dry chuckle from under his hood. "That's the excuse you came up with? Good thing you're not paid for your creativity."

Kevin spluttered, his skin darkening. "Now, Arlo. You know what we agreed—"

"I know," Arlo said bitterly. "You don't need to remind me. I'll be a good boy."

He stormed from the room, carefully keeping his face hidden. He couldn't hide his shaking hands though.

We all looked at each other in confusion. Normally, Jack would be tearing out of the room after Arlo, but he remained motionless against the wall. He didn't look at us, staring instead at the wall opposite.

If it wasn't for the muscle jumping in his jaw and the fists clenched by his sides, I would've thought he was unaffected.

Simon was the one to go after Arlo, and every time after that, it was either him or a band member.

Jack never chased Arlo again.

In the years since, they'd barely been in the same room together. Jack had seamlessly slipped into his role as my bodyguard, but I hadn't missed how he couldn't help but watch Arlo whenever we were out.

I'd tried to get what happened out of Arlo. We all had. But for someone who overshared everything about his life, that was the one area where he was frustratingly tight-lipped.

And Jack? I hadn't even dared to ask him. Talking to him about himself was like trying to untangle a ball of yarn. The more you pulled at it, the tighter it'd get.

Three years later, I knew little more about Jack now than I had then. He was good at his job, which was the most important thing. He demonstrated those skills now as he smoothly carved a path through the crowd. He paused occasionally, allowing me to sign the odd T-shirt or pose for a selfie.

At one point, he gestured for me to give him my coffee cup so I could have both hands free, but I hugged it to my chest. I didn't care that he was being nice. He could pry my caffeine away from my cold dead fingers.

I breathed a sigh of relief as we squeezed in through the glass doors at the front of the building.

Then I realised the fans had followed.

"Wait, Luca!"

"Come back!"

"Luca, sign my shirt!"

"Where's the rest of your security staff?" Jack barked at the lone guard standing at the desk.

"What staff?" he asked, staring bewildered at the horde of screaming teenagers flooding the lobby. "It's just me. Stuff like this doesn't normally happen."

Jack's jaw tightened. "Where's the nearest stairwell?"

"At the back of the building. But the lifts are closer, and there's less opportunity for anyone to follow."

Just then, the crowd caught up with us. Jack shot a protective arm around my shoulders, but it wasn't enough. I was being jostled from every direction, the noise threatening to deafen me. The nice impromptu meet-and-greet had taken a sinister turn. Hands grabbed my sleeves. Rubbed my hair. Pulled at my clothes.

Then someone shoved me hard in the back. I cursed, my professional expression slipping as my hot coffee spilt over my hand. Jack and the security guard yelled at people to step back. Instead of giving me space, the crowds moved in closer. I couldn't differentiate between individual faces. They were one baying mass, clawing in desperation as they tried to get to me.

My chest tightened as my breath sped up. My head was spinning. Couldn't move. Couldn't breathe. *Couldn't move. Couldn't breathe.*

"Get me out of here, Jack."

It took everything in me to get those stuttered words out.

Jack glanced at me and cursed. Leaning close so I could hear him over the cacophony, he said, "Keep your head down and keep breathing. In and out."

I ducked my head, trying to keep the panic from showing on my face. I didn't have anxiety attacks often, but once they started, I could do little to stop them.

I'd yet to have one in public, but hey, there was a first time for everything.

Jack positioned himself behind me, both his massive arms bracketing me. The lone security guard walked in front of him, cutting a path through the masses.

It was a painstakingly slow path. I kept my eyes on the ground, counting each tile we crossed.

A few more feet. Just a few more.

Then you'll be able to breathe.

Jack squeezed my shoulder, his mouth at my ear. "The lifts are straight ahead and on the left. When I say go, take two steps to the left and go around the guard. Do not stop until you're in the lift and heading to the twelfth floor. We'll hold back the crowd to give you time to escape."

I nodded once to show I understood. Sadly, it wasn't the first time we'd had to pull a stunt like this to escape fans. Individually, most fans were kind and respectful, but en masse like this? Mob mentality took over.

Tiny spots crowded the edges of my vision, and I shook my hands, trying to force the tingling sensation from them.

"Go now. Second lift. Not the first. Someone has just got in there."

I didn't respond, just followed his instructions. Stepping around the profusely sweating guard, I ran. Thanks to the exuberant performances we tended to put on, I was quick on my feet.

The noise increased behind me as the crowd realised they were being held back. *Fuck.* I had to get out of here before I went viral on TikTok for having an anxiety attack in the lobby of a building.

Think of the headlines that would bring. My anxiety disorder was something Kevin preferred to keep hidden. Given the years I'd spent doing CBT and the medication I used, it didn't cause issues very often.

Today, though, no amount of grounding techniques would be able to pull me back from the edge.

Everything around me blurred as I struggled to drag in oxygen. The gleaming silver doors of the lift were like a beacon, offering me sanctuary from the chaos.

But they were closing.

Lunging forward, I slammed my hand in to prevent them from shutting.

When the gap widened enough, I threw myself in. As the doors closed behind me, I leaned against the wall, trying desperately not to slide to the floor. I buried my face in my hands and tried to get my breathing under control.

Someone cleared their throat, and my stomach dropped.

Fuck.

I'd got in the wrong lift.

Chapter 3

Ollie

Somehow, I'd made it to Grosvenor Place, where the *Identity* offices were located, with a scant three minutes to spare.

Everything that had happened in my flat had been put in a little box. I'd buried the box in that place deep in my psyche where trauma eventually becomes dark humour.

Couldn't see me ever laughing about it, to be honest. Right now, I'd take just being able to erase the image of them fucking. Was brain bleach actually a thing? Because if it was, I needed to Amazon Prime a bucketful of the stuff.

I drove down the street, searching for parking. Great. Not a single fucking space. Even worse, some moron had abandoned his car in the middle of the street outside the building, blocking the road. It was a fancy piece of shit too.

"Entitled rich motherfuckers not thinking of us little people..." I slammed on my indicator, waiting for a gap in the oncoming traffic to go around them.

By the time I'd found a space on a nearby street, I was more than ten minutes late. Sweat poured down my back as I pounded the pavement. My tie felt like it was choking me. I wasn't used to wearing them. My current office was all about casual attire, but I hadn't risked not donning one for this interview. It was too important to let something as simple as my wardrobe fuck it up.

Not that it mattered now I was late. Talk about the worst way to make a first impression.

I didn't notice the crowd until I was a few feet away. Coming to an abrupt halt, I gawked at the horde of screeching people surrounding the door to the *Identity* offices. They were holding signs, waving flags, bouncing with excitement.

How had I missed them earlier? Probably because I'd been so focused on the car in my way. I glared at it for a second, like I could hold the owner personally responsible for the various ways my life had been fucked up today. It was still obstructing traffic, causing beeping horns coupled with much swearing.

An uptick in the shouting dragged my attention back to the melee.

"Luca! Luca, over here! Luca, please sign this!"

There was a gap in the crowd, and I glimpsed the man causing all the fuss. Luca Weston, lead singer of Caffeine Daydreams. Playboy, entertainer, idol. He'd built an entire career on his sultry voice and enigmatic stage presence.

Personally, I wasn't a fan of Luca and his band, Caffeine Daydreams, but Suzie was *obsessed* with them. Even if she hadn't been, you'd have to have lived under a rock to have missed the spectacular rise of Caffeine

Daydreams. They'd started out busking on the streets of Southampton before a video of them performing went viral on YouTube.

They'd swapped the town centre for sold-out stadiums.

And Luca? He was the face of the band. The one who appeared on billboards and magazine covers. His high cheekbones and full pouty lips made people of all genders sigh. He'd recently cropped his shoulder-length chestnut curls, much to the dismay of his fans. It made him look older. Moodier. There was no sign of the tattoos I knew covered his chest and arms, but I could almost picture them as I studied him from afar.

The thought drew me up short. Since when had I paid enough attention to a guy's body that I could picture it without trying?

I shook my head, forcing away the errant thought and focusing instead on Luca's ripped clothing. The band had been moving towards a more emotive sound in the last couple of years, so management had probably decided this image fit better than the curly-haired golden child he had been.

He was far from a child these days. Even at this distance, I could see that every inch of his lean six-foot frame was solid man. He had to be at least seven years older than me.

One of the most famous men in the world was smiling at his fans as he posed for selfie after selfie while a massive guard loomed over everyone.

And all I cared about was that he was in my way. Stupid fucking rock star adding yet more drama to my day.

The car had to be his. Made sense. Luca Weston

struck me as exactly the type of guy who wouldn't consider what problems he might cause other people. Stars like him didn't need to worry about little things like job interviews or being on time. He probably didn't care about getting a parking fine. He probably had people who dealt with all his trivial life matters.

Let's be real. Luca Weston was so famous that his people probably had people.

To me, though, he was just another piece of kindling on the burning fire of my life.

I slipped inside the building next door, making a beeline for the *Identity* building. Few people knew the two were connected. I'd had a temp job here once, so I knew there was a door that allowed you to pass between them. Terrible in terms of security, but they were owned by the same management company that was well-known in the city for being tight with cash. God forbid they should put something as simple as a coded lock or another guard there.

Regardless, it worked well for me. The quiet lobby was a blessed relief after the mayhem happening outside. That relief quickly dwindled when I stepped through the doorway into the *Identity* lobby. Annoyingly, Luca seemed to have finished his little tete-a-tete with his fans and was now entering through the front doors, his security detail barking something at the guard.

Through the glass windows, I could see the crowd surging forwards. Apparently, they weren't content with the time Luca had given them.

Shit. I needed to get out of here before they overtook the place. If I moved fast, I might make it to the lifts before they took over and barred my way.

Again.

I did exactly that, but fate was clearly determined to keep me from getting this job. I barely made it ten feet across the space before I was swallowed up by a mob of pheromones.

Cursing, I turned sideways and nudged my way through the crowd. Years of working as a bartender in a nightclub at uni had served me well, helping me weave through. It was slow going, but the lifts were in sight.

Just then, hot liquid splattered over my front.

"Shit," I hissed, pulling the wet material away from my skin. The burning sensation faded quickly.

The massive coffee stain blooming over my previously pristine white shirt was another matter.

My head snapped sideways, searching for the culprit. My gaze fell on the takeaway cup in Luca Weston's hand, and I had to bite back the urge to growl.

The motherfucker didn't even notice. His attention was on his bodyguard whispering in his ear.

Thirty seconds more, and you'll be in the lift. I turned away, more determined than ever to escape this hellhole. My chances of landing this job had undoubtedly been washed down the drain, but I wasn't a quitter. I'd keep going until the door was literally closed in my face.

By some miracle, I made it the rest of the way to the lift without further incident. Slipping inside and punching the number twelve on the panel, I tapped my fingers impatiently and willed the doors to close faster.

Come on, come on.

I sighed in relief when they started to glide shut, the sound of the chaos outside being cut off.

But before they met in the middle, a hand shot between them. They opened, revealing Luca Weston like

I'd never seen him before.

He was several shades paler than a few moments ago. A fine sheen of sweat covered his skin, and...was he trembling?

He didn't even notice me, collapsing against the lift wall and burying his face in his hands. His feet slid on the floor as though he struggled to hold himself upright.

What was wrong with him? I shifted. It went against every bit of my British DNA to acknowledge a stranger in the lift, but it didn't feel right to leave him in the dark. He clearly thought he was alone.

Unsure of what to do, I cleared my throat.

Great work, Ollie.

The effect on Luca was instantaneous. It was like someone flicked a switch. His hands dropped away from his face as he straightened. The smile on his face was a mere whisper of the one he used to charm his fans. It was easy to see the effort it was costing him, his eyes barely concealing his exhaustion.

"Sorry, I'm not in the mood for taking photos right now. If you DM me on Insta, someone can be in touch with a signed copy at a later date."

My eyebrows went so high they were possibly flirting with my hairline. "Do you just assume everyone who breathes near you is a fan?"

Luca gave a barely perceptible wince before flashing me a self-deprecating grin I didn't buy for a second. "Sorry. Pretty safe assumption when you're me."

I glared at the digital display showing which floor we were on, willing it to go faster. "Well, you can relax. The day I go weak in the knees for a celebrity is the day hell freezes over."

"Noted." Luca chuckled, and it was the first genuine emotion since he'd noticed me. I couldn't help but glance sideways at him as the lift ascended. I'd always figured the stunning green eyes shining in his publicity photos were enhanced using Photoshop. Seeing him now, that obviously wasn't the case. If anything, they might dull them in pictures. I'd never seen a colour like it.

That's a weird thing to notice about a guy.

Brushing it aside, I focused instead on his demeanour. He seemed calmer than when he'd first burst into the lift. His colour was returning to normal and his breathing was less laboured.

He still didn't seem...right though. He fidgeted with his bracelet, rocking up on his toes like he was fighting the urge to run.

Which was a bit hard to do in a confined space.

Pity settled in my stomach as I forced my gaze forwards. I recognised the signs of anxiety all too well. Growing up with my mum meant I was well-versed in spotting an oncoming anxiety attack. I'd known about grounding techniques before I'd learned to tie my own shoelaces. It was on the tip of my tongue to ask him if he was okay, but I bit it back. Given how hard he was trying to hide it, the last thing he probably wanted was some random stranger interfering.

Two floors to go. I took some deep breaths, running through potential interview answers in my head. I straightened my jacket, trying to cover the coffee stain and failing miserably.

I sighed. I didn't know why I was stressing out about it. I was now so late I'd probably blown what little chance I'd stood of getting the job anyway.

The display had just clicked over to the eleventh floor when it happened.

The overhead lights and the lights from the displays all went out. We were plunged into complete darkness. The lift ground to a halt, the emergency brakes screeching as they kicked in.

"What the fuck?" Luca exclaimed.

I grabbed the rail behind me, using it to keep me grounded. The darkness was so all-encompassing I couldn't see an inch in front of my face. "Must be a power cut. Don't worry. Lifts have backup generators. The emergency lights should kick on any second now."

The only response was a low moan that seemed to come from the floor. My eyebrows drew together in confusion. "Luca, are you okay?"

That was the moment the emergency system started up. The lights were dim, but it was enough to show that Luca clearly wasn't *okay*.

He was sat on the floor with his knees drawn up to his chest. His head was on his knees as he shook his hands furiously.

"Can't feel my hands," he whimpered, still shaking them. "Can't feel them. Can't..."

Muscle memory kicked in. I dropped to my knees, careful to give him space but close enough that he knew I was there. "You're having an anxiety attack, Luca. Focus on my voice. Can you do that for me?"

"Can't breathe," he moaned. Sure enough, his breath was coming in ragged pants. He yanked at his tight necklaces against his skin and pulled the collar of his shirt. "Can't breathe."

"Can I touch you?"

His nod was barely perceptible, but it was enough for me.

Moving fast, I reached around the back of his neck, unclasping the two chains and letting them fall into his lap. It took me another ten seconds to unbutton his collar and open the neck wide. Neither of those things was actually impeding his breathing, but rationality wasn't a factor when it came to anxiety attacks.

He was still breathing far too fast for my liking. Hesitating, I tried to decide whether to cup my hands in front of his face to help him stop hyperventilating.

That felt too intimate. Instead, I grabbed one of Luca's hands and put it on my chest, holding it there. Immediately I regretted it as electricity zipped through me. How had I thought having him touch me would be less intimate?

My heart was racing now. It had to be related to the situation. I was just in a heightened state because anxiety attacks triggered memories I'd rather forget. That was all it was. "Breathe with me now. In. Out. In. Out."

I took deep breaths, silently counting to seven as I inhaled and eleven on the exhale. "In and out. You can do it, Luca."

It took a few moments, but with encouragement, Luca began to mimic my breaths.

"Tell me five things you can see."

My chest ached at how fast he responded. He was familiar with this grounding technique, which meant it wasn't his first attack. "The tile floor. The wall. The bar. The doors. You."

We made our way through the rest of the list quietly, helping Luca using all his senses to ground him.

By the time we reached the end, his trembling had mostly subsided, a sure sign the worst was over.

"Still can't feel my hands."

Luca spoke so quietly that I almost missed it. Pulling his hand from my chest, I grabbed his other and rubbed them vigorously with my own. "It's the lack of oxygen. It'll feel better in a few minutes."

Luca didn't reply, but he also didn't stop me.

I didn't know how long we sat there, his head bowed and me kneeling beside him. My side began to protest the awkward angle, but I wouldn't let Luca go until I knew the attack had completely finished.

He cleared his throat. "Thank you."

"It's nothing."

He closed his eyes, his chin on his chest. "It's not nothing. You didn't sign up to deal with this."

"Neither did you."

That made his eyes snap open. They were so breathtaking that, for a split second, I forgot how to breathe. "What do you mean?"

What was Luca doing to me? Since when did I think any man was *breathtaking?* I forced a smile onto my face. "Pretty sure you didn't choose to have anxiety. Therefore, you didn't sign up to deal with it either."

His lips twisted into a rueful grin, and my heart just about stopped. "Can't argue with that." His gaze dropped south and uncertainty crossed his face. "You can let go of my hands now."

Shit. I hadn't realised I was still holding them. Dropping them like they were hot coals, I scooted away. I moved so fast that when my back collided with the wall opposite, I winced. "Sorry."

Luca looked bemused. "You don't need to apologise."

"But I was touching you."

"Is that a bad thing? Touching me?"

"Of course not," I said hastily. Too hastily. Great. Now he probably thought I was a homophobe. Which I wasn't.

No, but I was freaking out about how bad it *hadn't* been. How natural it'd felt to hold Luca's hands in mine. I groaned, dropping my head into my hands.

Seriously, how much was the universe going to throw at me today?

I definitely hadn't had enough coffee for this.

"What's your name?"

"Ollie."

"You know, Ollie, a lot of people would pay good money to touch me."

Luca's arrogant remark had me pulling my head out of my hands. One look at the soft grin on his face suggested he was teasing. Relief flooded through me as I realised he wasn't going to make a big deal over my obvious freakout. "Good to know. My car could do with a new set of brakes. Do you think I could charge your fans to touch my hands knowing they'd touched yours?"

He pretended to consider it. "They'd probably go for it, but you wouldn't be able to wash them until you'd made the money. Plus, then you'd have to deal with all the germs from strangers..."

I shuddered. "Yeah, maybe not. How about a lock of your hair? That'd probably go for over 10K on eBay."

"Only 10K?" Luca put a hand to his chest in mock outrage. "Honey, I'm worth *at least* twenty."

A small thrill went through me at the casual endearment before I stamped down on it.

"In that case, sod the brakes. I'm getting a whole new car."

"Why stop there?" Luca flashed me a grin, showing off his perfect Hollywood teeth. "You could shave my head and buy a house. Ooh, I bet some weirdos out there would pay a *fortune* for my nail clippings."

I made a mock gagging noise and held up a hand. "Okay, that's a step too far."

Luca's laugh filled the small space, the rich sound ricocheting off the walls, lighting something deep inside me. I frowned and surreptitiously pressed a hand against my forehead, checking my temperature. Nope, no fever.

I turned my attention to the man opposite me. Luca's legs were sprawled in front of him, his arms in his lap. To most people, he probably looked totally relaxed. But the aftereffects of an anxiety attack were easy to spot if you knew what to look for. It was the way he repeatedly clenched his hands, attempting to clear the last of the pins and needles. How his eyes darted around the space. The slight hitch in his breathing, like he had to remind himself to inhale deeply.

"Does it bother you?"

"What?" Luca's gaze turned to me, puzzled.

"That people genuinely would pay to get their hands on some part of you. I've heard of those bullshit auctions on eBay where someone sells a celebrity's T-shirt or something, and everyone goes wild. I'm sure that's happened with something you've owned or touched."

He shrugged. "I'm sure it has."

"Don't you hate it?"

His head tilted to the side. "That's a deep question for one stranger to ask another."

Shame flooded my cheeks. "Sorry. My mum was always telling me off for being nosey."

"It's fine."

He studied me suspiciously. "Fuck. Are you a journalist?"

I shifted slightly. "What makes you think that?"

Luca's face went completely blank, his limbs tight. "It's a pretty good guess, given the building we're in. And I think I deserve to know the truth due to what you've just witnessed."

He was right. He did deserve that. "Yes, I'm a journalist. But I won't tell anyone about anything that's happened here. I promise."

He folded his arms over his chest. "Why would you promise that? A story about a rock star having a meltdown simply because he got stuck in a lift would make you enough to buy five new cars."

"It wasn't a meltdown. It was an anxiety attack." My tone was harsher than intended, but I'd be damned if I let him downplay it. "And we both know it wasn't the lift that caused it. That was just the straw that broke the camel's back."

No, his anxiety had been through the roof the instant he'd entered. Unsurprising, given the intense display his fans had been putting on. It'd stressed *me* out, and I wasn't even the one it was aimed at.

"You didn't answer my question. Why won't you run the story when it'd benefit you so much?"

"Are you saying you *want* me to write a story about this?"

He huffed, rolling his eyes. "Obviously not. I'm trying to figure out your angle. I've never met a journalist who didn't have an angle."

I bit my lip. Talking about my mum wasn't something I did. Ever. Callum only knew about my childhood because he'd been there while I was going through it. Even Suzie didn't know.

An image of them that morning flashed through my mind. I focused on Luca instead. Tracing over his scowl. The light stubble on his jaw. His long fingers that were still twitching. I catalogued his features repeatedly until the image was erased and all that remained was Luca.

"It's because of my mum." I blurted it out fast. I'd seen him at his most vulnerable against his will, so offering him a tiny sliver of my soul seemed like a fair price. "She used to suffer from anxiety attacks and depression."

"Used to?" The question was soft, but the implication was heavy in the air.

I closed my eyes as I answered, hiding myself away. "Used to. She died by suicide when I was eighteen."

I'd never forget that phone call. Never stop blaming myself for leaving her alone while I went to university. Maybe if I'd been there...maybe if I'd seen the signs...

Maybe things would've been different.

Maybe.

A gentle touch on my knee had me opening my eyes. Luca knelt before me, his face solemn. "I'm so sorry. I know that doesn't make it better, but I truly am."

I swiped at my eyes. Damn, I needed to get a hold of myself. "It's okay. It was a long time ago."

Nine years, four months, and three days. It sure sounded like a long time, and that was what people *expected* you to say. They expected you to have moved on. To not still be picking up your phone and opening a text thread before remembering. To not be carrying on your life as normal, and then see something as simple as their favourite brand of tea and have the crushing weight of grief pushing you into the floor once more.

And just like that, telling Luca had ripped open that wound again. I needed to close it before it consumed me. See, this was why I kept my emotions locked tight.

Letting them out led to pain. I'd experienced enough of that to last me a lifetime.

It was like Luca could read my thoughts. "It doesn't matter how long ago it was. You're allowed to feel and acknowledge your pain. I haven't lost anyone close to me, but if I had, I don't imagine any amount of time would make it easier."

"No," I whispered, closing my eyes against the stinging tears. "It doesn't."

Luca stayed silent while I pulled myself back under control. His hand on my knee was the sole reminder that I wasn't alone. With anyone else, I'd be shrugging off the touch. But for some reason, his strong grip kept me grounded. It was an anchor in the churning sea of my grief, letting me feel it but not letting it pull me under completely.

Chapter 4

Luca

"Sorry," Ollie said eventually.

"You sure apologise a lot," I drawled, releasing his knee with a pat and retreating to the opposite wall. I wanted to hold on to him longer. Hell, what I really wanted to do after hearing that story was grab him and hug the shit out of him. But I'd already taken enough of a risk by touching his leg. Considering how he'd reacted earlier, it didn't seem smart to offer anything else, even if it was a platonic hug because he was hurting. "It's so British."

"Aren't you British?"

"Yep," I said. "But I've spent most of my adult years in the States. Over there, you only apologise if you have something to apologise for."

Ollie gave me a small smirk. "Must save a lot of time."

Now that I'd heard his story, I understood why he'd been so vehement in promising not to tell anyone. From how he'd struggled to get it out, I suspected it was information he didn't share with many people. To share it with me, a virtual stranger, simply because he wanted to put my concerns at ease, meant a lot. I cleared my throat. "Thank you for telling me that. I get it. I understand why you won't tell anyone."

"No one deserves to be judged for suffering from mental illness or conditions. And you don't have to believe me, but anything you say here will stay between us." Ollie's shoulders squared as he spoke with absolute conviction.

I shouldn't believe him about keeping everything private, but for some reason...I did. Not that I was expecting anything to happen. Even if this stranger had skin that looked like cream, just begging me to taste it. Or wore a shirt that stretched deliciously over his broad chest. Even the coffee stain didn't detract from the shape of his muscles under the material.

Couple that with his soulful hazel eyes, thick kissable lips, and primly styled blond hair...he made a pretty package I was *dying* to unwrap.

But that didn't matter. Given how quickly he'd pulled away earlier, he had to be straight.

"I wonder how long we're going to be in here," I said idly before something very obvious occurred to me. "Hang on, aren't we supposed to push a button and call for help?"

Understanding dawned on Ollie's face. "Bugger, you're right. I should've thought about it earlier, but I was distracted."

I winked, unable to stop flirting even though I knew it was a bad idea. "I am very distracting."

Ollie flushed beetroot red. Interesting. Was that because I'd embarrassed him? Or was it something else entirely...

Nope.

Ollie jumped to his feet and pressed the alarm button. It rang for a painfully long time before a bored-sounding operator came on the line. "Hello?"

"Hi, we're stuck in lift"—he glanced up to check the display—"*C* in the *Identity* offices in Grosvenor Square."

"Yeah, a power line has gone down in Millbrook. Half the city is without electricity."

I bit back a groan. An outage of that magnitude would mean we wouldn't be the only ones in need of a rescue.

"Do you have emergency lighting?"

"Yes."

There was a pause on the line. "But the lift doors haven't opened?"

Ollie looked over his shoulder at me in exasperation, and I snorted a laugh. "No. Hence the *stuck* part."

The level of sarcasm dripping from his tone was Oscar-worthy. I bit back a grin.

"The emergency generator should've automatically taken you to the nearest floor and the doors should've opened." Keys clacked on her end, followed by a sigh. "Unfortunately, it looks like the building owner hasn't updated the system in over a decade."

Ollie closed his eyes. "Any idea how long the power will be down?"

"Current reports are saying two to three hours. How many of you are in the lift?"

"Two."

"Is anyone hurt, unwell, or in distress?"

At that last one, he glanced back at me. I shook my head emphatically. I didn't want crews of emergency workers descending when there'd be other people needing them more. "No."

"In that case, it'll be a while before the emergency services can get to you." Some of the boredom in her voice was replaced by sympathy. "You'll just have to wait it out, I'm afraid."

"Fantastic," Ollie muttered, stepping back from the panel and taking his seat on the floor, long legs sprawled in front of him. "Looks like we should make ourselves comfortable."

He was so tense that it was on the tip of my tongue to offer to make him feel *really* comfortable. My cock plumped at the thought of the things we could do to pass the time.

I folded my hands in my lap, hiding the evidence from Ollie while berating myself. What was wrong with me? I normally had way better self-control than this. What was it about Ollie that had me feeling like a hormonal teenager?

He's *straight.* And even worse, he's a journalist.

Imagine the story he could write if I did make a clumsy move.

Trapped with Luca Weston: how the rock star everyone wants tried to seduce me in a lift.

That was the exact kind of headline Kevin wanted me to stay away from. Shame my libido didn't see it quite the same way.

"So, you're a journalist. Do you work here?" Maybe if I kept the topic centred around his profession, my dick would understand how pointless this sudden infatuation was.

"No." He laughed bitterly and checked his watch.

"I might've done, had today gone any differently. Given it's now almost an hour past my interview time, I think I can safely say the boat has sailed on that."

"An hour? We haven't been stuck in here that long. It can't have been that important to you if you weren't here early." I gestured at the large brown stain on his shirt teasingly. "And you've spilt coffee over yourself. Were you trying to make a fashion statement?"

Ollie's face turned purple. "Are you fucking serious right now?"

I tilted my head to the side and smiled softly. "I mean, the coffee stain does work. Really makes it seem like you put in the effort..."

"Let's set a few things straight, shall we?" He spoke through gritted teeth, and something in my stomach sank. "One of the reasons I was late is because a car was blocking the road and causing a build-up of traffic."

I flinched. Shit, I shouldn't have teased him. I opened my mouth to apologise, but he held up a hand to stop me. "Another reason was that the lobby was full of screaming fans, making it near impossible for me to get through."

The fire in his eyes practically sent out sparks as his temper grew. "And the coffee stain? I got that when *you* knocked into me, spilling your coffee over me and burning my chest. So thanks for that."

My blood ran cold as I scrambled across the floor to him. My hands were on his chest, hastily unbuttoning his shirt. "Oh my god, I'm so sorry. I had no idea. I swear, if I'd known, I would've got someone to get a first aider and offered to have your shirt dry-cleaned. Are you okay?"

"What are you doing?" he whispered.

I froze, my fingers twitching on the soft cotton. I raised my head to look at him, belatedly realising the move put my mouth mere inches above his. Christ, his eyes were even more captivating up close. "Umm...I was checking if you're okay."

Ollie's eyes dropped to my lips, and he cleared his throat. "I'm fine. You could've just asked instead of stripping me down."

"Oh fuck, you're right," I said, dropping the material hastily and hurrying back to my side. What was wrong with me? Where was the confident fuckboy everyone knew and loved? Apparently, he'd vanished the second he'd realised how deliciously tempting Ollie was. "Sorry, I panicked. I wasn't thinking."

"That's okay." Ollie sighed. "I'm the one who should be apologising. None of those things were your fault, not really. I'm sure you have a driver who chose to park there. You didn't ask your fans to hound you. Even the coffee can be blamed on them."

"Still feels like my fault." I twisted the bracelet round on my wrist, focusing on the intricate detailing on the beads. "You sure you're okay?"

"Here." Ollie knelt up, his eyes on me as he loosened his dark tie and unbuttoned the shirt slightly. He pulled it to one side, revealing a small red mark. I couldn't focus on it, my mouth watering at the expanse of creamy skin dusted with ash-blond hair. "See, nothing to worry about. It'll be gone by tomorrow."

"If you're sure," I said faintly, looking back down at my lap. If I stared at him any longer, he'd definitely think I was a creeper. "I am sorry. I'm happy to buy you a new shirt to replace it."

To my surprise, he chuckled. “No bother. It’s not like I’ll need an interview shirt any time soon. This was kind of a once-in-a-lifetime deal.”

“You should call them,” I said. “Let them know you’re stuck in the lift. It’s not like you can help it.”

He pulled his phone out and made a face. “That’d be a great idea if I had any signal.”

I checked my own. “Can’t even lend you mine. We really are cut off from the outside world.”

“Probably wouldn’t matter anyway.” Ollie huffed, shoving his phone back in his pocket. “Even if you hadn’t been here, I likely wouldn’t have made it. Not after what happened at home this morning. That was the biggest fuck-up of today without a shadow of a doubt.”

“Why? What else happened?”

He jolted like he hadn’t realised what he’d let slip. “Umm…nothing.”

His response was more intriguing than the original statement. “You don’t have to tell me.”

“It’s not that. It’s just…you’re a stranger.”

“Sometimes talking to a stranger is easier.”

His head thudded back against the lift. “It’s embarrassing.”

I leaned my arms on my knees and grinned. “Now this is getting interesting.”

“Not in the way you might think,” he muttered darkly.

“You don’t have to tell me,” I said. I couldn’t deny I was curious, but I wasn’t about to force him to open up. “But we’ve got a lot of time to kill, and you look like you need to get something off your chest.”

“Why do you even care?” He eyed me suspiciously.

"You're a literal rock star. Don't you have more interesting things to talk about than the shit heap that is my life?"

"That's the thing. Everyone always wants to talk about me." I lifted my hand up like I was holding a microphone.

"Are you and the band as close as you say you are? What's it like to be on stage? Do you like being famous? What's the story with Kai and Silas? Are they fucking or just close like they claim?"

His lips twitched. "As a journalist, I'd love to know the answer to the last one."

"No comment," I said with a smirk. "Seriously though...there's nothing going on there."

Even if Kai so obviously wanted Silas. Everyone, including our fanbase, could see that. The only one who couldn't was Silas himself. And until Kai got up the balls to confess how he really felt, nothing would change.

"But you see what I mean," I said with a gesture. "Everyone always wants to talk about my life, and I'm so fucking bored with it. No one tells me anything about themselves. I can't tell you the last time I had a conversation with someone about something other than music or the band."

"So because I'm trapped here, you want me to fill that missing void for you?"

I bit my lip. I had a void he could fill, but I was ninety-nine percent sure that wasn't what he'd meant. "Please, for the love of God, give me *something*. Anything normal."

He tapped his fingers on his thigh. "That's what you want? Normal?"

"Yes." I gave a mock groan, and Ollie shifted slightly. "Please. It's been so long that I can't even remember what normal feels like."

"Poor neglected rock star," Ollie mocked. "I feel so sorry for you."

I pouted. "You should. I'm spurned by the little people."

Ollie tried to keep a straight face, but the longer I stuck my lower lip out, the more he struggled. Eventually, his composure broke. His genuine laughter touched a place deep within, making me want to hear it again almost instantly. "I know you're teasing, but believe me, normal isn't all it's cracked up to be."

"Prove it," I said. My legs were starting to cramp, so I stretched them out in front of me. Because Ollie was sitting in a similar position, it took some manoeuvring to get comfortable. Eventually, I got there by spreading my legs wide, bracketing his limbs between mine. "Tell me about your fucked-up morning."

Ollie's hands twitched on his trousers. "I don't normally talk to people about this sort of stuff."

"Like we just established, I'm *not* normal. Ergo, you can feel comfortable telling me."

"Has anyone ever told you you're a bit annoying?"

I grinned. "Not since I became rich and famous. People tend to put you on a bit of a pedestal. But you feel free to remind me as often as you like."

"I'll make sure to tweet you a weekly reminder," Ollie smirked.

My good mood faltered slightly. That was right. Ollie wouldn't be able to tell me to my face because once we walked out of this lift, I'd never see him again.

That shouldn't matter. I met people on a daily basis who I would never cross paths with once the day was out.

So why did the thought of not seeing Ollie again make me want to punch something?

He fiddled with his tie, but I didn't push him further. It was up to him now if he wanted to confide in me about whatever bothered him.

"I caught my girlfriend in bed with someone else this morning."

My eyes bugged wide. "What? That bitch!"

He grimaced. "It gets worse. The guy fucking her? My best friend."

"Man, you weren't joking when you said it was fucked up. It's one thing for your partner to cheat on you, but with someone you trust? That shit's cold."

"Right? It wouldn't have been half as bad if it'd been a stranger, but Callum?" He shook his head in disgust. "He's been by my side through everything."

"What a fucking prick." My blood boiled that someone could treat Ollie that way, but I only allowed mild sympathy to show. "I'm so sorry."

Ollie blew out a breath, staring at the ceiling. The low lighting cast shadows over his features, hollowing out his cheeks and making his eyes appear darker. "It's okay. To be honest with you, the relationship with Suzie had probably run its course anyway."

I nudged his thigh with my foot until he looked at me. "That doesn't make it okay. Cheating is *never* okay."

He ran a hand through his hair. "Thanks. I do actually feel better now I've told someone."

"Don't you have someone else to confide in? Who

would you normally go to?"

He met my gaze levelly. "Callum."

"Well, shit." Now I really wanted to thump the guy. "Want me to take out a hit on him? I've never done it before, but I'm pretty rich. I'm sure I can make it happen."

As I'd hoped, my joke broke through Ollie's tension as he hooted a laugh. "Nah, but thank you anyway. Imagine the headlines if that story broke: *Rock star turned assassin: how Luca Weston took out a hit on a stranger to avenge the man he was trapped in a lift with.*"

"You're right. That's a bit of a mouthful." The amusement in my tone dried up as the phone call from earlier popped back into my head. "Although it might be a nice change from the recent articles about me."

Ollie gave me a quizzical look. "What articles?"

Ah. With everything he'd had happening today, he probably hadn't seen that I was blowing up on social media. Again. "Let's just say you aren't the only one who's been through a breakup in the last twenty-four hours."

"Jorge? I always got the impression things weren't that serious between you."

"What made you think that?" I was genuinely curious. Even though we hadn't been anything more than fuck buddies, Jorge had milked our 'relationship' for all it'd been worth in the press and on social media. Given that it was good exposure for his career, I hadn't felt inclined to stop him. "And just how carefully have you been following my career?"

Ollie gave me a withering look that made me chuckle. "Not me. Suzie. She'd definitely be one of those fans who'd pay through the nose for a lock of your hair."

Still chuckling, I nudged his leg with my foot. "You

need better taste in your partners."

"That's true," Ollie said before considering my earlier question. "I'm not sure really...I think it was the photos from your trip to Mykonos that first made me suspicious. Jorge was always pouting for the camera like he was on a shoot, while you looked like someone was standing just outside the frame pointing a gun at you until you smiled."

I winced, remembering the trip well. "God, that might've been better than what actually happened. Jorge bitched and whined the whole trip. It was supposed to be a relaxing break away between albums, but he kept insisting we ditch Kai, Silas, and Arlo to do impromptu photo shoots. I think he was one request away from Kai dumping him in the ocean."

"Funnily enough, that doesn't surprise me," Ollie said with a smirk. "Jorge strikes me as being...high maintenance."

"Understatement of the year," I said before catching myself. "All of this is off the record...right?"

Ollie's forehead creased. "I've already told you it is. You can trust me."

"Sorry," I muttered. "Maybe if I tell you the rest of the story, you'll understand why I'm not feeling so favourable towards the press right now."

And so I did. Everything from meeting up with Jorge to the way he'd dramatically flung his drink in my face. "So now I have my management breathing down my neck. Again." I shook my head in frustration. "Fucking Jorge. He even had the nerve to tell everyone I have a tiny dick. Which was a pointless move, given how many of my nudes have been leaked over the years. Still, you can guess which part the articles ran with."

Ollie's ears had turned red again. "Indeed. I'm sorry you had to go through that. It's bad enough dealing with situations like that in private...but knowing they're going to be scrutinised by billions of people? I don't think I'd like that either."

"No," I agreed. "It's something I knew would happen if we became successful, but I'd kind of pushed it to the back of my mind. I told myself that living in the spotlight couldn't *possibly* be as bad as everyone says it is. That it'd be worth it to live the life I'd always dreamt about."

"And now? Is it worth it?"

"No." I hadn't even realised how true that was until I said it. "No, I'm not sure it is. Don't get me wrong, I love my job. But how can I be myself with someone without wondering if one day, down the line, they'll be selling their story? Is it too much to ask that I find someone who wants me for me?"

"No, that's not too much to ask," Ollie said quietly. "Everyone deserves to be happy. To find that person who completes us. Who holds us up when we're falling down. Who cheers us on and pushes us to do better. Who lets us care for them when we need it. Who we can trust without question."

"Is that how you felt about Suzie?"

He snorted. "If only. When we first met at uni, I thought maybe one day we'd get there. But that day never came. Who knows, maybe Callum will be that guy for her."

"You don't mean that."

"I think I do." He gave me a tight smile. "Don't get me wrong. I won't ever forgive them for what they did to me...but I saw the way they looked at each other this morning. They might actually have a chance of making everything work now that I'm out of the way."

"I'm sorry."

"It's okay." His shaky breath said it obviously wasn't. "You know the worst thing though? The thing I can't get past? I kissed her this morning. Before I left, I leaned down and kissed her full on the mouth. Was she thinking about him then? Wishing it was his lips on hers instead? Or maybe she wanted to get it over with so I'd leave, and he could come over." He rubbed at his chest. "It hurts knowing that while I was thinking of her, she was picturing someone else. I know it's stupid, but all I can focus on is that was my last kiss for who knows how long...and she was thinking of him."

I moved onto my knees. What I was about to do was very, very stupid.

But I was going to do it anyway.

Anything to wipe that morose look from Ollie's face.

Ollie stared at me, his brows drawn in confusion. "What are you doing?"

I scooted a little closer and swung my leg over Ollie's lap so I was straddling him. I didn't put any weight on him, being careful to touch him as little as possible. "Something pretty idiotic. But let's face it, I'm not known for being clever."

"I don't understand."

"Listen, I know you're straight." I leaned in slowly, resting my hand on the wall beside Ollie's head. I kept moving until my mouth hovered only inches from Ollie's, not missing how his breathing hitched. "But why don't I kiss you?"

"What?" Ollie whispered, his eyes wide.

"Let me kiss you, Ollie. I'll kiss you, and I promise, you'll be the only one I'm thinking about."

Chapter 5

Ollie

I stared at the rock star straddling my lap and began to question my sanity.

Had I bumped my head this morning? Maybe I was flat-out somewhere in a coma. Perhaps this was some medicine-induced fever dream I would wake up from any moment.

If it was, I was pretty sure my cock wouldn't be hard as steel. The thin cotton of my trousers was doing little to hide my predicament. All Luca would have to do was scoot forward by another six inches, and he'd know what effect this was having on me.

The question was *why*. Why was my dick so hard that it was aching? Why did Luca's offer have my heart hammering and my palms sweating? Why did being pinned beneath him feel so right? I'd always been the alpha in the bedroom. I'd never considered letting someone else take control.

And suddenly, I was questioning why I hadn't.

"You want to kiss me?" Fuck, why was my voice

so squeaky?

Luca's head tilted sideways, a lock of his hair falling forwards. I had the sudden urge to reach up and brush it away. Would it feel as soft as it looked? "I do. I'm attracted to men, Ollie. And there's no doubt about it, you're a very attractive man. But I won't force you to do anything you don't want to."

"What about the camera?" Yes, I was searching for any reason other than just saying no.

Because if I was being truly honest with myself…I didn't *want* to say no.

Luca's eyes flicked up to the ancient device in the corner. "The light's off. Looks like they really skimped out on their backup generator capabilities." He turned back to me, his expression gentle. "It's okay. If you don't want to, we can forget I said anything."

"But why me?" No idea why my brain was more hung up on this fact than the idea of actually kissing a man. "You could have anyone."

"I could," Luca agreed, not taking his eyes off me. "But not everyone opens up to me the way you have. You have a problem. You can't stop thinking about the fact that your last kiss with someone else wasn't what you thought it was. I have the solution. Kiss me, and you won't doubt anything."

My hands trembled on the floor. I was straight. I shouldn't even be considering it. I opened my mouth to tell him thanks, but no. To my surprise, that was not what came out. "Okay."

Luca's mouth fell open in shock before being replaced with a dangerous smile. He leaned in, his hands braced against the wall on either side of my head.

My heart hammered as Luca drew closer. Suddenly the heat in his eyes was too much. It was making me feel things I didn't understand.

Things I hadn't been expecting.

I closed my eyes, my pulse racing as I waited for his lips to find mine. They were tingling in anticipation.

I might not know *why,* but there was no doubting I wanted this.

"I might've lied." Luca was so close that I felt his whispered words on my lips. "Call me egotistical, call me delusional...but I hope this'll make you doubt things."

I didn't have a chance to wonder what he meant before his lips closed over mine.

I'd expected his kiss to be harsh and brash. For him to attack me with the same confidence he had on stage.

That might've made it easier to handle.

But the soft sensual way he worked my mouth open? How his tongue teased and flirted with mine? The brush of his stubble against my lips?

Those things were my undoing.

I surged forwards, pushing myself as close to Luca as possible. I didn't care that his body was hard against mine. That I could feel his short beard burning my skin. That his cologne was unlike any perfume a woman would wear.

I didn't care that he was a man.

All I cared about was getting him closer and not letting him go until I'd had my fill.

Luca let out a small gasp of surprise as I buried my hands in his hair. It was as soft as I'd expected, and I couldn't resist running my hands through it, purring at the texture.

Luca didn't stop kissing me, but it wasn't

enough. His hands were still on the wall, and they were all I could think about. I pulled back, my eyes glassy. "You can touch me."

Luca's pupils were blown, his lips swollen. "You sure?"

I swallowed back the fear bubbling in my throat. "I'm sure."

He growled before his lips descended once more. His hands moved, one grabbing my jaw and the other finding my nipple with unerring accuracy. It pebbled under his touch. When he pinched it gently, I groaned into his mouth.

We were full-on making out now. All my previously held beliefs of being straight seemed laughable with Luca in my lap. My boxers were damp from the precum leaking from my cock. Releasing his hair, I slid my hands down until they were on his backside. It felt like the most natural thing to yank him forward, wanting to feel him against me.

The move had his groin hitting mine, and I froze.

Luca was hard.

And packing.

Suddenly the reality of what we were doing hit me. This morning I'd considered myself straight, and now my junk was happily introducing itself to another man's.

Obviously, twenty-seven was not too late to be learning new things about myself.

Luca pulled back a bit, studying my face. "You okay?"

"Yep."

The frown Luca gave made me think that perhaps I wasn't convincing enough. He went to slide off me, but I stopped him. "Wait."

He raised an eyebrow at me questioningly. "Is it… is it bad that I don't want to stop yet?"

Luca's face softened. "No. There's *nothing* wrong with that."

"Good." My voice might be shaky, but I was determined. For the next however long we were trapped here, I was going to forget about everything.

That Suzie had cheated on me.

How Callum had betrayed me.

That my plans for my dream job had gone up in smoke.

The fact Luca was a freaking rock star.

But most of all, I was going to forget that, before Luca, I'd never been attracted to a man.

We were just two human beings making each other feel good.

I tugged at his rear until Luca got the message and scooted forwards. This time when I felt his dick rub against mine, the fear was overridden by desire. I bit my lip as my hips canted upwards, seeking more friction.

Luca's eyes lit in understanding. He smirked, undulating his hips over mine and making me almost weep with pleasure. "This what you want?"

"Yes." I punctuated the word with a thrust. "More of that. And this."

My hand wrapped around his neck, and I pulled his mouth back to mine.

I had no idea how long we sat like that. We were lost in each other. All too soon, I felt my balls draw up tight. Pleasure zipped through me, and I knew I was getting close. "Stop."

Luca scrambled back off me so fast he tripped over

one of my feet and landed on his arse. "Ouch."

I couldn't help it. I laughed. Never before had I been on the brink of an orgasm and found something funny.

"Meanie." Luca scowled at me, making me laugh harder. It was one of those moments that tipped into hysteria. The more I tried to stop, the harder I laughed. Luca couldn't resist the humour, and his laugh intertwined with mine inside the small space.

Eventually, we got ourselves under control, wiping the tears from our faces as we grinned bashfully at each other. Luca's slid off his face, replaced with guilt. "I'm sorry. I shouldn't have pushed it so far."

I was baffled. "I don't understand what you're apologising for. I said stop because I was about to come in my boxers."

Luca's guilt transformed into a teasing smirk. "And that'd be a bad thing?"

I hated to burst our bubble with a reminder of the outside world, but I had to. "Given that the world's press is probably camped outside waiting to get the scoop on Luca Weston trapped in a lift, it's not a *good* thing."

"You don't want to be photographed with me, knowing they'd all speculate about who you are." Luca's tone had soured. "Got it."

"That's not it at all," I said, crossing my arms and glaring at him. "Aren't you the one who can't risk any more negative press at the moment? Surely fooling around with *a stranger,* regardless of who they are, wouldn't go down well with your management."

"You were…you were trying to protect me?"

"Yes," I said in exasperation. God, the utter confusion on Luca's face struck a chord in my soul. The idea that he automatically assumed everyone was out to take advantage of him was devastating. "I don't want you to get into any more trouble than you already are. But there's also no way I would be able to hold it back with that...thing you were doing."

Luca's face smoothed out, donning his confidence like a mask. "You liked that, did you?"

I rolled my eyes, pointing at my still-tented trousers. Even our little misunderstanding hadn't been enough to kill my erection. "Obviously."

He sat against the wall, one of his legs coming up for him to lean forward on. He was the picture of casual. His expression told a different story.

He looked like a predator preparing to pounce.

"You know, there's a few ways I can take care of that for you without making a mess."

My cheeks flamed as my brain helpfully filled in exactly how he might do that. An hour ago, I would've laughed at the thought. Right now, I was horny enough to be considering it.

"I'm not sure you're ready for some of them," he said, mischief sparkling in his eyes. "But my mouth on your cock? Maybe you're ready for that."

My brain said I was absolutely *not* ready for that. Unfortunately for my brain, it had been shoved into a safe and locked away by my cock. My cock that was now throbbing and leaking at the thought of Luca wrapping those talented lips around it. "Maybe I am."

Once again, I'd managed to surprise Luca. And just like the first time, it didn't take him long to recover. Before I'd even managed to drag in another shaky breath, he'd stood, crossing the small space in a single stride. He towered over me, his face serious as he surveyed me. "You sure you want this?"

I gulped. Fuck, I shouldn't. But I did.

I couldn't remember the last time I'd wanted something, *anything*, this badly.

And knowing that I'd never see him again once we were rescued gave me the confidence to do this. To take what I wanted.

For once in my life, to just...*feel.*

"Yes."

Luca studied me for a few minutes more before he spoke. "Stand up."

I should've been embarrassed by the speed at which I followed his command, but I wasn't.

Luca stepped closer to me. His hands went to my belt, and panic hit. Shit, was I really doing this?

"Here, maybe this will help."

And then his lips were on mine again.

He was right. With him kissing me, I forgot about everything else. Nothing else existed except Luca. He was like the most effective anxiety relief. If this feeling could be condensed into tablet form, I'd take it every day, knowing it'd relax me better than any medication could. It didn't even feel strange to be kissing someone the same height as me...it felt *right*.

I didn't even notice him freeing my cock from my trousers, but I sure as fuck felt the first time he gave it a stroke. I broke away from the kiss, my head hitting the wall with a thud. "Fuck."

Luca's smirk was knowing. "There's something different when it's a guy. Maybe it's because we grow up obsessed with playing with our dicks. Means we know all too well how to drive another man crazy."

Crazy was accurate. He ran his thumb over the slit, thumbing at the precum there, and I swear I saw God.

"I can get you off like this if you want," Luca murmured. "I've got some tissues in my pocket, which will solve the mess conundrum."

The thought was tempting. I'd never thought sex was that great, but a simple hand job from Luca was blowing all my preconceived notions out of the water. But if I was doing this, I wanted to do it properly. I'd always regret it if I didn't try it.

"No. I want your mouth."

Luca caught my bottom lip between his teeth, and I moaned. "Excellent choice."

He didn't take his eyes off me as he dropped to his knees. He slid his hands up my thighs. Even with us positioned like this, there was no questioning who was in charge. "Did you know my throat and mouth have been insured for two million pounds?"

"What?" His change of topic had thrown me.

Luca's smirk widened. "Yeah. Our record label is terrified of anything happening to ruin my voice. I like to think it's for other reasons too."

I was about to make a quip about his ego. But Luca ran his tongue up the underside of my shaft, and the words died.

And when he took me in his mouth completely?

I lost the ability to think.

Turned out that ego of his was well-earned.

He didn't rush. He explored every inch of my shaft like he was memorising it. Laving his tongue along the thick vein on the underside. Mouthing at my glans. Swirling his tongue over the head and dipping under my foreskin.

I didn't know what to do with my hands. On the rare occasion Suzie had gone down on me, she didn't like me to touch her. I'd never had an issue with it. Sure, I'd get off, but I'd have to work to get myself there.

With Luca, everything was different. He was dragging me towards my orgasm with alarming speed, and he'd barely got started. My fingers were scrabbling desperately against the lift wall as I tried to keep myself from grabbing him.

He leaned back, humming slightly as my cock fell from his lips with a pop. "You can touch me."

"What?"

He smouldered up at me. Moving slowly, he grabbed my wrists and placed my hands on his head. My fingers instinctively curled in his hair, holding him tight. "I'm not made of glass. You can touch me. I like it."

He didn't give me the opportunity to respond, sinking back down on my shaft while watching me from under his dark lashes.

I groaned, my hands flexing in his hair. He was sucking harder now, his cheeks hollowing as the head of my cock hit the back of his throat. "Holy fucking shit, Luca."

The man in question smirked as much as he could with my dick filling his throat. Never before had I thought I'd be doing this with a guy…and that he'd look so fucking gorgeous while doing it.

Luca cupped my balls in his hand, rolling them before sliding his fingers back to stroke over my taint.

"Fuck!" I didn't have time to warn him. My release hit out of nowhere, shooting down his throat. Luca didn't seem bothered, swallowing rapidly, making that addictive humming sound again.

It seemed to last forever. Normally it'd be over in a few seconds, barely worth the effort to get there.

Not only had Luca taken me to the summit so quickly, but the fall was so worth it. Every nerve ending felt on fire, like he'd doused me with gasoline before setting me ablaze.

It made me want to give him a box of matches and beg him to never leave.

"Sorry," I gasped, my chest heaving. "I should've warned you."

Luca was still teasing the slit of my cock with his tongue like he was searching out any lingering drops of cum. He leaned back slightly, his smirk wider than ever. "Nah. I like how you taste."

He gave the tip of my softening shaft a tiny kiss before tucking me back into my trousers and zipping them. I stayed dead still, gaping at the care and attention he was lavishing on me.

"Hmm," he said, poking at one of my knees. "Yep. Just like I suspected."

"What?"

He grinned up at me, and fuck me. That look on his face set a whole kaleidoscope of butterflies free in my stomach. "Looks like hell has frozen over."

I frowned at him. What the fuck was he talking about?

He stood, his tongue in his cheek as he boxed me in with his arms. "You said the day you went weak-kneed for a celebrity would be the day hell froze over. Correct me if I'm wrong, but those are some pretty weak knees you're sporting there."

My smile spread slowly over my face. "You're an egotistical little shit."

He brushed his still-grinning lips over mine. "I think you like that."

I did. There was a fine line between arrogance and confidence, and Luca straddled it beautifully.

He moved, and his erection brushed over my groin. "Uhh...do you want me to take care of that for you?"

I was stunned when that came out of my mouth. Was that just the British politeness instilled in me from a young age...or did I actually *want* to touch his dick?

"No." He gave me one more sweet kiss before tugging us both to the floor. "It's fine. I'll save it."

We sat beside one another, not a whisper of space between our bodies. Luca took my hand, wrapping his long fingers around mine like it was the most normal thing in the world. Which, for him, it was.

For me, it was something new. Something that had my breath catching in my throat and my heart beating faster.

What was happening to me? Why did this moment feel more intimate than when my cock had been in Luca's mouth?

Belatedly I realised I hadn't responded to Luca. "Saving it for what?"

He gave me a wry half-smile. "Well...that kind of depends on you. Either I'm going to go home and have the best yet very lonely jerk-off session while picturing how you looked while I was on my knees for you."

An image of Luca lying on his bed popped into my head. His cock in his hand, his head thrown back as he groaned my name.

I shivered. Huh. Didn't think the thought of

another man getting himself off would be appealing, but I was learning all sorts of things about myself today. "Or?"

"Or..." Luca's husky voice dropped to a whisper, accompanied by a flash of vulnerability in his eyes. "Or you come home with me, and I show you other ways I can make you weak at the knees."

Chapter 6

Luca

I knew as soon as I said the words that I'd pushed Ollie too far.

He stiffened, the blissed-out guy and his dopey relaxed grin vanishing instantly. "Ah, I don't think we should. I mean, this was great and all, but—"

"Forget it," I said gently, cutting him off. I didn't want to hear his reasons. His excuses for why he didn't want more. "I shouldn't have said anything."

This is why you shouldn't play with straight boys.

I huffed and ran a hand over my face. I'd learned that lesson already. It wasn't Ollie's fault he wasn't attracted to me. It wasn't his fault he was the first person in *years* to see *me*, not just Luca Weston.

Nor was it his fault my imagination had got carried away while I took him apart with my mouth. It always did like to go a bit wild, picturing things I should know were out of my reach by now. Envisioning lazy mornings waking him up with a blowjob. Seeing him smile at me from the wings of the stage. Throwing my all into every performance because I knew I'd be walking away from the spotlight and straight into his waiting arms. I should've learned by now to not get carried away.

The blame lay with me. Honestly, what had I been thinking? Picturing a whole future with him because he'd been *nice* to me? Because I felt a connection unlike anything I'd felt before?

Suddenly he was too close. Having him pressed against me and knowing I couldn't touch him again was the worst kind of torture. I couldn't just drop his hand and move though. That would be cruel after what we'd just shared.

Giving a fake yawn, I let go of his hand and stretched my arms over my head. Nope. That still wasn't enough. I could still feel him. Still smell him.

Fuck. He shouldn't affect me this much. It couldn't be healthy.

Jumping to my feet, I paced the tiny space and pretended to shake and stretch my limbs. "Man, I am cramped up."

"Uh-huh." Ollie's voice was thin, and he wasn't looking at me.

"Do you think it'll be much longer?" I bounced on my toes, eyeing the closed doors like I could open them through sheer will alone. Anything to be away from Ollie before I did something stupid—like go to my knees again and beg him to let me see him once we got out of here.

"Hopefully not," Ollie replied. He sounded far away, the hand I'd been holding slowly opening and closing.

I paused, staring down at it. Ollie glanced up and followed my gaze. He blushed hard, tucking his hand under his thigh. "Should we call them again?"

"No," I said with a sigh. I plopped to the floor, sitting opposite Ollie. That probably wouldn't make things easier, given that was where we'd sat earlier before I'd fucked everything up. "They'll be busy saving people who need them. We can wait it out."

Ollie nodded, a muscle in his jaw ticking. He didn't reply, closing his eyes and letting his head fall back against the wall.

It was too reminiscent of how he'd looked seconds before he came. I cleared my throat to get him to open his eyes. To look at me so I could remember why climbing back onto his lap was a stupid idea. "So…got any interesting plans for the rest of the day?"

His eyes snapped open, his gaze hot. Shit. Was he thinking about the plans I'd suggested? "Not really. I booked the whole day off for the interview. I'd planned on maybe taking Suzie out to lunch and then meeting Callum this evening."

I winced. "Yeah…maybe not. Does Suzie not work?"

Ollie snorted. "Not often. Well, that's not true. She works, but she can't ever stay in a job for longer than a week. Her CV is longer than most people's shopping list."

"How does she get by then? Do her parents still support her?" I knew a lot of people relied on their parents until their mid-twenties, but I couldn't think of anything worse. I liked to pull my own weight, even before we'd hit the big time. From collecting glasses to pizza delivery, I'd taken any job if it equalled a paycheque.

"Not her parents, no." Ollie sighed and raised an eyebrow.

I groaned as the penny dropped. "Fuck, Ollie. Not only did she cheat on you with your best friend, but she did it while you were supporting her financially?"

"Got it in one," Ollie said, rubbing his forehead. "Thing is, I never minded paying for stuff for her. I knew I was lucky because I'd found a job doing something I loved. It didn't seem right to tell her she needed to be unhappy doing something when I could provide enough for both of us."

"Was she grateful, at least?"

Ollie shrugged, and my hatred for the faceless Suzie increased. "I guess. She did bitch at me about the hours I worked, but I couldn't really turn down overtime when it was offered. Not if we wanted to make rent every month...oh fuck."

"What?"

"Rent," he said with a curse. "Both our names are on the rental agreement."

"Why would you do that if you're the one paying the rent?"

Ollie rubbed his head again. I itched to grab his hand and kiss the stress away. "She insisted. Said it was safer because if we ever broke up, she needed to make sure she had a roof over her head. I didn't argue because..."

"Because you didn't think you were going to break up," I finished for him. "I get why you did it, but that's fucking shitty. I'm guessing you don't think she'll move out then."

"Nope." His chin dropped to his chest, and he suddenly looked much older. "I don't think she will. She'll probably get Callum to move in and take over paying."

"Then he's an idiot too."

Ollie lifted his head, a tiny smile threatening to

crack through his dark mood. "You calling me an idiot?"

I pretended to consider it. "If it looks like one and talks like one, then…yeah."

As I'd hoped, the smile cracked through, followed by a deep chuckle. "Well, given I'm now probably single, homeless, and stuck in a dead-end job, I can't argue with you."

"You should call *Identity,*" I urged, returning to our earlier conversation. "If this is your dream job, you can't walk away from it."

"Yeah." Ollie's smile faded. "Maybe."

I bit the inside of my cheek. I wanted to encourage him. But he wasn't mine to push.

He was a stranger.

Even if he felt like anything but.

Something popped into my brain. "Hey, what about your dad? You said about your mum, but is he still around?"

"No." Ollie's face turned stony, his hands clenching on his lap. "He's not around. Hasn't been for a very long time."

Something heavy sat in my stomach. "Have you been on your own since your mum passed?"

He nodded once before coolly meeting my eyes. "I don't want your pity, Luca."

It wasn't pity I wanted to give him, but comfort. His no-nonsense tone told me this wasn't a topic for discussion.

"How about you?" Ollie asked, turning the subject back on me. "What are you up to for the rest of the day?"

I contained my sigh. I had no right to expect him to open up to me more than he already had.

But fuck, how I wanted that right.

Following his lead, I told him about the interview I

was supposed to be having with *Identity* before heading to London to meet the rest of the band. We were scheduled to shoot a music video for our upcoming single before flying to LA for show rehearsals.

We fell into an easy conversation. I found myself opening up to Ollie, telling him little details that might seem insignificant but were anything but. Things I'd never normally share with someone I barely knew, let alone a journalist. Like where my favourite places to eat in London were. How Arlo and I often teamed up against Kai and Silas for prank wars while on tour. The fact that I was exhausted by the constant media scrutiny.

That last one had Ollie interrupting me. "If you feel like that, why are you going to an interview today?"

I gave him a wry smile. "My feelings aren't taken into account. My manager thinks this is needed...especially with last night's escapades being splashed everywhere."

Ollie made a sympathetic noise. "After this though? Will you get a break from it all?"

"Yeah, for a bit. We've got five months until the tour starts. Kevin, that's our manager, is trying to arrange for a journalist to tag along. To document the whole thing from start to finish."

"And you don't want that," Ollie surmised. "Because you won't be able to relax knowing you've got the press watching your every move."

"Got it in one. That's the other reason Kevin made me come here today. He's hoping the person I'm meeting with will be able to *see the benefits* of the journalist being someone from *Identity*."

"Kevin's your manager, right? Why can't you just tell him no?"

I picked at a loose thread at the knee of my jeans. As with all the outfits I wore to media events, it had been preselected for me. It drove me fucking crazy how many of them had rips and holes. Considering how much they cost, you'd think they'd be in one piece. But no. Apparently, this was *fashion*.

Fuck, I was getting old.

"I wish I could," I said glumly. "But Kevin's been with us for years. We got royally fucked over by our first manager, and Kevin is a thousand times better than him."

"That's fair." Ollie pursed his lips like he was unsure if he should continue. "But if you're really uncomfortable about having press around you for the tour, you should put your foot down."

"Maybe." There wasn't any point explaining how the dynamic between Kevin and the band worked. We might pay him, but he was the one in charge. As a journalist himself, I half expected Ollie to try to convince me that having the press there wouldn't be invasive. That the benefits outweighed the negatives.

But he didn't. He just encouraged me to put myself first.

When was the last time anyone had done that?

"I want to see you again."

Ollie was silent for a few moments, his face progressively getting more crimson. Fuck, I wanted to know what he was thinking. What was he imagining to turn his cheeks such a gorgeous colour? "That's not a good idea."

"Why not?"

He fiddled with his tie, still blushing furiously. I'd bet my very extensive car collection that me being a guy wasn't what was holding him back. "You're…you. And I'm me. You're literally the most famous person on the planet right now. I'm…I'm a nobody."

"Not to me you're not."

Ollie finally met my eyes. "You barely know me."

That was irrelevant as far as I was concerned. I knew that letting Ollie slip out of my life as suddenly as he'd entered would always leave me wondering *what if*. "That's why you should see me again. So I can get to know you better."

Ollie was already shaking his head, and my heart sank. "No, I don't think so. It's not…I think you're great, but…fuck. I hadn't even *considered* fooling around with a guy until today. Obviously, I've got some shit to sort through in my head. But asking me to be seen in public with you? That's too much. I can't have my life and sexuality up for debate when I haven't even figured it out for myself."

"We don't have to meet in public." The resignation on Ollie's face was making me desperate.

He gave me a small smile. "Okay, say we do that. How long are you willing to hide? How long before word gets out? These things never stay hidden, Luca. You know that."

My heart sank. That was the one argument I had no comeback for. It was one thing to open myself to the spotlight, but to ask someone else to do it?

It was a lot.

Just then, the lights flickered on.

We both blinked at the sudden brightness, our arms jerking out to the sides when the lift began to move.

Neither of us stood. As the lift smoothly glided

upwards, we stared at each other.

There was so much I wanted to say to him. I wanted to persuade him to give us a chance. To tell him I'd felt more alive in the couple of hours we'd spent trapped in this tiny space than I had in years.

But he'd *just* got out of a long-term relationship.

He thought he was straight.

And I was out of time.

There was a quiet *ding*, and the metal doors slid smoothly open.

The cacophony of shouts and flashing lights shattered whatever had existed between Ollie and me. It seemed as though every press member within a twenty-mile radius was waiting for us in the corridor. Cameras were going off everywhere like they were hoping the doors would open to reveal Luca Weston in yet another scandalous position.

A little while ago, they would've done.

I stumbled to my feet while Ollie did the same. His lips were in a grim line as he took in the sheer number of people battling to try and shove forwards to get into the lift.

Then he did the last thing I expected. Reaching out to grab my arm, he yanked me behind him, stepping forwards so his slightly bigger frame shielded me.

"Back up," he barked. "Give him some space, for fuck's sake."

If anything, the press went wilder. Shit. While Ollie's protective behaviour was enough to give me butterflies, it was the one thing guaranteed to open him up to scrutiny.

"Maybe you should let me go," I said quietly, staring at the tense lines of his broad shoulders.

"Not until I know you're going to be safe," he said through gritted teeth. "Don't you have security or something?"

"Move!" As if Ollie's question had summoned him, I heard Jack's firm voice cutting over the din. "Back up unless you want to be escorted from the building."

With a lot of grumbling, the press slowly backed away. Jack appeared, his face stoic. The only giveaway that this situation was more stressful than usual was the small lines at the corner of his mouth.

He also wasn't alone. Bustling after him, out of breath and covered in sweat, was Kevin.

Judging by the scowl on his face, he wasn't loving the fact I'd managed to get more press attention mere hours after he'd told me to lay low.

It wasn't like this situation was my fault. One of my fans or someone who worked in the building must've tipped off the press that I was trapped.

Even with the appearance of Jack and Kevin, Ollie hadn't moved. Still shielding me from the press, he waited like a statue as Jack cleared a path.

I watched over his shoulder as Kevin took in Ollie's protective stance. His scowl developed into a sneer, and suddenly, I wanted to switch our positions. I wanted to hide Ollie from that look. To keep anything negative in my life from tarring him.

Then Kevin's gaze met mine, and I could read his thoughts clear as day.

It's obvious something happened here. I can see it, and so can the press.

Why are you always getting yourself into these situations?

Can't you go one day without fucking up?

If anything gets out, you'll fuck up negotiations with the label.

Panic filled me. I'd told Ollie so much. Given him insight into my life that I never gave *anyone*. Small details people would pay a fortune to get their hands on.

And that was even before we got into the fact I'd gone down on him. Seduced him into wanting a man despite him never wanting one before.

Just imagine what people would say about that.

What the fuck had I been thinking? Ollie was a *stranger.*

Kevin drew closer, his eyes narrowed. Before he could speak, I stepped around Ollie and held my hand up to stop Kevin. He paused, and I could see in the set of his mouth what he expected me to do.

Taking a deep breath, I turned to face Ollie, speaking in a low whisper so no one would hear. "I need you to sign an NDA."

Ollie's eyes widened. "What?"

"A non-disclosure agreement," I whispered quickly, all too aware of the many eyes watching us. "Promising you won't tell anyone about what happened in there."

"I know what a fucking NDA is," Ollie hissed. "I told you that you can trust me."

I could feel Kevin's gaze burning into the back of my neck. "I know, but I can't rely on that. I need you to sign it. Please."

That was the moment. I saw it happen. Saw the change shift on Ollie's face. The instant that whatever tentative hope I might have for our future shattered.

Ollie nodded sharply, stepping back to put some distance between us. "Sure. If that's what you need."

The impassive mask he wore was like a kick to my gut. But this was for the best...right?

I opened my mouth to apologise. To take what I'd asked back. But that was not what came out. "Kevin here will collect your details and arrange the documentation."

A muscle jumped in Ollie's jaw as he looked past me. "Great."

I needed to leave. The longer I stayed here, staring at this man, the more the rumours would grow.

But I couldn't bring myself to do it.

"Ollie..." I stepped closer, my voice dropping pleadingly. For what though? What did I want from him?

"Leave it," he said sharply. He still wasn't looking at me. "You need to go."

Jack's hand gripped my shoulder. "He's right, Luca. I've got the press held back, but they won't stay long."

"Okay." I drank in every detail of Ollie, knowing it was the last time I'd do so. "It was great to meet you."

"You too."

Then, like he couldn't resist the temptation any longer, his gaze met mine. The hollowness he'd exuded earlier was back.

I hated that I'd put it back there.

But with Jack leading me out of the lift and Kevin swooping in to clear up my mess, there was nothing I could do.

Nothing except leave and hope the memory of Ollie would vanish from my life as suddenly as he'd entered it.

Chapter 7

Ollie

Five months later

Hours after everyone else had left, I closed my laptop and stretched. There was no reason for me to be here this late, but I still felt the need to prove myself. No matter how often Becky, my department head, scolded me for putting in unpaid overtime, I couldn't let it go. Not when I knew how damned lucky I was to get a second chance at my dream job.

I'd been so surprised when *Identity* called the day after the whole lift…incident. Once I'd handed over my contact information to Luca's manager, it hadn't even occurred to me to go to the *Identity* offices and explain the situation. The whole encounter with Luca seemed to have removed my ability to make logical decisions. Which was probably how I ended up coming down his throat and then signing an agreement vowing not to go to the press. I'd barely heard the threats about what would happen if I broke the agreement his creepy manager had flung my way. I'd been too busy watching Luca disappear from my life and wondering what the fuck I should do now.

In the space of one morning, everything in my life that I'd thought I'd known had been flipped on its head. My relationship. My closest friendship. My career path. My living situation.

Even my sexuality.

But none of that mattered as much as watching Luca leave, knowing I'd never see him in the flesh again.

So no. Even without the NDA or threats, I wouldn't have told anyone anything about that day. It was sad that Luca hadn't trusted me, but I understood where he was coming from. I'd been mad at the time, but looking back at it now...I got it. His whole life was lived in the spotlight. People taking advantage of him was probably something that happened regularly. It made sense he'd assume the worst of me too.

It made sense, but it hurt, especially after how I'd opened up to him.

But that was all in the past.

Part of me had wondered if I'd hear from him. I'd told him I didn't want to see him again, but nothing about Luca suggested he gave up easily. Especially since his manager had my contact info.

But when my phone rang the following day, it hadn't been Luca on the other end of the line. Instead, it'd been Becky from *Identity,* offering me another chance at my dream job.

Determined not to have another repeat, I'd arrived over an hour early to my interview.

And I'd taken the stairs.

My interview had been surprisingly short. It was more of a meet-and-greet than the grilling I'd expected.

What had been even more shocking was that they'd hired me on the spot. I'd walked out of there in a daze, clutching the contract like a lifeline.

I'd been in such a fog that I hadn't realised I'd stepped into the same lift until it started moving. Memories from the day before had assaulted me. Luca teasing me. On his knees. His full lips wrapped around my cock.

That was when it hit me that I had no one to call. No one to celebrate my news with.

My only living family member, my arsehole father, may as well be dead as far as I was concerned. His treatment of my mother growing up still haunted my nightmares.

He'd lost the right to updates about my life the second he'd raised a hand to her. Not that he seemed to want any. I hadn't seen hide nor hair of him since the day he stormed out when I was thirteen.

Good fucking riddance.

Months had passed since the day I'd landed the job, and my life had moved on. Not massively, but enough to give me hope for the future. I'd made friends with one of my coworkers, Riley. We weren't as close as I had been to Callum, but that was okay. I was still stinging from his betrayal almost half a year later. Time had allowed me to recognise how toxic my relationship with Suzie had become. Now I could look back on it and be grateful that part of my life was done.

But losing Callum hurt far more than losing Suzie. It'd be a long time before I trusted anyone to get that close to me again.

Packing my few bits into my bag, I swung it over my shoulder and made my way down and out to my car. Not only had this job come with a much higher salary than I'd anticipated, but a company car too. Even more shockingly, when Becky discovered I was staying in a Premier Inn while flat hunting, she'd sent me information on a company-owned building. I'd never heard of a business offering their employees housing, let alone at a reduced rent rate. I'd said yes without even viewing it. It could've been a studio on the top floor of a concrete tower block, but anything was better than room 226 in a budget hotel. If I'd been kept awake by one more couple having an extra marital affair, I would've likely committed murder.

Fortunately, it was better than I'd dreamt. Far nicer than the flat I'd shared with Suzie. Nicer even than any hotel I'd stayed in.

I'd walked into a fully furnished two-bed flat with massive floor-to-ceiling windows in the living room and a kitchen fancy enough to give a chef a wet dream. The furnishings wouldn't have looked out of place in a John Lewis store, all matching and shit. If that wasn't enough, the building had a doorman and a gym, for fuck's sake. The second I'd seen it, I'd phoned Becky, convinced they'd made a mistake. Even with my generous salary, the place was wildly out of my price range. It was obvious there'd been a cock-up.

To my shock, Becky had assured me the amount quoted was correct. She said something about the company owner having more money than sense and was serious about employee benefits. I was sceptical. If anything, it was probably one of those dodgy tax evasion schemes I'd seen on the news. But hey, if they wanted to put me up in a luxury pad for a pittance, I couldn't afford to say no.

Five months later, I still had to pinch myself when I entered. Growing up with nothing, I'd always wondered how rich people did it. Did they walk into rooms and just not notice their surroundings?

I wasn't rich, but this was a far cry from what I'd known as a child. Maybe that was why I struggled to believe this was all mine. Or maybe it was because it wasn't really. I was at the mercy of the company owner. At any time, they could decide to sell or increase the rent to match market value.

Then I'd be fucked.

That was the other reason I worked so hard. I wasn't going to do anything to put my new standard of living at risk. I was going to be the best-damned employee *Identity* had ever seen.

Grabbing a can of Tiny Rebel beer from the fridge, I filled a glass before flopping on the sofa and pulling out my phone. My finger hovered over the Uber Eats app. I really should order some food because I hadn't made it to the supermarket this week. Now that I'd upped my hours at the gym from sheer boredom, I needed to not skip meals.

Instead, I clicked the icon beside it and opened Grindr.

Just like I had every night since the week after I met Luca, I flicked through profile after profile.

And just like every other time, I closed it without doing anything.

Swigging from my beer, I clicked the TV on and selected *Air Crash Investigation* out of habit. Some people thought it was weird that I relaxed by watching this show, but given those same people thought it was normal to fall asleep listening to true-crime podcasts, I wasn't bothered.

Coming to terms with the fact I was less straight than I'd believed hadn't been a huge stumbling block for me. I mean, sure, it'd taken some time to get used to. Hours lying awake, revisiting the memory of Luca on his knees, my cock in his mouth. Evenings spent watching gay porn and realising it wasn't just Luca who turned me on. Maybe sex hadn't been my issue, but the people I'd been having it with.

Maybe it would've been trickier if it had happened at another time or if someone other than Luca had been responsible for opening my eyes. But with my life in chaos, accepting I was attracted to men was one of the easier things to get my head around.

Refusing to acknowledge this part of myself wasn't an option. That'd be like admitting I was ashamed of what happened between Luca and me. Like I hadn't lain awake wishing it could happen again. Imagining what it might be like to take him in my mouth and return the favour.

That was the thing that had me tossing my phone aside every night. It wasn't that I didn't want to hook up with guys…it was that those guys weren't Luca.

Which was stupid. I was lusting after Luca Weston, same as approximately a few billion other people. The difference with me was I didn't want him because he was a rock star.

I just wanted *him*. Luca. The guy who got me to open my soul with a few simple words. The stranger who taught me things about myself I'd never realised. The man who showed me his vulnerabilities. Who allowed me to help him.

But he didn't exist. Not really. That was a snapshot

of Luca. A side he'd shown because of the situation we were in. His behaviour when the real world crashed in had demonstrated how little we'd work in reality.

I downed the rest of my beer. There I went again, making the situation more than it was. Luca had asked me for a hookup, not a relationship.

Like I'd summoned him with my thoughts alone, a Google alert pinged on my phone. I shouldn't check it. I shouldn't even have the damned alert set up.

Luca was my addiction, one I wanted desperately to kick. Keeping tabs on him like this was unhealthy, feeding my obsession over a man I'd met once. I was on the precipice of turning into one of those stalker fans, building up a whole future for us based on a single encounter.

I knew all of this...but I couldn't help myself.

I grabbed the phone and clicked on the notification. I prepared myself for the worst, to see headlines about Luca's latest fling. There'd been nothing yet, but that didn't ease the knot of anxiety.

Extra dates added for Rude Awakenings: Caffeine Daydreams' stadium tour! Tickets go on sale at 10:00 a.m. tomorrow.

I tapped the sides of my phone. So far, I'd resisted the urge to buy a ticket. To go and see Luca in the place where he thrived the most would only make my obsession with him worse.

No. I couldn't do it. It was too risky. It was bad enough that I caved every night. I'd go to bed, determined not to think about him. Then before I knew it, it was three a.m., and I was scrolling through social media, drinking up videos and photos of him like a man dying of thirst. And I hated it because not one of them was of *him*. The big smiles he gave his fans weren't anything like the ones he'd given me. When he played up to the crowd, rolling his hips and peeking suggestively from under his eyelashes, it was wrong. I could see it for the act it was.

None of these videos compared to the Luca I'd met in the lift.

I finished my beer, staring unseeing at the drama unfolding on the television. What was I doing with my life?

All those hours wasted thinking about a man who probably didn't remember my name.

"Sorry, can you repeat that?" Becky tilted her head to the side, making her dark hair fall like a curtain over her face. "Which part do you need me to repeat?"

"Let's try all of it." I shook my head, trying to clear the buzzing sound filling my ears. "There's no way I heard you correctly."

"I think you did," Becky said mildly, amusement dancing on her brightly painted lips. "Caffeine Daydreams have agreed to let a journalist profile them while on tour. We've decided to send you."

"Why me?" I blurted.

Becky rocked back in her chair, scrutinising me with a piercing gaze. "Why aren't you jumping at this? This is the sort of opportunity most journalists at your level would *kill* for. It'll put your name on the map, opening all sorts of doors for you. We aren't talking a single article here. This will be an in-depth look at every aspect of their life on tour. Your work will have top billing in not one but *six* of our editions. Is this really the sort of thing you want to turn down?"

Fuck. I couldn't tell her the truth—that the thought of being in the same space as Luca for a sustained time period made me want to dance and vomit simultaneously. Fortunately, I had years of experience when it came to schooling my emotions. "That's what I don't understand though. Surely an opportunity like this would be better suited for a more senior staff member? I don't want to tread on anyone's toes."

"Are you saying you can't handle this?"

I winced internally. The last thing I wanted was Becky thinking I wasn't capable of something like this. Because let's be real, if it was any other band on Earth, I would already be out the door and planning the focus of the first piece. "No, of course I can."

"Excellent," she said with a brisk nod. "You've got a meeting scheduled with the band and their management in London first thing tomorrow morning. You can take the rest of the day off to get yourself organised. The itinerary has been emailed to you. You'll need to prepare to be away for six weeks."

"Six weeks," I echoed numbly.

"Yes." Becky's attention had been caught by something on her computer. "One article a week."

"Wait," I blurted as another argument occurred to me. "You need to send someone else. I've...met Luca before. Trust me, he won't want me there."

"That's not possible." Becky frowned at her screen, her fingers tapping at the keyboard. "They requested you specifically."

It was a struggle to keep the shock off my face. Luca had asked...for me? Why? After the way we'd left things, I couldn't imagine why he'd want to be trapped with me for six weeks. "Are you sure?"

Becky turned her attention away from the computer with a sigh. Folding her hands on her desk, she studied me seriously. "They didn't just request you, Ollie. It's part of the deal. If you aren't the one I send, we lose the contract. It's you or no one, I'm afraid."

My stomach flipped. "So that's the reason why you've chosen me. Not because you think I'm the best person for the job."

"Not necessarily." Becky pursed her lips. "Your name is actually one that would've been put forward for consideration. Your work speaks for itself, and I would've championed you being one of the front runners."

"But I wouldn't have been the one you chose," I surmised.

"No." She gave a tight smile. "And that's not a reflection on your ability to do this—and do it *well.* But you were right when you said this type of opportunity would normally go to a more senior staff member..."

"Not one who's only been here five months," I finished for her. "Yeah, that would make more sense."

"Ultimately, I can't force you to go. But if you don't, we lose the whole deal. Caffeine Daydreams has always been...wary around the media. You'd be granted a level of access to them that's totally unprecedented."

Suddenly the reasoning for why Luca wanted me there made perfect sense. I'd seen him through a panic attack, fucked around with him, and listened to him.

And once I stepped out of that lift, I hadn't said a word. Sure, I had an NDA, but people broke those all the time.

Luca wanted me because he could trust me to be professional. To respect his limits with what could and couldn't be published.

Relief warred with disappointment. Of course he wasn't insisting I go just for the chance to see me again. Other than deciding I was the one for this job, he probably hadn't given me or what happened that day a second thought.

Could I really do it though? It felt like I'd be opening myself up to a world of pain. My obsession with Luca wouldn't be cured by spending time in his company.

But maybe…maybe if I drew strict boundaries, I could make it work. After all, I'd be there in a professional capacity. So long as I thought of Luca as the subject of a story, and nothing more, there wouldn't be an issue.

That was what Luca would be expecting anyway. He'd reached out to me in a professional capacity, not a personal one.

I'd be the most professional damned journalist he'd ever met.

"Ollie?" Becky's voice cut through my thoughts, making me realise I'd been sitting in silence. "Will you do it?"

I had to. I couldn't fuck it up for the company.

That was why I said *yes* before practically running from her office. I didn't stop until I hit the toilets, splashing water on my face and trying to get my shaking hands under control.

That's the reason, I told myself sternly. Water dripped from my pale skin as my reflection stared back at me wide-eyed. *Not because you want to see Luca.*

If I repeated it often enough, maybe I'd start to

believe it.

Leaving the toilets, I ran smack-bang into Riley. Before I met him, I thought accountants were quiet and restrained folk.

Riley proved that stereotype wrong on our very first social. He'd taken to the stage to bellow out "Don't Stop Me Now" by Queen and followed that up by leading the conga line.

I didn't know what expression I wore, but whatever it was had my new friend steering me into an empty meeting room. "What's happened?"

I smoothed down a wrinkle in my shirt, trying to calm myself. "I'm going on tour with a band. Going to be doing a full profile with six articles."

Riley's face lit up, smiling so big that his cheeks lifted his wide-rimmed glasses slightly. "Ollie Winters! Why don't you look happier? That's fantastic news! Which band?"

I took a deep breath. "Caffeine Daydreams."

Riley's smile fell away, his blue eyes widening. "Shit."

"Exactly."

Riley ran a hand through his short dark hair. Being gay, he was someone I'd gone to for advice while coming to terms with my sexuality. It had taken many lunches, many nights out, and a lot of Dutch courage before I finally felt comfortable enough to open up to Riley.

Even though I'd never told Riley what happened with Luca in that lift, I hadn't managed to hide the fact I had a massive crush on him. "How do you feel about that?"

"I don't know," I groaned. "What if I see him and can't act like a professional? Or, even worse, what if he pretends he doesn't know me?"

"Or," Riley countered, "what if everything goes smoothly and your career skyrockets? Let's be real, Ollie. Junior journalists *never* get opportunities like this. Can you really afford to turn it down?"

"No." It was the same conclusion I'd come to while in the toilets. "But I'm still...freaked out."

He squeezed my shoulder comfortingly. "It would be weird if you weren't. But I have a feeling this tour will change your life in the best possible ways."

Chapter 8

Luca

"Will you quit pacing?"

I stopped, turning my glare on Silas. "Sorry, am I not allowed to *move* now?"

"There's moving, and then there's wearing a path in the floor," Silas drawled. His long legs were sprawled in front of him, his blond hair artfully arranged in a carefree way that had probably taken him hours. With his lean physique and bright-blue eyes, he looked like he should be wielding a surfboard instead of a bass guitar. "Sit down before you scare the guy off."

"Who died and made you king?" I retorted.

"Back off," Kai shot back. I'd never been attracted to any of my bandmates, but even I could concede that Kai was one of the most beautiful male specimens to grace the planet. With his flawless dark skin, chiselled jawline, and soulful brown eyes, he was the whole package. He merely had to walk through a club to have men falling at his feet. Shame the only guy he wanted was the one who'd never see him that way. "Don't take it out on Silas because someone pissed in your cornflakes this morning."

I debated continuing the argument just to work out some of my tension, but with the way Kai was now glaring at me, it wasn't worth it. Dropping into my seat, I gave Silas a half-smile. "Sorry, man."

"No harm, no foul." Our perpetually easygoing bassist spread his hands. "Just saying, if your guy walks in to see you about to go off like a loose cannon, he'll run in the other direction."

I pinched the bridge of my nose. "He's not *my* guy."

"So you've said." Silas grinned. "But, come on, you've not *looked* at another person since you met this Ollie fella. And all the trouble you've gone to to make sure he—"

"Silas," I said warningly. We might be alone in the room, but who knew who might be listening in from outside. Even worse, if Ollie walked in and heard the wrong thing, my whole plan would be fucked before it even got started. I may have crossed several lines, interfering in his life the way I had. It hadn't stopped me though. Not when I knew how much happier Ollie was due to my...meddling.

"Fine." Silas winked, leaning back in his chair. "But he's gonna work it out. He'd have to be a prize fool to not realise how you feel about him."

From the corner of my eye, I saw Kai wince. Sympathy twisted in my gut as he shoved back from the table and busied himself with the coffee machine in the corner.

"Mind you," Silas continued, oblivious to what had just happened, "he'd have to be a fool to get involved with you in the first place."

"Haha," I said dryly. I checked the time on my phone for the thousandth time. "Why isn't he here yet?"

"He will be," Kai said, his voice rich and deep as he slid a coffee in front of Silas before returning to his chair. His expression was still hard, but when Silas grinned happily at him in thanks, it softened.

Silas sipped his drink and hummed contentedly. Kai watched him for a beat longer, the bleak yearning clear in his eyes. He seemed to sense me watching him, turning his gaze to me and shaking his head slightly. I bit back a sigh but didn't say anything. I'd learned a long time ago to not interfere with those two.

I checked my phone again, and Kai spoke. "Relax. We're early. Arlo isn't even here yet."

Like his words had summoned him, the door slammed open and our drummer stormed in. Ignoring us all, he made a beeline for the coffee station. Once he'd made himself a drink and piled a heap of pastries onto a plate, he returned to the table. Only then did he acknowledge us. "Where's your grumpy security guard today?"

His question could've been aimed at any of us. Even if he hadn't passed Silas's and Kai's guards in the hall, we would've known it was me he was speaking to. "Jack's downstairs with Kevin, waiting to greet Ollie."

Arlo grunted, tearing a danish in two. "Lucky Ollie."

I exchanged a look with Kai. "You know, if you want to switch back, we can discuss it with Kevin."

"Nope." Arlo's response was curt as he scowled down at the pastry like it'd done something to offend him. "Like I said before, there's no point. Jack doesn't want to be around me, and the feeling's…mutual."

Well, that was a load of bullshit. Before I could

push the issue further, the door opened again. I was on my feet in a second, my heart pounding.

Kevin entered first, speaking over his shoulder to someone. I bounced on my toes, impatient to get a glimpse of the man I hadn't been able to stop thinking about.

This was it. The moment I'd been waiting for. Either I was going to see him and realise I'd been building it all up in my head. That I'd imagined the intense connection between us. Or I was about to turn my whole life upside down if that was what it took to get him to take a chance on me.

Kevin stepped to the side, and he was there.

His blond hair was shorter than that day in the lift. If I wasn't mistaken, he'd packed on some more muscle since then too. God, I ached to strip him down to see him in all his glory. Dressed in a sharp blue suit that brought out the colour of his eyes, there wasn't a coffee stain in sight.

He was everything I remembered...but yet so much more. I wanted to get closer to breathe him in. To sniff him to see if he wore the same cologne. To stroke my hand over his jaw just to see if he'd shiver like he had that day in the lift.

I did none of those things. Obviously. That sort of behaviour led to a restraining order.

"Caffeine Daydreams, this is Ollie Winters from *Identity*. Ollie, this is the band."

My bandmates gazes slid to mine, even Arlo's. Waiting for me to speak. To take advantage of this moment they *knew* I'd been waiting for.

But I was frozen. I couldn't do anything other than gawp at Ollie.

There was an awkward pause before Silas got up from his chair, the others scrambling to follow.

Ollie's smile was strained as they introduced themselves and made small talk. It was nothing like the one I remembered him giving me in the lift. This one was tight, barely there. His gaze shuttered and his tone clipped.

I couldn't stand it. That was what got my feet moving, shoving my bandmates aside until there was nothing between Ollie and me except ten inches of air and a boatload of tension. "Hello again, Ollie."

That fake smile slipped from his face. He sucked in a shaky breath, rocking onto his heels like he was fighting to not take a step.

I had no idea if that step would've been forwards or backwards. Ollie shook himself, and I could almost see him transform into another person before my eyes. "Mr Weston, lovely to see you."

I eyed the hand he held out. "Mr Weston?"

That's how you wanna play this?

"Yes. I'm very grateful for this posting, and I intend on doing the best possible job I can."

His eyes were hard, his unspoken message clear. Ollie was setting professional boundaries.

Too bad for him that I'd never been good at respecting those. I couldn't challenge him on it, not with Kevin looking on. If our manager even got the slightest whiff of the real reason I insisted on Ollie being here, he'd fire him like a shot.

Taking his hand with mine, I made sure to rub my thumb over his skin. Ollie's lips parted slightly, and I smirked in response. "Good. I look forward to us spending *many* hours together."

Ollie blanched, pulling his hand from mine and taking a step back. "I'm sure that won't be necessary. I know tours can be taxing, and I want to give you the space you all need to relax. My methods won't be invasive. I'll be able to gather all the necessary material without you even realising I'm there."

"Nonsense," Kevin boomed, his arm slipping around Ollie's shoulders. "For the next six weeks, you're a part of the family. Besides, if they know you're watching, they won't be able to get up to their usual mischief."

From the corner of my eye, I saw Silas scoff. We hadn't behaved brilliantly in our youth, but we were in our mid-thirties now. Our partying days were behind us.

Well, apart from Arlo, that is. Even if he wasn't a couple of years younger than us, that fucker didn't appear to be growing up any time soon.

Kevin was still wittering on, but I'd stopped paying attention. My eyes were narrowed on where his arm was still slung around Ollie's shoulders. The longer he held on to him, the more I focused on how Ollie's demeanour changed. How his smile grew pained. The way he shuffled on his feet like he wanted to remove himself from Kevin's grip without offending him.

I, on the other hand, had no qualms about offending him. Temper licking at my bones, I took a step forward. "Kevin, you need to—"

Jack slid between us so fast I hadn't even seen him approach. "Luca's right. We need to get moving. There's press outside, and we need to be at the airport in thirty minutes. Kevin, you go with Arlo, Kai, and their guards. The rest of us will accompany Ollie, Luca, and Silas."

There was a bustle of movement as everyone began

to file out in the order Jack instructed. I didn't move until Kevin dropped his arm and stepped away from Ollie. The man in question gave an imperceptible shudder before lifting his chin and wiping the expression from his face.

I was so busy studying him, wondering how he could flick his emotions off so easily, that when Jack whispered in my ear, the sound made me jump. "Hold it together. Lose it in front of Kevin, and he'll make it so you won't see Ollie ever again."

My head snapped around. In all our years working together, Jack had *never* cautioned me to behave in one way or another. Nor had he ever said anything negative about Kevin. "What do you mean?"

Jack glanced over my shoulder for a second before dipping back to me. "Just trust me. Don't let Kevin know how you feel."

He stepped back, indicating for everyone to leave. Ollie didn't look at me as he hurried after the others.

I stared after them, disappointment sinking like a stone in my stomach. That wasn't how I'd expected our reunion to go, but at least Ollie didn't seem to hate me. I wouldn't blame him if he did, not after I showed him how much I trusted him by shoving an NDA down his throat and then ignoring him for five months.

A small sniff behind me made me whirl around as I realised I wasn't alone. Leaning against the wall, his hood for once fully pushed back, leaving his haunted face on display, was Arlo. His face was pale, his dark curls were limp and hanging over his forehead. He wasn't looking at me. No. He was staring at the door through which Jack had just disappeared.

"You okay, man?"

Arlo's hands went to his hood, snapping it back over his head. "Yeah. Let's get going."

I never knew what to say to Arlo…or any of the others. For a songwriter, you'd think it'd be easier to find the words.

But there was only one person I'd found them easy with.

Now, I had six weeks to learn if it'd been a fluke. If it was, we'd part our merry ways at the end of it and go on with our lives.

And if it wasn't?

Then I'd do whatever it took to make Ollie mine.

To my dismay, by the time we got downstairs, Ollie had jumped in a different car. Even worse, I boarded the private jet at Heathrow to find Ollie already sitting next to Marta, one of our makeup artists.

I scowled as I took in their bent-together heads. A soft smile was on Ollie's face, leagues away from the tight ones he'd offered earlier. He didn't look up as I passed, but given how his shoulders tightened, he knew I was there.

I could've taken any of the several empty seats on the plane, but I didn't. Instead, I dropped into the one across the aisle from him, facing the back of the plane. It put Ollie right in my line of sight.

As the jet taxied the runway and got into takeoff position, I couldn't stop watching Ollie and Marta. She giggled, her hand toying through her hair as she whispered to Ollie. If she scooted over another few inches, she'd be in his lap.

Ollie grinned at her indulgently, his quiet comments making her laugh louder and louder. My fingers dug into the arms of my chair. Since when was Ollie a stand-up comedian? The guy was funny, but come on.

Suddenly a chilling thought hit me. Something I wished I'd considered before hatching this madcap scheme. Did Ollie still consider himself to be straight?

All this time, I'd hoped he'd take one look at me, and we'd pick up where we left off. That this tour would allow him to see me in all my glory on stage while getting to know the *real* me backstage.

But what if that wasn't going to be the case? What if that day in the lift was nothing more than a blip on his sexuality radar?

Or even worse, what if he had decided he was interested in men…just not me? What if he was already in a relationship with someone?

Given the way he was entertaining Marta's advances, I could probably write the latter off.

The longer I watched Marta giggle and flirt, the more my jealousy rose. Kai tried to engage me in conversation a couple of times, going so far as to kick my foot to try and get my attention. I waved him off, unwilling to take my attention off them.

The first time Ollie glanced up and saw me watching, his cheeks heated. The second time, he glared at me for a second before dragging his eyes away.

He didn't look at me again.

It took an infuriatingly long time to reach cruising altitude. Part of me was tempted to undo my seat belt early so I could drag Ollie into the back and give him a piece of my mind. Unfortunately, I'd seen too many episodes of *Air Crash Investigation*. My jealousy wasn't a good-enough reason to take the risk.

Finally, the stewardess's chipper voice came over the loudspeaker, telling us we were free to move around the cabin. Why they bothered to use the loudspeaker on such a small aircraft was beyond me. I was moving before she finished speaking, crossing the aisle and glaring down at the giggling couple.

Marta noticed me first. Jolting away from Ollie, she crossed her legs and gave me a breezy smile. "Luca? Is everything okay?"

"Peachy," I said through a gritted smile. "Just wanted to give my journalist here the grand tour."

Ollie took his time lifting his gaze to meet mine.

"Oh, don't worry. I can do that." Marta was already unsnapping her belt and beaming at Ollie. "Come on, you won't *believe* half the stuff they have on this thing."

"No," I barked, wincing as several heads twisted in our direction. I gave Marta one of my press smiles, the one that had won me *Best Smile* awards.

Also known as the one that was fake as fuck.

"I mean, it's fine. It'll give us a chance to get to know each other before everything gets chaotic. Right, Ollie?"

Ollie swallowed. "Right."

Stepping back so he could get up, I cut my way down the aisle, hoping he'd follow. Kai shot me a worried look as I passed, while Silas's was more of a *what the fuck are you doing?*

I avoided them both. At this point, I had no fucking idea. I'd been expecting Ollie to come in and... well, not fall at my feet. But maybe slip back into the flirty banter and deep conversations we'd had in the lift.

What I hadn't expected was this level of cold professionalism.

One thing was certain, I had a shit tonne of grovelling to do if I wanted any hope of a future with him.

Entering one of the two bedrooms at the back of the plane, I stood close to the door until Ollie came in. Once he was over the threshold, I closed the door and flicked the lock.

The sound had Ollie freezing in the middle of the room. "What are you doing?"

Leaning against the door, I shoved my hands in my pockets and smirked. "Looking at you."

Ollie bristled, folding his arms over his chest. "Look, Mr Weston..."

"Luca."

He stiffened. "I'm not going to call you that."

I pushed away from the door, stalking towards him. "Really? Got some problem with saying my name?"

"No," Ollie breathed, stumbling away from me. "But it's better if we keep things...professional."

His back hit the wall, and I was on him in an instant. My hands were on either side of his head, boxing him in. "Didn't feel very professional that day in the lift."

"We weren't working together then. This is different."

"Is it?" I licked my lips, and Ollie's eyes dipped, following the movement. I smirked. "Feels the same to me. Small space. Can't get out."

"This time, I work for you."

"No, you work for *Identity.*"

Ollie's gaze was unwavering, but his body trembled. "I'm not losing my job just for the sake of having a fling with you."

I leaned forward, ghosting my breath up his neck until I reached his ear. "Who said I want a fling?"

Ollie, the little fucker, did something completely unexpected. Thrusting his hips forward, he rubbed his groin against my very hard cock. "Maybe you should tell your dick that."

I chuckled. "Oh, I want you, Ollie. Make no mistake about that. That's not the real question here."

Ollie's chest was moving faster. I leaned back so I could see his face, and the desperation there threatened to break me. His voice trembled as he spoke. "It's not?"

"No, the real question is, who's this for?" Moving my hand from the wall, I dragged it slowly down his front, giving him ample time to tell me to stop. But he stayed silent. I pushed under his waistband, gripping his shaft firmly. "Is this for me? Or for *her*?"

Ollie stiffened, understanding dawning. "Wait…is that what this is about? Are you jealous?"

I slowly stroked him, memorising the way his head fell back against the wall. "Jealous? That depends."

"On what?" Ollie gasped, his eyelids drooping as I rubbed my palm over the head of his cock, slicking it with precum.

"On you. Tell me, is she the one you'd rather was in here with you?"

Ollie lifted his chin. "Maybe."

My own breathing was increasing, my head dropping to Ollie's shoulder. "Is she the one you'll lie awake thinking about tonight?"

"Yes."

"Liar," I hissed. "Admit it. Tell me the truth."

"Damnit." His hips were thrusting now, his dick fucking into my fist. "It's you. Ever since that day in the lift. It's always fucking *you*."

"In that case, I'm not jealous." That was a lie. I was fucking jealous of anyone who got to breathe the same *air* as him. "So long as it's my name you say when you come."

Ollie's lips tipped into a wicked grin. "Sure thing… Mr Weston."

A growl slipped, and I yanked my hand from his trousers. Ollie's grin fell immediately. "Shit, no, don't stop…"

"Oh, I'm not stopping. I'm going to drive you so fucking crazy it's going to take every ounce of your self-control to stop from screaming my name."

Tweaking one of his nipples, I hovered with my lips an inch from his. "If you want this to happen again, you better say my fucking name. You remember it's me on my knees. Me turning you inside out."

I dropped to my knees, triumph racing through me at Ollie's sudden gasp. Loosening his cock from his trousers, I held the tip towards my mouth.

Looking up at him, I winked. "Just don't say it too loud. Unless you want everyone to know what I'm doing to you."

Chapter 9

Ollie

Oh my god, it was happening again.

Had I imagined this so often that I'd manifested it into reality? That had to be the reason. There was no other explanation for why Luca was sucking me into his mouth.

Groaning around my shaft.

Rolling my balls in his hand.

Making me feel so good I wasn't sure which way was up.

"Right there," I moaned as he tongued my glans. I had no problem touching him this time. Wild horses couldn't stop me from winding my fingers through his hair. "That's it."

Luca pulled off my dick for a second, smirking up at me. "So…not so straight?"

I rolled my eyes, using his hair to tug him back towards my cock. "Obviously not. But maybe you better make sure."

He chortled but returned to his task.

Turned out that saying his name as I came wasn't an issue. Stopping everyone else from figuring out what we were doing was. I shot down his throat with my teeth clamped onto my fist to keep me quiet.

After, Luca stood with a quiet chuckle. Examining my hand, he gently kissed the indents my teeth had left behind. "We need to figure out a better way to keep you quiet if we keep doing this."

"We shouldn't."

He was quiet for a second, his green eyes serious. "Are you still in love with Suzie?"

The laughter that barked out of me was far too loud. "Jesus, no. I don't think I've been in love with her for a very long time. That door is well and truly closed."

"Good." Luca hummed, dropping my hand and instead cupping my face. "So that's not why you don't want to do this again?"

I closed my eyes to escape the intensity of his stare. "No. I'm not saying I don't *want* to. I'm saying we *shouldn't.*"

"That's never been a good-enough reason for me to not do something."

"Why am I not surprised?" I opened my eyes to find Luca studying me softly. "I don't get it though. Why did you bring me here?"

He let me go abruptly and turned away, scowling into a mirror on the wall at the damage my fingers had done to his hair. "I didn't."

He set about fixing his hair while I watched his reflection carefully. "Really? Then why did my boss tell me the deal would only go ahead if I was the assigned journalist?"

Luca tensed. "She wasn't supposed to tell you that."

I stepped closer, purposefully invading his space. Luca might've had the upper hand when we came in here, but one thing about me was I liked to get the truth. It was what made me such a good journalist. I was like a dog with a bone when I could tell someone wasn't giving me the whole story. "Why me, Luca? Was it just because you wanted to hook up again?"

"No." He fiddled with his shirt, his head bowed.

I echoed his earlier statement. "Liar."

He spun around to face me. "It wasn't that. If that's all I wanted from you, I would've called you before now."

"Then why didn't you?"

I hadn't realised how much it bothered me until the question slipped out.

Luca's lips parted in shock before he swallowed. "You told me not to."

I had? Shit, I couldn't be mad at him for respecting my boundaries. "Okay, so why am I here now?"

"Two reasons. First, Kevin *insisted* we needed to have a journalist covering this tour. The only concession he'd agree to was that I could pick who. You already know I have…you know…"

"Anxiety attacks?" I asked gently, reaching out to touch his shoulder. "It's nothing to be ashamed of."

"I know that." He gave a shaky laugh, brushing it off in a way that told me he *didn't* know. "I'm not expecting that to happen, but I trust you won't cover anything if it does."

"Of course not."

"Plus, if I have to have someone hanging around us constantly, I want it to be someone I'm comfortable with."

Surprise slid through my veins. "You feel comfortable with me?"

"Obviously."

Butterflies kicked off in my stomach at his quick response. Like it was the easiest question in the world for him to answer. "What was the second reason?"

I'd barely finished speaking when the plane hit a patch of turbulence, the floor dipping under our feet. It threw Luca off balance, sending him flying towards me. Instinctively, I opened my arms and caught his weight.

The plane righted itself, and suddenly Luca and I were only inches apart. I couldn't stop myself from tracing over the sharp lines of his face. The light freckles dusted over his nose. The flecks of amber in his eyes.

Every time we'd touched, Luca had been the one in control, but this was different. Now it was me holding him, my mouth leaning over his, already dying for another taste.

A loud laugh from beyond the door slammed me back to earth, reminding me of where I was and how much I had to lose. Luca wasn't any guy. He was the most famous musician on the planet. And for the next six weeks, my career—my entire life—relied on behaving like a competent professional.

I wasn't going to throw that away for a fling with Luca. What if all he wanted was one night? I wasn't sure I could do that, not with how obsessed I already was with him. For all I knew, Luca could be like all those player rock stars you read about—bedding a different person in each city. What if I slept with Luca, then had to watch him take other groupies back to the hotel?

I wouldn't be able to stand it.

I dropped my arms away from Luca, taking a stiff step back. "Apologies, I overstepped."

"No, I don't think you did," Luca drawled like he didn't care about my dismissal. He wasn't fast enough to hide the flash of hurt in his eyes.

I couldn't do this. I needed to get away from Luca before I did something stupid...like tackling him onto the comfortable-looking bed and humping him like some feral animal. "I better get back to my seat."

Luca smirked, but it did nothing to detract from the warning he gave. "If I see you flirting with Marta again, I'll drag you back here and pin you to that bed until you can't think of anything but me."

I gawped at him. Why the fuck did that sound so appealing? Why did it make me want to go back out there and turn on the charm with the pretty makeup artist just to see what Luca would do?

Not trusting myself, I nodded curtly before turning to leave. I made it to the door before Luca called out my name. "Don't you want to know the second reason?"

"Yes."

Luca leaned over my shoulder. When had he even come up behind me? He nibbled on my earlobe, and I had to bite my lip to avoid moaning. My cock started to stiffen again, Luca having apparently destroyed my refractory period. "That's a shame. I think I'll keep it to myself for now."

"Why?"

"Because I know it'll drive you crazy, which will make you come back for more."

"You're overestimating how invested I am in what makes your brain tick."

Luca's chuckle made my blood heat. "I'm really not. But that's okay. You're also not ready to hear my other reason. One day, I hope you will be."

My head swam, trying to make sense of what the fuck Luca was talking about. Adjusting my semi so it wasn't obvious, I took a breath and left the room.

Before I did something else stupid.

The first stop of the tour was Rome. I practically pressed my whole face against the window as our car zipped through the city streets. Grief hit me unexpectedly as I wondered what Mum would think of all of this. Whenever she was in a good head space, she'd describe all the places she wanted to visit.

I hated that she'd never had the chance.

She lingered in my thoughts as I drank in the brief glimpses of another culture, a layered tapestry woven into the streets alongside cafés and office buildings. There'd be no time for sightseeing before we were on the move again, so this was my only opportunity.

Before now, the furthest I'd travelled was to Poland on a school trip to Auschwitz when I was seventeen. That was the only reason I had an in-date passport, and it was up for renewal in a few months. I hadn't been planning on getting a new one.

But maybe I should. Maybe I should travel more. For Mum.

For me.

Thankfully, I'd managed to slip into a different car to Luca, riding instead with Arlo and his guard. Something told me that not being in a confined space with Luca so soon was a good thing.

Arlo seemed as content as me to sit in silence. Unlike me, he ignored the city views, instead scrolling endlessly through his phone. His knee bounced constantly. Was he anxious? Or was it a habit?

I'd done a bit of brushing up on the other band members overnight, but I hadn't learned much. I knew Arlo was the youngest of the four at thirty-one, four years older than me. Like the others, he'd grown up on a council estate, the launch into fame transforming his life in an instant.

If Becky could see me, she'd probably be fuming that I wasn't trying to extract information from Arlo. I couldn't bring myself to flip into journalist mode, not when he was intent on keeping to himself. Besides, I'd promised these guys their space. I wasn't about to go back on that.

We had to coexist peacefully for the next six weeks.

If Luca didn't tempt me into insanity first. Something about him opened the tightly locked box where I kept my emotions. He made me feel out of control. Just look at what happened in that lift. And no, I wasn't referring to the sex.

I was referring to how *easily* I opened up to him. How natural it felt to let him see the version of me that I tried to keep hidden away.

There was one question burning at me that I knew Arlo could answer. "Don't you guys have a tour bus?"

Arlo snorted, answering without looking up from his phone. "Used to. We trashed it one too many times. Plus, now that we're all older, we need our own spaces. The jet and hotel rooms work better for everyone."

By the time I let myself into my hotel room, I was exhausted from overthinking it all. I fell face-first onto the double bed, ready to escape the Luca-focused confusion swirling in my brain.

It was going to be okay. I could do this. I'd go to the shows, make notes, and ask a few questions. Return to my room, eat dinner, and crash for the night. Wake up the following morning, write, travel, rinse and repeat.

That was my plan. It left no space to be alone with Luca. To get myself into any other scenarios that would tangle the situation more than it already was.

Because no matter how much I might want a future with him, there was no way I would let that happen. And I wasn't going to throw away my whole career and add another scar to my heart for the sake of a casual hookup. Because I think that was what I'd be for Luca.

Replaceable.

I couldn't go through that again.

However, a new day immediately revealed the flaw in my iron-clad plan to shield my body and heart.

I hadn't accounted for Luca's sheer bloody stubbornness.

The itinerary called for outfit fittings for the band this morning, followed by a full tech rehearsal this afternoon. While I'd planned to attend the rehearsal, there was no need for me to go along for the fittings. I'd wanted to use the free time to catch up on emails while drinking my third cup of coffee. The Italians might not put much stock in tea, but they made a great cappuccino.

I'd only been away from my desk for a couple of days and the email backlog was already building. I'd barely made a dent in them when a knock disturbed me. I opened the door to find Luca leaning against the doorframe, looking fucking edible. How he managed to make a simple T-shirt and jeans combo so mouthwatering was beyond me. He didn't speak. Just let his gaze rake over me, lingering on the skin revealed by my loosely tied robe.

I fought the urge to pull at my robe. Whether I wanted to close it or open it further for Luca's gaze was anyone's guess. "Can I help you?"

"Why aren't you dressed?" His eyes travelled further down my exposed skin and my cock twitched between my legs.

I cleared my throat. "I know you're not familiar with the corporate world, but answering emails from a hotel room doesn't have a set dress code."

"I mean, neither does accompanying me this morning." He lifted a finger, dusting it lightly along the opening of the robe, careful not to touch the skin beneath. "If this is what you want to wear, then I'm all for it. Can't promise to behave myself though, so it's up to you."

"I'm not accompanying you." I stepped back, and Luca's hand fell to his side.

"Oh, but you are. Didn't your boss tell you? You're going to be my shadow for the next six weeks." He gave me an innocent grin. "How else are you supposed to learn *everything* about me?"

I sighed, realising this was an argument I wouldn't win. "Give me ten minutes. I've showered already, so I just need to chuck some clothes on."

"Great." Luca beamed, pushing on my door and

stepping over the threshold. "I'll wait in here."

He took my seat at the table, ignoring the open laptop. Stretching his long legs out in front of him, he crossed his feet at the ankles and helped himself to my coffee. God, what would happen if I went and ran my hands up his thighs? I'd never sat on a guy's lap, but Luca looked strong enough to hold me. I could straddle him and...

My brain screeched to a halt even as my dick continued to stiffen. This was why I needed space from him. Being in close quarters with him seemed to remove the levelheaded adult I normally was and replace it with a hormonal version of myself that I hadn't been even as a teenager.

Flustered, I pulled my robe tighter, double knotting it. "Why do you need to wait in here?"

"Security risk," he said, shooting me a wink. "Isn't that right, Jack?"

I spun around and poked my head out the door. Jack, Luca's hulking security guard, was staring impassively at the wall opposite. He didn't respond to Luca's question, nor did he acknowledge me.

"Does he really need to wait in here?" I whispered desperately.

Jack turned his head slightly, giving me a long-suffering look. "No. But it's easier if you go along with it. Trust me."

Shutting the door with a muttered oath, I pointed at Luca. "Stay there."

He wriggled his eyebrows over my coffee cup. "I think I like you bossy."

A flirty quip about how I liked to boss him around danced on the tip of my tongue. I swallowed it back at the last second, knowing that if I did say something, it would only encourage him. And I knew that if he flirted with me, I might end up with my dick in his mouth. Again. But fuck, it was hard being this close to him and remembering why I shouldn't go there. "I'm going to get dressed."

Luca didn't seem disappointed by my response. If anything, it seemed to amuse him. "Need any help with that? I've been told I'm an *excellent* stylist."

I rolled my eyes, grabbing an outfit from my case and heading for the bathroom. "I don't know how it works for you *rock stars,* but I've been getting myself dressed since I was a child."

He grabbed my wrist as I walked past, pulling me to a stop. "Getting dressed isn't my speciality. Getting people undressed, however..."

That remark was a wake-up call. If his reputation was anything to go by, Luca had no difficulty getting people into his bed. I couldn't risk being used and then possibly discarded. Not when I'd have to see him day after day for the rest of the tour. It was bad enough we'd already messed around twice. That'd given me enough material to agonise over for several months.

If I took him to bed, I didn't think I'd ever get over it. Five months had passed, and I'd managed to get over a six-year relationship.

But that lift incident? Definitely not over that.

Peeling my arm from his grip, I didn't respond to his comment. Luca seemed to have a way of twisting my words, leading me down a path I wasn't ready to walk with him. Perhaps ignoring him as much as I could was the way to get through this.

I couldn't look back at this tour as the time I got

my heart broken. I wouldn't.

I just had to be strong enough to keep Luca at arm's length.

Chapter 10

Luca

Whatever ground I'd gained with Ollie disappeared into the wind as the day went on. I didn't know what I'd said this morning to make him close up, but since then, he'd gone out of his way to ignore me.

It was driving me crazy.

I wasn't used to people avoiding me. Not to sound big-headed, but I was *Luca Weston*, for fuck's sake. I normally couldn't pay people to stay away from me.

But perhaps that was one of the reasons why I was drawn to Ollie. It'd been a long time since someone had made me chase them.

I didn't plan on letting Ollie outrun me.

Apparently, I was the only band member he was avoiding. He'd spent the morning chatting with Kai and Silas, their conversation lively as they warmed up to him. I'd had to stop myself from storming over and inserting myself every time one of them laughed.

Right now, I was being mic'd backstage, ready for the sound check, while Ollie and Arlo conversed quietly in a corner. Their heads were bent together, Ollie's notebook held loosely in his hands as he focused intently on what Arlo was telling him.

I glanced sideways and realised I wasn't the only one watching them. Jack stood beside me, arms folded over his chest and his gaze unreadable.

"I don't think they're flirting."

Jack stiffened. "I didn't think they were."

"Really?" I nudged him with my arm, twisting so the sound technician could clip the mic pack on my hip. Everyone here had signed an NDA, but even if they hadn't, they knew discussing what was said backstage was a one-way ticket to ending their career. "Then why are you staring at them like you're two seconds away from throwing Arlo over your shoulder and dragging him back to your cave?"

Jack snorted. "No, that's how *you* look while staring at Ollie. Me? I'm just happy Arlo is opening up to someone."

Before I could respond, he turned on his heel and marched away. His words had guilt and shame curdling in my stomach as I tried to recall the last time Arlo had confided in me. Shit. I couldn't remember. He'd been pulling away from us all so slowly I hadn't even noticed how far he'd gone.

Arlo gave a bark of laughter, Ollie grinning in response. Instead of jealousy, I felt...relief. Five minutes alone with the most closed-off member of the band, Ollie had him laughing.

"Who's ready, mother and fatherfuckers?" Silas whooped as he entered the room with a disarming grin.

I rolled my eyes, thanking the sound technician as she finished working on me.

She focused on Silas next, who lit up at the sight of the perky redhead. His grin eased into a flirtatious smile we'd all seen far too often. Lifting his shirt with one hand, he yanked it over his head in a practised move, puffing out his muscled chest.

The techie blushed, smiling and ducking her head as she taped the mic wire to his skin. He spoke to her in a low tone, too quiet for any of us to hear, but there was no missing the fact he was hitting on her. Her increasingly giddy giggle suggested he'd got himself set for his after-show celebrations.

Kai entered, his attention landing immediately on Silas and the techie. There was a brief flash of pain before he smoothed it away. Turning on his heel, he stormed back the way he'd come from, the water bottle in his hand crushed beneath his grip.

I was tempted to go after him, but I knew that wasn't what Kai needed. If he wanted company, he'd seek it out. But otherwise, he liked to process his emotions alone.

It wasn't like we didn't expect it. After all, Silas did the same thing at every show. His so-called *bromance* with Kai was something both Silas and the fans revelled in. Silas thought the fan theories about them being a couple were hilarious. He'd laughed about it so many times without knowing how much his reaction killed Kai. Even worse, he leaned into it on stage. The fucker would grind against Kai and generally drive him wild without realising it...before going home to fuck whatever girl had caught his eye that night.

I had no idea how Kai coped. I'd sat with him one too many times, keeping him company while he sought solace in a bottle of whisky. For someone who rarely spoke, those nights were ones when I couldn't shut him up. Not that I wanted to. We'd all fallen for a straight boy before. It was never an easy thing to get over.

And for Kai? It was damn near impossible. He couldn't avoid Silas. Couldn't stay away from him on stage, couldn't ignore him off it.

They were best friends, had been since they were kids. Arlo and I had tried to persuade Kai to either tell Silas how he felt or put some distance between them. I had no doubt that if Silas knew the impact his actions had on his best friend, he'd be horrified. He was as protective over Kai as Kai was over him.

But Kai wouldn't tell him. If we brought it up, he told us to fuck off. Every. Time.

Ollie evaded me the entire time we set up for the sound check. Disappointment and frustration filled me as I took to the stage, looking over the empty stadium. Tonight it'd be full of screaming fans, unable to take their eyes off us.

I didn't want that. Well, I didn't want *only* that. I wanted someone who couldn't take their eyes off me.

And as stupid as it might seem, given how he behaved around me, I wanted that person to be Ollie.

As Arlo tapped out the opening beat to "Tease", I saw a flash of movement from the corner of my eye. Ollie was in the wings, his arms folded over his chest. His expression was inscrutable. To an outsider, he probably looked like a consummate professional, cataloguing the goings-on on stage in preparation for his first article.

But as I lifted my mic and belted out the first note, his eyes held mine.

With no audience other than Ollie to perform

for, I turned to face the wings. This song was sultry. Sexy. Hungry. For a sound check, we normally kept it perfunctory, hitting the necessary notes but holding back the true performance until the concert kicked off.

But there was none of that now. Not with Ollie watching me like it was costing him everything to look unbothered.

This is where I thrived. It might not be who I really was, but I was arrogant enough to know I was good at my job. Like they knew what I was doing, the rest of the band stepped up to the plate, giving a performance worthy of awards. The backtrack allowed me to slip fully into my role. I gyrated my hips to the music, sucking on my thumb before running it down my chest…just to watch Ollie's eyes darken as he followed it. He was remembering it all. How it felt to have my hands on him. How I'd run my fingers up his thighs. How I'd taken him deep into my throat.

The song trailed off. I grinned at Ollie, preparing to nab him before he could disappear. Before I could take more than a step, Kai began knocking out the notes to a song we weren't even playing on this tour.

I spun on the spot to frown at him. He raised an eyebrow at me, continuing to lazily strum out the chords. Behind him, Silas picked up the tempo, with Arlo jumping in on the drums.

Okay…I had no idea what my bandmates were up to, but apparently, we were giving "Something" a go.

With a shrug, I turned my focus back to Ollie, throwing my all into the song. As I let the lyrics wash over me, the familiar words easily sliding from my lips, awareness began to prickle at the base of my neck.

"Something" was slower, more personal.

I'd written it a few years ago after going through a particularly horrendous anxiety attack alone. At the time, I'd pictured some faceless stranger next to me. Someone who might sit beside me as I pulled myself back together. Someone to tread water with me when I tried not to drown.

Now though, I wasn't picturing a stranger.

That was fucking terrifying.

As I lifted my mic to sing the final lines, the lyrics hit home like they never had before.

All because you do something to me
Something that stops me being lonely
Something that makes me need you
For the love of all that's holy
Say there's something
That makes you need me too

The final line left my lips, and I let the mic fall to my side. During the song, I'd crossed the stage to be closer to Ollie.

I stared at him with my chest heaving. Ollie's lips were parted and his arms hung loosely at his sides.

The stage was bustling with workers and my bandmates, but for all the attention Ollie and I paid them, we might as well have been the only ones there.

I took a step towards him, lifting my hand. "Ollie, can we—"

Just then, Kevin appeared over Ollie's shoulder. His calculating eyes darted between the two of us, suspicion dawning.

I dropped my hand, hardening my face into nothing more than disinterest. "Ollie, do you need anything from me before the show tonight?"

Ollie stiffened, oblivious to the audience we'd gained. "No, Mr Weston. I've got enough material for today."

I gritted my teeth at the name. Fuck, I'd never hated the sound of my surname as much as I did when it slipped from Ollie's lips. "Excellent. Please excuse me."

Without waiting for a response, I shouldered past the confused journalist, nodding curtly at Kevin as I passed.

"Thought I told you to play it cool," Jack muttered as he joined me backstage. "What the fuck do you call that?"

I took the bottle of water he held out, guzzling half. "Don't know what you're talking about."

"Really? Because during that first song, it looked to me like you were thirty seconds away from launching into a strip show. Last time I checked, you're a member of Caffeine Daydreams, not Magic Mike Live."

I scowled at my suddenly chatty bodyguard. "Do you want to talk about how things *look*? Because I gotta say, I've got a *lot* of opinions where you are concerned."

Jack slammed his mouth shut and regret rolled through me. "Shit, Jack. I'm sorry. I shouldn't have said that. That was crossing a line."

"It's okay," he replied automatically, his gaze over my shoulder. I didn't need to look to know he was watching Arlo. Again. "But this is why I'm telling you to be careful. The last thing I want is for you to end up like me."

My brow furrowed. I dropped my voice, aware of the many people around us. "Listen, Jack. If Kevin is stopping you from seeing Arlo, I can—"

His expression cooled. "Now you're stepping over a line."

I held up my hands in apology. "Okay, I'll leave it."

Just then, Ollie crossed backstage, giving me a tight nod as he passed. I winced internally. No doubt my hot and cold flashes were fucking with his head.

They were certainly fucking with mine.

Inspiration struck. "Hey, will you be watching me from the pit tonight?"

"Yes, like always." Jack eyed me warily. "Why?"

All our guards normally observed the crowds from different points in the venue, with Jack taking the front of the stage. He liked to claim it was because it put him closer to me.

But we all knew it wasn't me he did it for.

"Tell Ollie he's to join you," I said, staring at the tight set of Ollie's shoulders as he retreated into the distance. "He'll have a good view from there."

"He'd have a better view from the seat he's been allocated. You know, the one the venue has provided."

I ignored the pointed note in his voice. "I'll feel better knowing he's got you next to him."

"What's he got to worry about? It's not like he's famous."

"Please, Jack?" I dragged my attention from where Ollie was sitting, making notes. "What if it was Arlo? What if he wasn't famous? Would you want him out of your sight and reach during a massive event like this?"

Jack glared at me, his jaw working. Eventually, he blew out a sigh. "Fine, I'll keep him with me."

"Thanks, man," I slugged him on the arm. "I appreciate it."

"You sure he's worth it?"

I turned back to Ollie, delighting in how his hand flew over the page, his face creased in concentration.

"Honestly...I don't know him well enough to answer that. But I hope he is. My gut says he is. Sometimes that's got to be enough to take the leap."

Chapter 11

Ollie

Luca was fucking with my brain.

Watching him during the sound check was a revelation. Sure, I'd seen videos of him performing, but this…was different.

He was performing for *me*. Despite everyone watching, I was the one he gave all his attention to. The one he didn't take his eyes off.

That kind of attention was dangerous to someone like me. I'd lived my life surviving on the barest scraps. What Luca was offering was a full five-course meal.

But a meal like that wouldn't last. Before I knew it, I'd be back to living off scraps, my body aching now it knew what it was like to be truly satisfied and fulfilled.

If I thought watching him perform the first song was bad enough, it was nothing compared to the second. When Kai started playing the opening to "Something", Luca obviously hadn't been expecting it.

I'd heard the song before. Even if it hadn't lived in the charts for many weeks, listening to Caffeine

Daydreams' back catalogue was the guilty pleasure I gave in to during the darkest hours.

That and jerking off to thoughts of the lead singer on his knees for me.

So yeah, I knew the song. But as Luca rasped the lyrics, his eyes asking for things I dared not believe, I heard it in a way I never had before.

When it finished, he stepped towards me, and I found myself hoping. Despite everything...every reason why I shouldn't go there, I stepped towards him.

Only for him to snap into professional mode. Of course I'd read the situation wrong. As a journalist, you'd think I'd be better at reading people. Fuck, given my upbringing, I should be better.

But everything about Luca threw me off.

After his brush-off, I'd kept a low profile for the rest of the day. Even though my article wasn't due until the end of the week, I'd already gathered enough material from the other band members to get writing. This piece would focus on the build-up to a show, covering everything from their prep to how their dynamics worked on and off stage.

Their official dynamics, that was. Although I knew my editor would have my balls, there'd be no mention of the tension lingering between Arlo and Luca's bodyguard. No reference to the longing looks Kai threw at Silas whenever his back was turned.

And certainly nothing related to what had passed between Luca and me during the sound check. But that was more because the connection was all in my head, a product of my obsession and overactive imagination.

Honestly, thinking about it now, the way I'd

stripped Luca with my eyes made me blush.

When the crowds began filling the stadium, I tucked my laptop away. The band was chilling in the so-called green room, munching on Maltesers and M&Ms. Arlo and Silas had extended invitations for me to join them, but I'd refused. I wasn't going to fuck around with Luca behind closed doors only to have him treat me with disinterest in public.

Maybe I was being too harsh. After all, I was the one who'd told him we needed professional boundaries.

Could I really be mad at him for taking me at my word?

"Where are you going?"

Jack's surly expression had me phrasing my answer as a question. "Umm, to my seat?"

He grunted. "Plan's changed. You'll be watching from the front of the stage with me."

I shifted on my feet, torn between wanting to be professional and reluctant to be up close while drooling over Luca on stage. "Who authorised this?"

Jack raised an eyebrow. "Who do you think?"

It seemed Luca wasn't done fucking with me today. "Of course he did. Okay, lead the way."

I trailed after Jack as he wound around the barriers to a small gap at the front of the stage. The pit was crammed full of fans of all ages. Like with all Caffeine Daydreams' shows, there were various hilarious signs and countless T-shirts bearing the familiar band logo. Even with nothing but an empty stage before them, they were leaning over the barriers, their excitement palpable in the air.

Not that the stage was going to be empty for long. The supporting act, an upcoming pop-punk group called

Eden Project, was filing out and grabbing their instruments.

The enthusiastic roar from the crowd had me grinning. A band as big as Caffeine Daydreams could have their pick of support acts. But I'd heard from Arlo and Silas that they always chose artists on the brink of breaking into the limelight. It was apparently something Luca had insisted on from the beginning, claiming their launch into stardom had been based on luck as much as talent. And that now they'd hit the big time, it was their responsibility to help give other artists the same opportunity.

While Eden Project was good, I couldn't help counting down the minutes until Luca took the stage. I shouldn't want this. Watching him perform during the sound check had been one thing, but this? In his element?

It was going to drive me crazy.

Eden Project left the stage to cheers and hollers. The lights dimmed and the stage crew ran to switch out the instruments. All around me, the buzz of anticipation increased as the fans waited for Caffeine Daydreams to appear.

The lights cut out, plunging the arena into darkness. An excited hum began to rumble over the stadium.

There was a strum of a guitar.

The tapping of drumsticks.

Then the sound of Luca's husky voice rolled through the speakers.

Don't worry about me, darling
You've always had me on my knees
Because your love is a poison
Yet you're still the one I need

On the final word, the lights went up, and the roar of the crowd almost frightened me off my feet. Jack put his hand on my shoulder to steady me, but I barely noticed him.

All I could see was Luca.

His white cotton shirt hung open, his skin golden under the spotlights. Against his chest sat the necklaces I remembered loosening that day in the lift. Tight faux-leather trousers wrapped around his long legs, so tight I was convinced you could see his dick imprint. Dark liner made his eyes pop, the green looking more surreal than ever. His hair was mussed like he'd just stepped out of the shower and roughly towel-dried it.

Or like he'd been on his knees while someone ran their hands through it.

My blood rushed south at the thought, my balls pulling up tight. *Get it together, Ollie.*

Luca had his hands around the mic stand, singing into it like it was his lover and the lyrics were the dirty things he wanted to do to them.

When the chorus kicked in, Luca yanked the mic from the stand and sauntered across the stage. His arrogant smirk had his fans going wild. They threw hats, flags, and even a plastic cup or two.

There was no denying this was Luca in his element. He wasn't one of those stars who shunned the limelight. He *thrived* in it. This might not be the real Luca, but it was a persona he donned like armour. A persona he clearly loved.

Like everyone else, I knew all the words. I tried not to sing along, but I couldn't help it. I could've blamed it on the energy pulsing through the arena, but it wasn't that.

It was all Luca.

He worked the crowd like the pro he was, dancing

suggestively, bending over and singing to fans. Blowing kisses and just generally having everyone melt under his attention. Luca was the king of the stage, and he knew it, strutting across the space—sex dripping off him with every step he took.

But that wasn't what had my mouth watering, my fingers itching to explore him. No, that was all down to the expression on his face. The fierce joy that lit him from within as he gave the song his heart and soul.

After the first song, he returned to the mic stand, pushing his hair off his face as he grinned at the crowd. "Hello, Roma!"

They screamed back in response, making Luca chuckle deeply into the microphone. "Looks like we've got a rowdy lot here tonight. Are you ready to make them hear you all over the city?"

I winced at the wall of noise that hit me. Beside me, Jack rolled his eyes. Unlike me, he had earplugs in. That was smart. I should probably invest in a pair if I wanted my hearing to survive intact.

Not for the first few shows though. I didn't want to miss a second of Luca in all his glory.

Luca introduced the band members like the audience didn't have their names written on signs, T-shirts, and in a few cases, their chests. I barely paid attention to any of them, unable to look away from the frontman.

Luca hadn't so much as glanced at me, which was a good thing. It meant I didn't need to worry about the fact I was openly drooling over him.

Because how could I not? There was something enigmatic about watching him perform. It wasn't his fame. It wasn't even the actual performance.

It was just...him. His love for life made me want to pin him to a flat surface and try the things I'd only seen in porn.

As the concert went on, I found myself dancing along to the music, shouting the words as loudly as the fans behind me. Jack's mouth twitched with laughter, but I didn't care. I highly doubted he'd tell any of them about this when he barely seemed to speak a full sentence at a time.

I was having *fun*. For the first time in...fuck. I didn't even know how long.

The tempo increased as Arlo smashed out a familiar beat. My mouth dried in response, knowing what was coming. This was the song Luca had tortured me with during the sound check.

"Tease" was exactly what it sounded like. It was filthy, dirty, desperate. All the things Luca made me feel.

Had I watched him perform it in the dead of night, remembering how it felt to have his hands on me?

Yes. But I'd never admit it aloud.

Luca pulled the mic free, crossing over to the side of the stage I was on. He stopped dead in front of me, the words falling like poisoned honey from his lips.

His hooded gaze didn't leave mine as he dropped to his knees. Sweat glistened along his chest and abs.

Don't say you don't want me, baby
Because you know how I'll take that maybe
And tease you until you can't think
Until you're ready for me to sink...

The crowd took up the final part of the lyric as Luca sucked a finger into his mouth. As they chanted *'lower, lower, lower'*, that fucking tease ran his finger slowly down his body. His thighs spread wide, his hips gyrating like he was fucking someone.

I was frozen in place, utterly transfixed by Luca. There might as well have been an empty stadium behind us, given all the attention either of us was paying them. There was just the two of us for a heartbeat, the tension stretching to a breaking point.

His hand stopped at the button of his trousers, and I sucked in a breath. My eyes flew up to Luca's in alarm, only to see him wink.

In one lithe movement, he jumped to his feet, singing the next verse as he strode to the other side of the stage.

A bottle of water was pressed into my hand. I glanced up to see Jack glaring at me with a pinched expression. He leaned close so I could hear him over the music. "You look thirsty."

I nodded in thanks, trying to calm my flaming cheeks.

"You need to be more subtle," Jack said before turning back to the stage.

"There's nothing going on," I shouted back.

Jack clapped me on the shoulder. "If there's not, there will be. Just be careful. That's all I'm saying."

Unsure of what to say, I drank some more water. Luca was back in front of me, but the teasing from earlier was missing now. Instead, he raised an eyebrow as he sang, like he was asking me if I was okay.

I gave him a thin smile in response.

No, I wasn't okay. I was a fucking idiot.

Because Jack was right. Nothing might be happening right now, but it was going to.

I didn't know who I'd been kidding, but there was no

way I would be able to resist Luca if he came at me again.

I didn't want to.

I was going to do this, knowing it was wrong. That it would lead to pain for me. I wouldn't be able to get involved with Luca without feelings entering the mix. If we were caught, I'd be risking my entire career.

So yeah, I was a fucking idiot. Because I knew all of that as well as I knew my own name.

Yet I was going to do it anyway.

Because even a taste of Luca would be worth any risk that followed.

Chapter 12

Luca

It'd been a struggle to pretend I wasn't performing for Ollie. To keep myself down at the other end of the stage, knowing the one I really wanted watching me was within reach.

That was the smart thing to do. Jack's warning rattled around in my brain, clashing obnoxiously with the memory of Kevin's suspicious face as he'd eyed Ollie and me during the sound check.

I got on okay with our manager, but ever since he'd switched Arlo's and my security detail, I'd been cautious. I'd even gone to Arlo to ask if he wanted us to find new management, but he'd been adamant the switch was what he wanted.

If any of us had learned otherwise, we would've fired Kevin in a heartbeat. He was here to manage our business, not our personal lives. He already interfered too much for my liking, but there was a line he didn't cross… as far as we knew.

Since Arlo was insistent that nothing like that had happened, we'd let it go.

But with what had occurred today, my hackles were raised. Ollie was understandably concerned about protecting his job and reputation, and I respected that.

What Ollie *didn't* know was just how secure his job was. He could rock up to the office two hours late every day and not even get a disciplinary.

I couldn't tell him how I knew that though...not without confessing what I'd done. Why I'd done it was beyond me. I knew he thought he still would've missed his chance without me making him even later, but I couldn't live with that on my conscience.

But I didn't want him getting a bad rep as a journalist. If it got out he was fucking around with someone he was writing a story on, that would have repercussions even my long reach couldn't take care of.

When "Tease" had come on, a light had flicked briefly over Ollie's face, illuminating his expression.

Hunger.

Yearning.

Desperation.

I couldn't help myself.

Sauntering over, I'd stopped right in front of him and dropped to my knees. At this point, it had to be a familiar sight for him, but the way his mouth dropped open like it was the first time made lust roar through me. The height of the stage put my crotch at his eye level. I ran my hands down my body and gyrated my hips, keeping my eyes on him the whole time. Did he know I was imagining fucking him?

Given how his pupils were blown and his chest heaved, he had to have *some* idea.

And by the looks of it, those ideas had to be *good.*

When my fingers danced over the button to my leather trousers, Ollie's gaze cut up to mine in alarm. I bit back a chuckle. No, I wasn't about to flash a stadium of fans, not even to impress Ollie. But it was cute that he worried.

Winking at him, I jumped to my feet and returned to the other end of the stage. Kai raised an eyebrow at me, but his attention was quickly diverted when Silas chose that moment to lean in close to share his mic. Their bodies pressed together, and Kai forced an easy grin.

I was the only one who could see it was fake as fuck...well, me and Arlo, given the way our drummer scowled and hit the high hat a touch too aggressively.

Kai was dying inside. If he didn't do something about this situation soon, it would affect the rest of us.

Speaking of not letting things affect us, I spent the rest of the show pretending Ollie didn't exist. It was either that or yank him on stage so I could dance all up on him and feel his hands on me.

Yeah, that wouldn't make this situation better.

After the show, there was the usual meet-and-greet for fans who'd purchased VIP tickets. Jack arrived, but Ollie was nowhere to be seen. I raised an eyebrow at him in question just to get a shrug in response.

Was he hiding from me again?

I thought something had passed between us when I'd been on stage...but maybe I'd been wrong. Honestly, this whole arrangement was starting to feel like a fuck-up. Yes, Ollie and I had connected that day in the lift. But that was a long time ago. If Ollie didn't feel the same as I did, there was no point in pursuing this.

A chilling thought occurred to me as I reflected on the hungry way Ollie had watched me on stage. What if Ollie wanted to use me to...experiment? After all, he hadn't said anything about being with other guys since me. What if he was looking for a fling while I was after a relationship?

I kept my smile up for my fans, but my mood darkened the longer the night stretched on. By the time I let myself into my hotel room, I had plans that involved my hand and a bottle of Jack Daniels.

Closing the door behind me, I flicked on the light and froze.

I wasn't alone.

Perched on the edge of the table was Ollie. He'd unbuttoned the top of his shirt, and I couldn't help but linger on the skin and hair revealed there. He was smirking, but there was an underlying nervous current to it. Like he was aiming for confidence but got lost on the way.

"Didn't realise breaking and entering were on the syllabus at journalism school."

Ollie's lips twitched. "I wouldn't know. Didn't go to journalism school."

"How'd you get in here?"

Ollie lifted his hand, showing my room key clasped between his fingers. "Jack."

I raised an eyebrow. "Jack gave you a key."

"In a manner of speaking." Ollie tilted his head to the side. "Would it surprise you to know I was something of a pickpocket back in the day?"

I surveyed Ollie from head to toe, taking in everything from his Oxfords to his pristine white button-down. "Umm...yeah. Kind of."

"Let's just say I didn't have the best upbringing. I'm not proud of it, but sometimes the difference between having food or going without was how many pockets I picked."

A chord struck in my chest. I took a step closer. "You're not the only one who grew up poor."

He gave me a small smile. "I know. I read an interview you gave about it a few years ago."

I lifted my chin. "Council estate, born and raised. Mum still lives there. I offered to buy her a house anywhere, but she didn't want to move from there. She has a community around her. So, I bought her house from the council instead."

Ollie studied me. "You're a good son."

I shrugged self-consciously. "It's no more than she deserves. In her words, she'd rather have three cruises a year than a swanky pad."

We laughed softly before the sound ebbed away, leaving something heavier in its place as we stared at each other.

"Why are you here, Ollie?"

His fingers twitched against the table. "Is it okay that I am?"

"Yes." My voice dropped an octave. "But that's not what I asked."

Ollie's eyes cut to the side as he blew out a breath. "I'm not...I'm not good at this."

"This?" I took a step closer, my heart in my throat as I voiced my fear about being an experiment for him. "What, being with a man?"

"No. Well, technically, yes, that's new too. But I meant more..."

His voice trailed off as I shrunk the distance between us. I was now standing between his thighs, my legs brushing against his. "More what?"

"Talking. Emotions. That sort of shit."

I put a finger under his chin, tilting his face upwards. "Is that why you came here? To talk?"

He swallowed. "No."

I ran my thumb over his bottom lip. He parted them obediently, his tongue tentatively flitting over the pad before sucking it in.

Fuck me. What I wouldn't give to feel him do that to the head of my cock. Removing my hand, I stroked down until it came to rest loosely around his throat. "What do you want, Ollie?"

"Everything. I want it all."

Our mouths clashed together like his words were a starting pistol. There was nothing delicate about this kiss. It was a brutal, desperate coming together. My hand tightened around his neck as the other wound in his hair. His hands roamed over me like he couldn't decide what he wanted to touch first.

Ollie tried to pull me down into his lap, but I had other ideas. Without breaking the kiss, I half lifted, half shoved Ollie until his back hit the table.

Crawling on top of him, I blanketed his body with my own. Our kisses were hungry, a fucking mess of lust and need. I ground against Ollie's groin, making him kick his foot out with a curse. Something crashed to the floor, but we ignored it.

Breaking from Ollie's lips, I kissed my way down his chest, my hands tearing his shirt open. Buttons pinged off in every direction.

"I'll buy you another," I mumbled between kisses. "As many as you like."

"I don't care," Ollie gasped, shoving on my

shoulders to get me to rise. "Get fucking naked. Now."

Another time I might've made a quip about his bossiness. Not now. Not when he looked at me like I was the answer to a question he thought he'd never solve.

He lifted himself from the table, shoving off his shirt before helping me tear off my own. "Faster, faster," he chanted.

Blood pounded through my head as we tore at our clothes like animals. I couldn't remember ever feeling this desperate. There was nothing finessed about it.

Just carnal need driving us, making us think of nothing but touching.

Finally, we were naked. I didn't waste a second, dropping back down on Ollie and seeking out his lips. His hairy calves tangled with my own, his big arms coming up to wrap around me, pulling me tighter.

He was holding me so close that, with anyone else, it would've felt suffocating.

Not with Ollie.

I felt protected. Cherished.

Safe.

Small whimpers broke free from his lips as we rutted together. In the back of my mind, I worried about how Ollie might feel about getting naked with me. It was one thing to let a guy blow you. It was another thing entirely to strip off and rut against him.

It didn't seem to be a problem though. Given how Ollie's hand was now caressing my arse, his fingers flirting with my crease, he was up for taking it further too.

I shifted my right leg upwards in an attempt to give Ollie the access he needed. A loud creak had us freezing before chuckles broke free.

"Let's move this to the bed," I said, kissing the end of Ollie's nose.

"Okay," he said, almost shyly. His mouth twitched like he wanted to add something else but was holding it back.

"You sure?"

He nodded, his smile growing. "Sure."

Sliding off the table, I ran into the bathroom to grab a condom and some lube. When I returned, Ollie was reclined on the bed, his hand lazily tugging his cock.

I held my goods up to Ollie. "Am I being presumptuous?"

"Fuck no," he rasped. "Only question is, who's going to wear it."

I paused. "Is that...do you...?"

"You know, I would've thought a Grammy award-winning songwriter would have an easier time coming up with words."

I scowled as I straddled him. "Can't blame me for being thrown. We haven't...talked about it. Guys who are experimenting aren't usually volunteering to be the one getting dicked down."

Ollie rolled me in one movement so he was the one on top, glaring at me. His fury was as palpable as his desire. "You're not an experiment, Luca. I'm right here in this with you, and I want to try everything. Are you in this with me?"

Okay, I'll admit it. Ollie being all domineering was definitely working for me. "Yes."

"Good." He leaned down to nibble along my jawline. "Now, I might not have done this with a man before, but I'm nothing if not a quick study."

"Wait." I grabbed his hair, using it to pull his head up so I could see him. "You haven't been with another guy since me?"

"No, Luca. I haven't been with *anyone* since you."

Then his mouth was on mine, erasing all my conscious thoughts. I wanted to tell him that I hadn't been with anyone either. But he might think that was weird. After all, he'd been getting over a long-term relationship.

What was my excuse? I couldn't admit to him that the only thing I'd gotten off to since that day was the memory of his face as he came undone under my mouth.

He'd take out a restraining order. I certainly had for far less than that.

Ollie's hand circled around my cock, and I inhaled sharply.

"Huh," he said, sounding dazed. "It feels different."

My lips twitched. "Because it's not attached to you?"

Ollie rolled his eyes. "No, prick. I've had a lot of time to imagine this, and…it's not what I expected."

"In a bad way?"

"In the best way."

With a growl, I rolled us again so I could pin Ollie underneath me. Precum was sticky between us. I had no idea who it was coming from, and I didn't care. "How do you want to do this? I'm vers, so I'm happy with either."

Ollie's hand grabbed my cock again, his thumb toying with my foreskin. "Can I top? You're…bigger than I expected."

I gave a mock gasp. "You're telling me you didn't look me up on the internet?"

Ollie's blush gave me away. "Well…not your nudes. Everything else, yes. But no, I wouldn't do that."

That was...surprisingly refreshing. Especially given how many of them had been leaked over the years. Maybe my standards were on the floor after over a decade in the limelight, but the fact Ollie purposefully hadn't sought them out made me fall for him a little more.

"You can have a whole album full of my nudes if you like." I stroked my hand along his chin, enjoying how his five o'clock shadow bristled under my fingertips. "Just say the word, and I'll be your muse."

Ollie's face softened and he pulled me down for a tender kiss. This was as good as the furious desperation of earlier, but in a different way. Before, he'd kissed me like it was his one and only chance.

Now, he was taking his time, like he knew there'd be many more opportunities in future.

I wouldn't lie. I knew which one I preferred.

Words I couldn't yet speak bubbled up within me. Not wanting to send Ollie running, I distracted myself by grabbing the lube and clicking the cap open.

"What are you doing?"

"Umm, prep?" Just how little did Ollie know about anal sex?

He rolled his eyes. "I know *what* you're doing. I meant, why are you doing it instead of me?"

"Oh," I said stupidly, holding out the bottle to him. "I didn't realise."

Ollie squirted some lube onto his fingers like a pro, his hand immediately wrapping around me to seek out my hole. He stroked and probed the puckered skin tentatively like he was testing what to do.

It was nice that he was being gentlemanly, but I was done with waiting. If we took too long, he might start having doubts. He was telling me he wanted this, but I couldn't help but worry that he'd change his mind any second.

I'd rather he do that after I'd had him inside me. At least then, I'd have this memory to look back on. I pushed back on his hand, continuing until his finger was knuckle deep.

"Oh my god," Ollie moaned. "You're so tight. How the fuck am I supposed to fit in there?"

"You will." I chuckled, bending to kiss him and open myself up more. "And it's going to blow your fucking mind."

Chapter 13

Ollie

M*ind-blowing was right.*

That was all I could think as my cock slipped past the tight ring of muscle and into Luca. He'd tried to rush me through the prep, shoving down on my hand as much as possible. I'd refused to let him. I knew he thought that the longer we took, the more I might doubt that I wanted this, but nothing could be further from the truth.

There was nothing I was more certain about than Luca.

If I had my way, I'd explore every crevice of him. I wanted to run my tongue over the grooves between his abs. Bury my face in his groin to inhale his musk. Feel the weight of his cock on my tongue.

There'd be time for all that later…if Luca wanted it. I just needed to show Luca that this wasn't an experiment for me. If he wasn't ready to listen to my words, I'd show him with my body.

My hands went to Luca's hips, all my muscles tensing. "Luca. Oh my god."

He froze. "Is this okay? Sure you want this?"

My response was to lift my hips, pushing myself deeper into him. He let out a low moan, his head falling back. "I'll take that as a yes."

"Damn right, you will." Sitting up slightly, I put my arms around Luca and pulled him down so he lay against my chest. "Stop thinking, Luca. I want this. I want you. If I change my mind, I'll speak up."

"Sorry." Luca gave me a wry smile, his hips shifting in infinitesimal movements, taking me deeper with every rotation. "You aren't the only one who's had a lot of time to imagine this."

My chest burned at the intensity of Luca's gaze, but I kept my face blank, fighting to keep my emotions under control. "Tell me when I can move."

Heat flicked over Luca's face. "Now."

I started with small thrusts, marvelling at how tight and hot Luca was. His hole was strangling my cock in the best possible way.

Even better than that was the way Luca touched me. His hands never stopped moving, his lips only lifting from my skin to let out a moan.

I changed my angle slightly, and Luca went wild, a loud groan tearing from deep within. "There, right there."

Thrusting my hips up, I made sure to catch the spot again and again. Luca's cock was making a sticky mess against my stomach, and fuck, I loved it.

This. This was everything. Everything I'd been led to believe sex was supposed to be. Frenzied. Passionate. Tender.

It was all of that and more.

"My turn," Luca gasped. Pushing on my chest, his

large hands wrapped around my wrists, pinning them to the sheets on either side of my head. "Keep your hands there and don't move."

My cock twitched at the easy way he took control.

"Buckle up, baby," he murmured. "I'm gonna ruin you for everyone else."

He already had. Didn't he know that?

Rising on his knees, Luca pulled off until just the tip of me rested inside him. Then without warning, he dropped back down.

"Fuck!" I squeezed my eyes shut, willing myself not to come yet. "Luca."

"I love the sound of my name on your lips," Luca whispered huskily. "Let's see if we can make you say it a few more times, shall we?"

He started to move, his wish coming true almost instantly. His name fell from my lips like a sinful litany.

Luca. Luca. Luca.

Luca rode me like it was his sole purpose in life. His body had a sheen of sweat, his muscles tensing as he plunged down on me again and again.

"I can't hold on," I gasped. I didn't want to lift my hands from the bed, not when Luca had told me to keep them there. "Please. Let me touch you. I need it."

Luca's eyes were wild as he nodded frantically. "Yes. Ollie...touch me. Oh god...touch me."

My hands were on him in a second. One curving around his hip and the other wrapping around his length. It took three solid strokes before he shot his load. His cum jetted from him, splashing over my chest.

Like he was marking me.

That thought sent me over the edge. Spots filled

my vision as the most intense orgasm of my life rocked through me. My hands went to Luca's hips, holding him tight as I emptied into the condom.

Fuck. That was everything.

Luca lifted himself off me with a wince. "Shit, are you okay?"

He grinned at me, and it was full of happy laziness that warmed me from the inside out. "Oh, I'm better than okay."

He grabbed the condom before I could, knotting it and dropping it in the bin with a few swift movements.

"I could've taken care of that."

"I know, but now you don't have to." Luca's simple statement made my chest pull tight. He grabbed two bottles of water and popped them on the nightstand. He disappeared into the bathroom before returning with a damp cloth in his hand. I watched in amazement as he carefully cleaned the cum off my chest before tossing it aside. Then he flopped down on the bed, pulling the sheets over us, making sure I was covered. Each of his movements made my chest tighten further until I felt like I couldn't breathe.

"So...did I ruin you?"

Ruin me? Fuck, Luca had the power to *break* me. And I wasn't even talking about the sex. When was the last time someone had done something as simple as look after me because they could?

Forcing those emotions away before they got me into trouble, I plastered an easy grin on my face. "Nah. I think we need to try it a few more times to be sure."

"Oh, of course," Luca said with a mock-serious expression. "For science."

Just then, there was a pounding on the door, followed by a familiar voice calling out. "If you're finished, open the fucking door."

Luca frowned at me quizzically. "Has Jack been knocking long?"

"How would I know? Everything stopped existing the second you put your mouth on me."

I loved how he thought I'd paid attention to anything outside him during the last...

Well, five months, if I was honest.

Luca let loose a growl, grabbing the back of my neck and yanking me to him roughly. I groaned at the feel of his lips under mine. His light scruff brushed against my skin, making it burn in the most delicious way.

Unfortunately, before we could go any further, the knocking started again.

"Luca, I'm serious. Open the door before I break it down."

Cursing, Luca let go of me and shoved off the bed. Grabbing a towel from a chair, he wound it around his waist before stalking towards the door. He glanced back at me.

"What?" I asked, sitting up. "Do you want me to hide?"

"Fuck no." Luca snorted. "Just making sure you're covered. Jack's seen me naked more times than I care to count, but I want to keep you all to myself."

I lay back on the pillows with a blush, making sure the sheet covered me. I shouldn't like Luca being possessive over me.

I shouldn't. But I did.

Luca yanked the door open, his body filling the

frame. "What?"

"Jesus, Luca. Haven't you heard of putting some clothes on before opening the door? What if paps had been out here?"

I could imagine Luca smirking at that. "Like you'd let them on my floor."

"I take it you're fine then. I heard noises and panicked," Jack said. He peered over Luca's shoulder, immediately spotting me in his bed. His eyes narrowed. "Did you take Luca's key card?"

"No," Luca said smoothly, closing the door around him so I was hidden from sight. "I gave him one."

I bit my lip to contain my grin at Luca's blatant lie.

"Then where's mine?"

"You must've lost it." Luca yawned obnoxiously. "Are we done? I have some things to get back to."

"Fine," Jack bit out. "But next time, don't come up to your room without me. It's a security risk. You can't just wander off. This time it was Ollie, but it could've been anyone waiting in here."

I didn't know what made me do it, but I got up from the bed and crossed the room. Using Luca's body to shield my nakedness, I slid my arm around his waist. Luca jumped slightly before relaxing into my hold.

I met the guard's stern look unflinchingly. Maybe I should be worried about Jack telling someone...but if Luca trusted him, I would too. "Don't worry, Jack. I plan on waiting in Luca's hotel room every night until he tells me otherwise. Whatever city we're in. Anyone who wants to get to Luca will have to go through me first."

Something like respect flashed in Jack's eyes. "Fine. But I'll still escort Luca up here and make sure he's safe."

"Of course," I said. "I want Luca safe too."

Jack studied me for a moment longer before turning back to Luca with a sigh. "Want me to get him his own room key for your suite going forward?"

"Please," Luca said, flashing a grin at Jack as he started to close the door. "Saves him from going to the trouble of stealing yours every night."

The door clicked closed on Jack's outraged face. I let out a laugh, but the sound was swallowed by Luca's mouth. He twisted us around, pinning my back to the door as he devoured me with hungry kisses.

"Did you mean it?" he asked when he eventually pulled back, his eyes searching mine. "About being here every night?"

My chest tightened, the fear of being hurt rising again. But I pushed it away. I wasn't going to let myself fall in love with Luca. I would enjoy this time with him, knowing it'd be a cherished memory for me to look back on. "I do. I'll be here until you tell me to stop."

"What about your job?"

I bit my lip. Ah. That. The thing I'd been purposefully ignoring since Luca dropped to his knees before me on the stage. "Well...if we get caught, I'll get fired, I guess."

"No, you won't." Luca pecked me on the lips. "But if it's easier, we can keep this quiet while we're on tour."

That made sense. Once the tour was over, we would be too, and there'd be no fear of this leaking and coming back on me. "Thank you."

A yawn caught me off guard, reminding me of the stupidly late hour. Sex with Suzie had always been a shamefully short affair, with me trying to get us both off as fast as possible so it was over and done with.

Turned out that sex with Luca was much…longer.

And somehow, not long enough.

"Come on, sleepyhead, time for you to get your beauty rest." Luca tugged me to the bed, yanking back the sheets and indicating for me to get in.

I wavered. "I can go back to my room if you'd prefer?"

Luca's nostrils flared as he took a step closer. "Get your arse in my bed now. And don't even *think* of sneaking out in the morning. If I don't wake up with you next to me, I'll be beyond pissed."

I bit my cheek to hold back a massive grin. It took so much effort to keep my expression placid when, in reality, I wanted to jump up and down on the spot. But that'd make Luca laugh.

And not in a good way…more in a *what the fuck have I got myself into* kinda way.

I got into the bed, sighing quietly when Luca pressed tight to my back.

Yeah, I could get used to this.

I couldn't though. Not when letting people in meant you got hurt.

But I could pretend.

Just for a little while.

Chapter 14

Luca

My alarm went off far too early the next morning. Shutting it off, I turned my attention to the man in my bed.

Normally I kissed my one-night stands farewell at the door, never letting them stay the night. Even with Jorge, the only time we'd shared a bed was when we travelled together.

But things were different with Ollie. I *felt* differently about him. It might be stupid to pin all my hopes of settling down on the man snoring beside me, but honestly? Right now, it was hard to picture anyone else in his place.

I wasn't saying I was in love with him or anything…it was way too fast for that.

But for the first time ever, I could *see* myself falling. Fuck, I hoped Ollie would be there to catch me.

The man in question stirred, his eyes opening blearily. "Morning."

"Morning." I brushed a kiss over his lips. Then I

remembered my medication. Sitting up, I popped a pill from the packet I kept on my nightstand and swallowed it with a sip of water from the bottle I'd put next to it the night before.

Ollie watched me lazily, a touch of curiosity in his eyes. I flashed the packet in his direction. "SSRI. I take one a day to keep my anxiety under control."

"Smart," Ollie said with a yawn. "Mum was always better when she took hers. She never stuck with it though. She thought taking them was...weak or something. I don't know."

I sighed. That was such a common misconception. The stigma surrounding medication for mental health conditions was so damaging. "That really sucks. I'm so sorry. It's frustrating that people are judgmental about antidepressants. Like, if I had diabetes and needed insulin every day, they wouldn't bat an eye. But because the condition is in my mind, that's somehow different?" I shook my head in frustration. "It's a ridiculous attitude."

Ollie ran a hand idly over my thigh. "Preaching to the choir. Seriously, though, it's good you keep on top of it."

"It's how I've got to be. I've learned the hard way that I can't just ignore it and hope it goes away." I grazed my knuckles along Ollie's chest, goosebumps chasing my touch. "Have to say, waking up in bed with you is almost as effective as the medication. Did you sleep okay?"

"Like a log." He lifted his own phone from the nightstand and groaned. "Could use a few more hours though. Aren't rock stars supposed to sleep the day away?"

I snorted, climbing out of bed and putting a cup under the fancy coffee machine. Thanks to the brief time I worked in Hell on Earth—AKA soft play—I was au fait with how to work it. Couldn't have parents being uncaffeinated while their demonic spawn ran riot through the play centre. This suite came with a butler to do this sort of thing for me, but I never bothered. There were some luxuries I gave in to, but letting people wait on me when I was perfectly capable of doing it myself was not one of them. "Not while we're on tour...especially not one with as many stops as this one."

"Yeah." Ollie stood and stretched, his joints popping. The lines of his naked body reminded me of the night before. How his muscles had rippled as I rode him. The way his lips looked when he'd shouted my name. I'd had a lot of sex in my life, something I wasn't at all ashamed of.

But nothing had come close to what Ollie and I had shared.

"Luca?"

I jumped guiltily, Ollie's voice pulling me from my reminiscing. "Sorry, what did you say?"

He rubbed a hand on the back of his neck, making his bicep bulge. My mouth dried out. "Don't you ever wish you had more time to explore the sights?"

I forced myself to focus on the coffee. If I didn't, there was a chance I'd end up taking Ollie back to bed just so I could explore his body in the daylight.

As I didn't fancy having to explain to Kevin *why* we'd missed our flight, I needed to not be looking at Ollie right now.

"Not really," I said, answering Ollie's question. "During our first few tours, our management arranged several sightseeing outings and stuff like that. Now, I kind of feel like I've seen it all, especially in the big cities like this."

"Makes sense," Ollie said, staring out the window wistfully. Then he jolted before turning to me with a thin smile. "Guess I better go back to my room so we can make a move."

"Wait." I put the cups to the side and pulled him into my arms. "Have you not been here before?"

He gave a bashful shrug. "No, but I've not been anywhere, really. Except for Poland on a school trip. But this has been great—I'll definitely come back one day to see more."

"Shit, I wish I'd known. Maybe we could've taken in some sights."

Ollie's eyes bugged out of his head. "No, that's not why I was saying it. Honestly, simply being here is awesome. I saw so much just on the drive alone."

I mentally began flicking through the future tour stops, a brief plan coming together in my head. "Maybe one day I'll bring you back here."

"I can bring myself back," Ollie said, leaning forward to nuzzle my neck. "I don't need you paying my way, thank you very much."

I winced. Okay, that didn't bode well.

Changing the subject, I smoothed my hands over Ollie's rear. "Shower with me?"

His eyes darkened. "I don't have any clothes. And I need to pack."

"That's easily fixed." Releasing Ollie, I strode across the room and picked up the phone. The butler assigned to me answered immediately. In a few sentences, I'd arranged for Ollie's belongings to be packed and delivered to my room.

I wouldn't have the butler wait on me…but I

was prepared to utilise them if it bought me a few more minutes of privacy with Ollie.

Ollie was gaping at me. "Did you just…?"

I grabbed his hand, grinning at him over my shoulder and pulling him towards the bathroom. "Just roll with it. If we hurry, we can combine our shower with orgasms."

Ollie put an arm around my waist, lifting me clean off the floor and carrying me into the bathroom. "Why didn't you say so?"

Ollie was back in professional mode. From the moment we stepped out of my room to greet Jack to boarding the jet at Fiumicino, he didn't let his demeanour slip. He was polite, distant, controlled.

It was driving me crazy.

Not that I'd expected anything different. For fuck's sake, I was the one who'd said we'd keep up appearances while on tour. Then, once all the articles were released, we could take our relationship public.

So long as that was what Ollie wanted…

I held it together until Ollie boarded the plane, deep in conversation with Marta. He walked down the aisle without even glancing in my direction. My scowl deepened with every step he took. Kai was saying something to me, but I couldn't hear him past the blood rushing in my ears. All my attention was on the far-too-pretty makeup artist and the man I'd taken to bed the night before.

Without breaking their conversation, Ollie took his seat and began buckling. Marta beamed as she slipped into the one next to him, tossing her hair over her shoulder.

It was the hair flick that did it.

Unbuttoning my belt, I crossed the aisle. It took more effort than usual to find my charming smile. "Hi, Marta. We need to switch seats."

Ollie's head snapped up, his lips twitching like he was fighting a smirk. "Problem, Mr Weston?"

I took a steadying breath. Fucker knew *exactly* what he was doing, calling me that. "Yes, actually. I won't have time to do the interview later, so we need to do it now."

Ollie's eyes flashed as he caught on. "Not a problem. I'm happy to fit you in now."

My cock thickened. Yeah, I'd love for him to fit me in too.

"Sorry, Marta." Ollie gave her a warm smile that made me want to straddle his lap and shove my tongue down his throat. "Do you mind swapping with Mr Weston so I can conduct his interview?"

The pinched lines around Marta's lips implied she did mind, but she could hardly say no. "Not a problem."

I stepped back as she gathered her things, ignoring the knowing looks from my bandmates. Fortunately, Kevin was deep in conversation with Jack, oblivious to everything happening at this end of the plane.

Marta ran a hand over Ollie's shoulder, a flirty smile on her face. "I'll catch up with you later."

Ollie stiffened, and it made me want to smack her hand away. "Thanks, Marta. I'm sure I'll see you around."

Marta didn't take my seat, instead choosing to sit with the other stylists like she usually did.

"She likes you."

"And I like you," Ollie said matter-of-factly, staring

at the safety card like it held all the secrets of the universe.

"You do?"

His gaze cut sideways. "I would've thought last night would've answered that for you. Especially with what I said to Jack."

That was true. I chanced a brush over his thigh. "Still nice to hear it."

"I can't..." He sighed. "I'm not good at this, Luca. I told you that."

"What do you mean? What are you not good at?"

"This." He gestured helplessly. "Talking about feelings and stuff. I've spent my whole life trying to feel as little as possible, then you come along and..."

His voice trailed away. "And what?"

"And...you're making me feel *everything*. It's too fucking much, Luca, and I don't know what to do about it." He sighed, rubbing a hand over his face. "This isn't the time nor the place to be having this conversation."

"It's not," I agreed. The seatbelt sign clicked off, indicating we'd reached cruising altitude. "Come on."

Ollie followed me silently as I got up from my seat and headed for the bedroom at the back of the plane. Kevin and Jack looked up questioningly as we passed.

"Just heading back here to do the interview," I said breezily. "Too noisy out here."

Kevin nodded before going back to his laptop. Jack narrowed his eyes like he was warning me to be careful.

Ollie closed the door behind us, immediately looking at the spot where I'd blown him a few days ago.

I dropped onto the bed. "You going to stay there?"

"Yep." He shoved his hands into his pockets, one of his feet going against the door.

"Why?"

"Because if I come over there, we won't get any talking done."

"I can behave myself."

His eyes were hooded as they swept hungrily over me. "But I can't."

My blood rushed south, and I had to adjust how I sat to account for my rapidly swelling dick. "That's not necessarily an issue. There are many ways to join the mile-high club. I'm more than happy to help you meet *all* the criteria."

"How selfless of you," Ollie quipped.

I smirked. "Always."

Ollie's smile faded into a grim line, his voice dropping to a whisper. "What are we doing here, Luca? Is this just a fling while we're on tour?"

"Is that what you want it to be?"

"Yes...no. I don't know." Ollie slumped back against the door, his hand covering his eyes. "I can't think straight when I'm around you. I was so determined to keep you at arm's length, and then I saw you on that stage, and—"

"Wait." A stone of dread settled in my stomach. "Is that why you came to me last night?"

Ollie pulled his hand away, his brows drawn in confusion. "I mean, yeah. You were flirting with me on stage...right? And seeing you perform...I knew it was pointless trying to resist you."

"Right," I echoed hollowly. I got to my feet, straightening my shirt so I had something to do with my hands. "You saw the rock star everyone else sees and decided to have a taste. Got it."

There was a faint ringing in my ears as I walked up to Ollie and attempted to shove him aside so I could leave. I'd been so foolish thinking Ollie might be different. All it had taken was one performance for the real Luca to be erased from his mind.

Ollie refused to move, understanding dawning on his face. "Luca, that's not what I meant."

"Don't stress about it, Ollie. I'm used to it."

I tried to push him aside again, but he didn't budge. "Can you move?"

Ollie moved, but not how I was expecting. Grabbing my arm, he twisted me until my back hit the wall. His arm came up across my chest, pinning me in place. "No. You're not leaving until you've listened to me."

I sighed. "Save it. I've heard every variation of this story. They all boil down to the same thing—you didn't want me until you saw me on stage. You didn't want *me* at all. You wanted Luca, frontman of Caffeine Daydreams."

"Are you going to let me finish?" Ollie demanded. "Because I've got a few things I want to say."

Reluctantly, I raised my gaze to meet his. I was expecting to see maybe shame or regret at being found out...but instead, there was anger.

It was the most emotion I'd seen from him since that day in the lift. It shouldn't have turned me on, but it really did.

Maybe I was broken.

"What I meant was *seeing you in your element* made me want you. When you perform, you're happy... free. This weight you carry around with you otherwise is lifted. It was one of the most beautiful things I'd ever seen. But it would've been the same if you were a teacher revelling in delivering a lesson. Or a writer who'd finally found the right words. If you're happy in what you're doing, you...glow. That's what I meant. It has *nothing* to do with your fame. If anything, your fame massively puts me off pursuing anything with you."

I swallowed, scarcely daring to hope.

"I won't lie and say it's not also because of the way you move your body," Ollie continued, the fury in his eyes replaced by humour now that I was listening to him. "Especially with the way you were eye-fucking me from the stage. What were you hoping for when you did that?"

My cheeks burned. Turned out I was the one who needed to feel shame and regret. "That I'd persuade you to join me in my bedroom after the show. I'm sorry, Ollie. I shouldn't have assumed you wanted me for my fame...especially when you've given so much evidence to the contrary."

"It's okay," Ollie said, lifting his arm and winding it around me. "I get it. You've been burned before."

"I have. But still, I should be better."

He kissed me soundly, his tongue leisurely exploring my mouth. When he pulled away, he pecked my lips once more like he needed another brief taste. "Maybe. But I've been burned too, Luca. I know how hard it is to open up after something like that."

"I know." What Ollie had been through was worse. He'd been betrayed by not only his girlfriend but his best friend. "I'm sorry I reacted like that."

"It's okay." He cupped my face with his hand. "Maybe we could...take this slow? We've got six weeks to explore together."

I swallowed the urge to make it more official.

Now that Ollie had confirmed he wasn't after my fame, nothing was holding me back. But he was right. We'd both been burned and needed time to open up to each other.

Which was fine. It wasn't like we were putting a deadline on this. We were just...taking it slow.

"Sounds good," I said finally, running my hand down to palm Ollie's shaft. "Now, fancy a repeat of last time?"

He nudged me back until I was against the wall again. "Actually, I was thinking this time it could be the other way around."

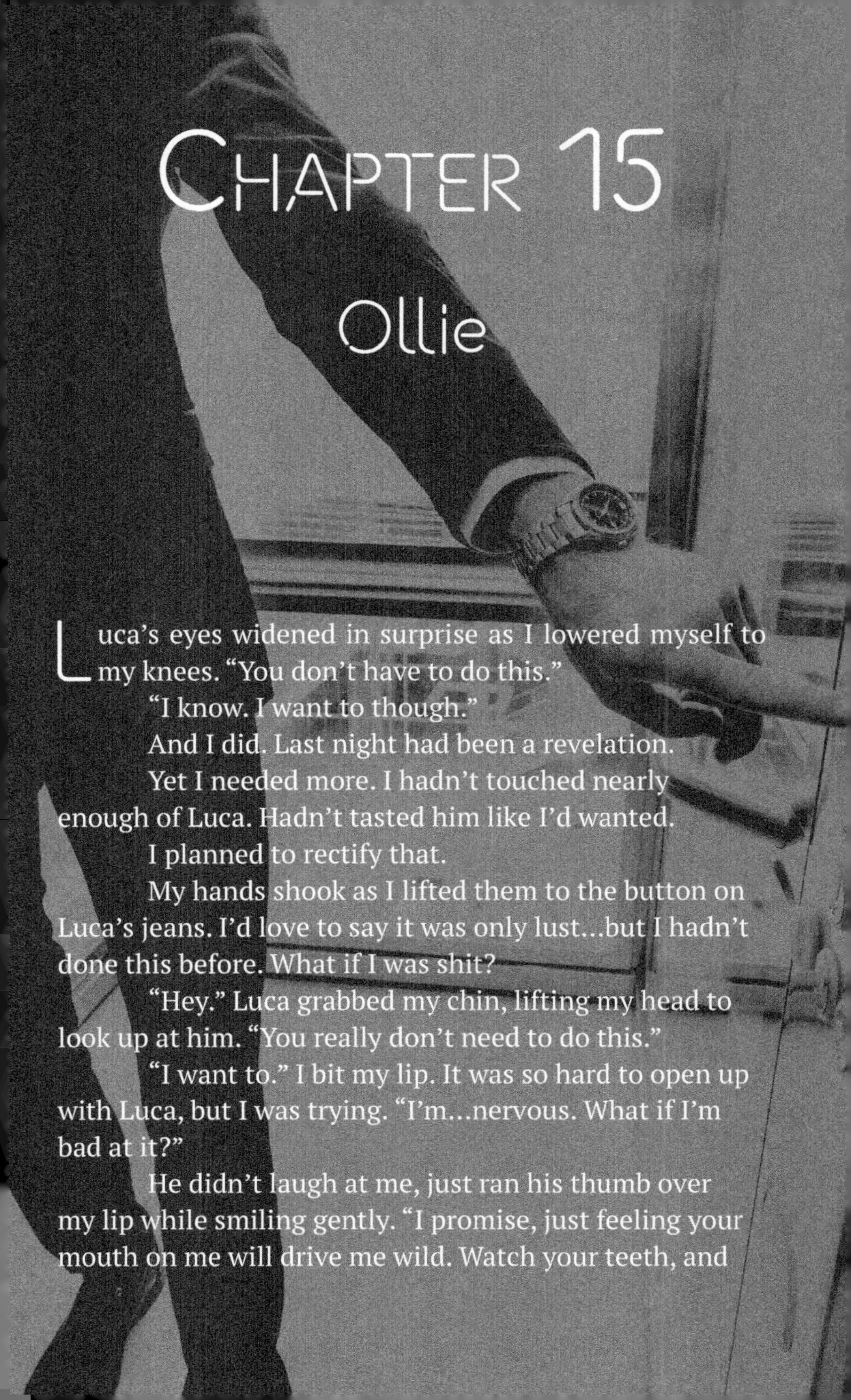

Chapter 15

Ollie

Luca's eyes widened in surprise as I lowered myself to my knees. "You don't have to do this."

"I know. I want to though."

And I did. Last night had been a revelation.

Yet I needed more. I hadn't touched nearly enough of Luca. Hadn't tasted him like I'd wanted.

I planned to rectify that.

My hands shook as I lifted them to the button on Luca's jeans. I'd love to say it was only lust…but I hadn't done this before. What if I was shit?

"Hey." Luca grabbed my chin, lifting my head to look up at him. "You really don't need to do this."

"I want to." I bit my lip. It was so hard to open up with Luca, but I was trying. "I'm…nervous. What if I'm bad at it?"

He didn't laugh at me, just ran his thumb over my lip while smiling gently. "I promise, just feeling your mouth on me will drive me wild. Watch your teeth, and you'll be fine."

I nodded, unzipping Luca's fly. Having watched him get dressed this morning, I'd known he was going commando. A small fact that had driven me so crazy I'd chosen to take a separate car to the airport.

I hadn't thought keeping a professional distance would be difficult. But knowing what Luca looked like when he came undone was making that impossible.

And the jealousy he'd shown with Marta?

Fuck, I shouldn't like that. But I did.

Luca could have anyone. *Anyone.*

But he wanted me.

Stroking his shaft, I studied every inch of it. Like I'd noticed last night, he was…big. Bigger than me, for sure. It wasn't just the length that had my hole twitching, but the girth. I could only imagine how that would feel pressing against my rim. Stretching me wide, almost to the breaking point.

I couldn't wait to find out if my imagination was correct.

For now, I'd have to settle for figuring out how to fit him in my mouth.

Tugging his foreskin back to reveal the head of his cock, I leaned forward to run my tongue over him. Luca hissed above me, his hands grabbing my hair.

His reaction made me feel braver. Opening my mouth wider, I took the first few inches into my mouth. His cock was heavier on my tongue than I'd expected. My lips were stretched wide already as he filled my mouth. I ran my tongue around him, experimenting with different pressure and memorising his taste.

Luca was cursing quietly above me. I glanced

from under my lashes to see his hooded stare fixed on me. "Perfection."

Glowing under his praise, I tried to take him deeper. Too fast. His cock bumped against the back of my throat, triggering my gag reflex.

Luca used my hair to pull me back off him. "Easy. You don't need to deep-throat me the first time. Or ever."

"Porn makes it look so easy." I swiped at my watering eyes.

Luca's lips twitched. "Please tell me you're not basing all your gay knowledge on porn."

"Where would you prefer me to learn it? From hookups?"

Luca's expression darkened as his hands tightened in my hair. "Fuck no. You'll learn everything you need to know from me. No one else."

Fuck. If I got any harder, I might actually die.

"Wrap your hand around the base," Luca said huskily. "Jerk me off at the bottom while you wrap your pretty lips around the top."

Had I ever been called pretty before? I didn't think so. Wasn't something I thought I'd like...but Luca being the one to call me that? While I was on my knees for him?

Turned out I liked it a lot.

Doing as he instructed, I fell into an easy rhythm. I alternated between running my tongue over him and sucking until my cheeks were hollow. It wasn't a tidy blowjob by any stretch of the imagination. Drool ran down my face, mixing with Luca's precum to drip to the floor.

"Ollie," Luca gasped, his fingers twitching against my head. He wasn't controlling my movements, just reminding me that he was there. "That's so good, baby.

Fuck. Yes."

I doubled down on my efforts, determined to taste him before someone came exploring to find out what was taking so long. Luca didn't make me wait long, his breath hissing out. "Pull off, or I'll come in your mouth."

Butterflies rolled in my stomach at Luca's thoughtfulness…not a sensation I expected to get while giving another man a blowjob. My hands went to his rear, stopping him from pulling backwards.

Luca gave a low curse as he filled my mouth. I swallowed hastily. It was more bitter than I'd expected but not unpleasant. When he finished, I ran my tongue around the head of his cock, collecting any remaining drops.

Strong hands tugged my hair gently until I was standing. Luca took my mouth hungrily, clearly not caring that I tasted of him. His hand slid down to palm my erection, squeezing it gently through the material.

Just then, there was a knock on the door. "Mr Weston? It's time to take your seats for landing."

Luca squeezed me once more before slipping back a step, eyes full of dangerous promises.

"Later."

"I'm counting on it."

Later turned out to be many more hours than either of us had thought. Luca had barely gotten inside the room before I was on him, tackling him to the floor as we attempted to wrestle each other's clothes off.

When Luca's naked cock touched my own, I swear

I went cross-eyed. If I thought humping against him was good, it was nothing compared to when he spat in his hand and wrapped it around our cocks. He jerked us to completion with nothing more than precum and that bit of saliva.

And it was bliss.

But my favourite time came after. We were in bed, our legs tangled together as we lay facing one another, sharing a pillow. Despite our exhaustion, neither of us could bear to sleep just yet.

I studied the lines on Luca's face. The hard stubble contrasting with his soft full lips. His long eyelashes I was sure people envied him for. The ever-present crinkles around his eyes that paid testament to how often he smiled and laughed.

He was perfection.

"Tell me what you're thinking," he breathed.

That you're beautiful. That I can't remember ever being this happy before. That I can't imagine a time when I won't want you.

The end date of the tour loomed big in my mind. Would Luca even want to continue this after? My familiar walls slammed down, and I flinched.

A shadow passed over Luca's face, something hardening in his eyes. My chest tightened. I knew what Luca wanted from me. I should try and open up. Try and tell him how I was feeling.

But when I opened my mouth, that was not what came out. "Tell me how you and the band met."

There was a beat of silence while Luca clearly considered whether to push me.

Please, half of me whispered.

Please don't, the other half screamed.

Fortunately, Luca went with my subject change. "It didn't happen all at once. Kai and Silas, well, they'd been friends since they were like...thirteen? Twelve? I'm not really sure, but they met when they were young. They lived on the same council estate."

"You didn't grow up on the same estate?"

"No," Luca said. "Thank god. Don't get me wrong, my estate wasn't great...neither was Arlo's. But the one Kai and Silas grew up on...it's the kind of place that gives council estates a bad name."

"How did you meet them?"

"College. I met Silas first. We had a class together."

"Music?"

"No," he snorted. "Believe it or not, philosophy."

I pictured the laid-back bassist. I could see Silas debating Plato and Aristotle. Luca though? "Really?"

He dug a bony finger into my ribs, making me squawk. "Hey, I can chat shit as much as the next person."

I raised an eyebrow at him until he rolled his eyes. "Fine. I needed a fourth subject, and it had the highest pass rate at the college. At the time, I planned on going to university. Like Kai, I knew the best way off the estate was a good education."

"What would you have studied at uni?" I asked curiously, running a finger down his arm.

"Probably aerospace engineering," he said. "I've always been fascinated by planes, and it's a well-paid career. That was what was most important to me."

As someone who'd also grown up in poverty, I understood exactly where Luca had been coming from. It wasn't wanting to be rich but wanting to know you had money to cover your bills. That you'd open the fridge knowing you wouldn't be confronted with empty shelves. That if someone invited you out for the day, you wouldn't need to think up an excuse that wasn't *I can't afford it*.

I gestured at the ridiculously opulent hotel room. "Well, you might not be an engineer, but I think you've done okay for yourself."

His laugh was throaty. "Oh, you can say that again. Honestly, this was never even a thought when we first started playing together. After Silas and I became friends, he invited me to hang out with him and Kai. The two of them used to hang out in Silas's garage, jamming on their instruments. When they realised I had a decent singing voice, they roped me into their sessions. It was...fun. After a while, we used our free periods to book out one of the college's music rehearsal rooms because we loved it so much."

"When did you meet Arlo?"

"It was a total fluke. He was in his final year of secondary and taking a tour of the college. He got separated from the group and found himself in the music building while we were playing. According to him, he watched us for half an hour before building up the courage to knock on the door and ask why we didn't have a drummer."

I grinned at the soft nostalgic light in Luca's eyes. "I'm guessing he offered himself up as tribute."

"He did. Before we knew it, we had a fully formed band. Arlo might've been two years younger than us, but you'd never have known it. Before long, we were no longer satisfied playing with only walls as our audience. We started busking on street corners and in dingy pubs."

"And now you're playing stadiums," I said, lifting his hand to kiss his knuckles. "That's a hell of a leap."

"It is," he agreed, but now his smile was tinged with sadness. "Sometimes I miss those early days. Just four guys hanging out with their instruments. No one else to please or worry about. Just...us."

I didn't know what to say to that. I'd watched their easy camaraderie on the tour and envied it. But even though their long-standing friendship was obvious, there were clear wedges. The things they'd left unspoken seemed to stand like sentinels between them.

Like the way Kai moved around Silas as if he was his centre of gravity. Or how Arlo and Jack pretended they weren't constantly watching each other.

I brushed my thumb over Luca's lower lip, and the quiet sadness in his eyes was immediately replaced by lust.

He rolled on top of me, pinning my wrists to the mattress with his hands.

"Enough talking," he murmured, nosing along my jaw. "Let's discover if I know any other ways to make you weak in the knees."

Chapter 16

Ollie

The next two tour stops passed in a blur. With three shows in Berlin and two in Amsterdam, the band barely had time to breathe in between. Not only that, but they were so busy doing press before the concerts that I didn't have much opportunity to speak to them.

Well, all of them except Luca. I had the chance to talk to him every night when he met me in his room after the show. But not much time was spent talking during those short hours between nightfall and dawn. Just a desperate introduction to all the ways Luca could give and receive pleasure.

Each night brought a new discovery that, added together, revealed one overwhelming truth about myself.

I wasn't disinterested in sex, so long as said sex involved Luca.

During the day, we kept our distance as much as possible. I didn't go to sound checks anymore, choosing instead to sit backstage and work while Luca and the others prepared. I wasn't sure if it was my imagination, but I could've sworn Kevin was cagily watching Luca and me whenever we were in the same space. The last thing I wanted was for Kevin to discover the truth and feed it back to my boss.

There was something about Kevin I couldn't put my finger on. He didn't seem to pay attention to how the band was doing, only speaking to them when he needed to bark orders or reprimands. It left me confused. Wasn't he supposed to work for them, not the other way around?

With Luca filling my nights, I needed whatever time I could grab backstage to write. We were now going into the third week of the tour, having arrived in Copenhagen the previous afternoon. Yet another beautiful city I wanted to come back and visit. Becky had raved about my first two articles, which was a huge relief. Having not covered anything like this before, I wasn't sure how good I'd be at it. Fortunately, my imposter syndrome was forced to sit quietly in the corner. Becky had sent me a screenshot of the website showing me just how successful the first article had been. Who knew if that was down to my writing or the popularity of Caffeine Daydreams. Whatever it was, it was enough to have Becky and the higher-ups raving, which had me relaxing a little.

I'd also heard from Riley a few times, which had been…nice. Just general chit-chat messages, checking in. We'd grown close, but it shocked me to realise I actually missed hanging out with him.

While I steered clear of sound check, the actual shows were a different story. No excuse would've been good enough for me to miss it, given what my role was.

And I didn't want to miss it.

With the screaming crowds and dim lighting, I was

free to ogle Luca on stage as much as I liked. Now that he knew *why* I found his performances so hot, he played up to it even more. I didn't even bother attempting to go to my allotted seat anymore. Luca and Jack made it clear that I was to watch from the pit...and who was I to complain, given it gave me the best possible view of Luca living his best life. The fucker didn't make it easy, however. He flirted with me constantly, his gaze finding mine from whatever side of the stage he happened to be on. And when "Tease" came on? He did exactly what he'd done the first night.

Dropped to his knees before me and drove me fucking wild.

He'd done it so often that the crowd had begun to expect it. The opening chords would ring out over the stadium, and the fans would roar, chanting one word like a desperate prayer.

Kneel. Kneel. Kneel.

And so he would. Every fan in the vicinity behind me believed he was doing it for them. But it wasn't them he was looking at as he sucked his finger into his mouth and ran it down his bare chest.

It was all for me.

Tonight was extra tough. Having discovered how much I enjoyed his bare chest, Luca had decided to forgo his shirt entirely. He'd even poured some water over himself, the liquid cascading down his pecs before rippling over his abs in a way that made me desperate to get back to the hotel room.

When he bent over in front of me, his tight trousers pulling around his delectable rear, I actually whimpered. I thought the noise from the stadium would cover it, but the marginally amused look Jack shot me suggested it hadn't.

I checked the time on my phone for the tenth time in as many minutes. Was time actually going slower?

There was another reason it was dragging on…and it was currently pressed against my prostate. Luca and I had fucked around in practically every conceivable way.

Except one.

Turned out I was a *big* fan of anal play. I didn't know how I'd made it to twenty-seven without discovering this whole new realm of pleasure, but fuck was I grateful Luca had introduced me to it. He could find my prostate with unerring accuracy. Pretty much every night, I came with either his fingers or tongue buried inside me.

I was desperate for him to fuck me. He'd been working me open gradually over the last week, insisting we didn't rush. Given his size, I didn't push the issue too much.

But now I was ready. I'd snuck out to the red-light district during our stop in Amsterdam. It had taken no time at all to hunt out a sex shop. Once I'd overcome my intense embarrassment, the lovely lady who worked there helped me select this plug and everything I needed to…prep.

Using work as an excuse, I'd returned to the hotel during the sound check. After reading a few articles, I'd prepped before taking the most thorough shower ever.

My cock had been rock hard before I'd even opened the lube to coat the plug. Just the thought of what I was about to do had me throbbing.

And knowing Luca would later pull it out to replace it with his shaft?

That had me grabbing my dick and giving it a few

solid tugs.

I'd stopped before I came. I'd wanted to save it for later. It'd make the waiting all the more delicious.

That was what I'd thought then. Several hours later, watching Luca power through the final song, I wished I'd just jerked one out in the hotel. There was so little blood in my head that there was a strong possibility I might faint.

Imagine how that conversation with Jack would go.

"You okay, Ollie? Do you need a doctor?"

"Nah, it's fine. I've just got a boner so epic it's actually trying to kill me."

Seeing as I'd literally rather die than have to admit that, I tried to think unsexy thoughts.

Toenail clippings.

Clogged plugholes.

Dead Mum.

That last one worked best. *Sorry, Mum.* I thought about her as Luca finished the concert, wondering what she would've thought about the life I was living now. Knowing her, she would've been thrilled I was seeing the world. The sole thing she'd wanted for me was to not feel trapped.

Like she'd always felt.

There was no fear of that happening.

Once the show was done, slipping away from the hubbub backstage and into a waiting car was easy. Jack had continued to make good on his promise to get me a room key, meaning I didn't have to resort to my…unusual life skills.

By the time Luca managed to extricate himself from the palaver that seemed to follow every show, I was ready. Given the band's exhaustion after a performance, it struck me as odd that they were expected to hang around for so long afterwards. It wasn't just the fan meet-and-greet either. Kevin always seemed to have some jumped-up VIP he expected them to hobnob with.

The more time I spent with Kevin, the more my guard went up around him. Some days, he barely seemed to register the band was there unless he needed something from one of them. Luca didn't seem to have any issues with the guy...but still. My instincts hadn't failed me yet, and there was something about Kevin that made me wary.

The beeping sound of the door unlocking yanked me from my thoughts. Spreading my legs a little wider, I popped my hands behind my head and lay back. The hours in the gym had paid off. My muscles were more defined than ever. Though that wasn't why I'd gone. There was only so much *Air Crash Investigation* and *Modern Family* I could watch during my free time. Sure, I'd hung out with Riley, but there was no denying that losing Callum and Suzie had left a gaping void in my life.

The gym had filled it.

Luca froze as his gaze fell on me. His hand was outstretched, like he'd been about to throw his key on the table but had gotten distracted.

I bit my lip, trying to contain my smirk. Reducing Luca to stunned silence was an achievement.

Talk about an ego boost.

"Hello," I drawled, letting my knees fall even wider. "As you can see, I started without you."

His dark gaze dropped, his pupils dilating when he saw what rested between my cheeks. "You sure?"

I didn't answer him with my words. Instead, I

reached a hand between my cheeks and slowly extracted the plug. The aching sense of emptiness it left behind was odd. I was seconds away from losing my cool and begging Luca to fill it.

Luca gave a shuddering exhale. He began to strip quickly. "Stay there. I'll be as quick as I can."

I teased a finger around my opening before slipping it inside, making Luca whimper. "Hurry."

Toying with myself carefully, I hovered between the line of arousal and desperation.

I wanted Luca to be the one to push me over.

After the quickest shower known to man, Luca stalked out of the bathroom. After quickly rubbing a towel over his hair, he chucked it to one side before sliding his body over mine.

"You're still wet." I laughed. The sound rapidly morphed into a groan as Luca's hand wrapped around our cocks and gave a leisurely squeeze.

"Don't care," Luca growled, kissing his way up my neck. "You can't expect me to waste time when you're *literally* spread out here, waiting for my cock to fill you."

I whimpered as his hand tightened. He gave a dangerous chuckle. "What's got you so hot, Ollie? My hand? My dirty words? Or are you imagining the way my cock is going to stretch you wide?"

"All of it," I gasped, trying to buck into Luca's grip. "It's all driving me fucking crazy. Jesus, Luca. Don't make me wait."

He shifted his weight to his knees. I was about to protest, but the words died on my tongue as the rough pads of his fingers circled my rim. "How long did you have that plug in?"

"A few hours."

Luca groaned. "Don't tell me you were wearing it the whole time I was on stage."

I stared down at him with hooded eyes. "Yep. Every time I moved, I felt it push against my prostate. When you started thrusting your hips in front of me, I almost fucking fainted just imagining how this would feel."

"I'll make it so good, I swear."

I sat up so I could grab his wrist and pull him in for a kiss. "I know, Luca."

He kissed me once more before settling back on his knees. His hand pulled back for a second before it returned. The cool lube made me squirm as Luca slid a finger into me. "Fuck, Ollie. You're so loose already."

Luca crooked his finger, hitting my prostate dead on. I groaned, my hands digging into the cotton sheets. "I'm ready. I promise."

"You're ready when I say you're ready." Luca added another finger, scissoring me open. "I'm not risking hurting you. Not for your first time."

It seemed to take forever before Luca was satisfied, donning a condom before hovering over me. He forced his tongue into my mouth for a dirty, claiming kiss. "How do you want me?"

"Like this," I panted against his lips.

"It might be better for you to be on top the first ti—"

I clamped a hand over his mouth. "You asked me how I want it. Now follow through."

He licked my palm, making me reflexively yank my hand back. "Ew."

"Funny how you don't say that when I lick you in other places."

Luca knelt between my thighs. His dark hair was mussed around his head, still damp from the shower. He looked like a fallen angel as he guided the head of his cock to my rim. My whole body instinctively tensed against the intrusion.

"Relax, baby," Luca murmured, grabbing my flagging erection and stroking it back to life. "Bear down. Let me in."

Inhaling deeply, I did as he said. I'd had the same issue with the plug earlier. I just needed to get Luca past the first few inches.

Luca was significantly bigger than the plug. Even with the tortoise-like speed he used to ease himself in, I felt like I was being split in two.

Finally, I felt the tight curls at the base of his cock brush against my arse.

"Are you okay?" Luca was leaning over me, studying me with careful eyes. If it wasn't for how he gritted his teeth, I'd have had no idea how hard it was for him to hold back.

"Yes. Move."

Slowly, ever so slowly, Luca pulled his hips back. As he sank back in, his cock brushed against my prostate.

I whimpered as the discomfort shifted into something infinitely more pleasurable. "Again."

Luca repeated the move until I couldn't hold back my moans. My dick was now hard between us, sticky precum trailing and catching on Luca's abs as he worked me over.

I'd never felt anything like this before. I could feel Luca everywhere, but somehow it wasn't enough. My fingers scrabbled against his back, one hand on his arse as

I tried to pull. "Harder. Please, Luca."

Luca's hair fell over his forehead as he looked down at me. "You sure?"

"Yes," I hissed, grabbing him and yanking him into me. "Give it to me, Luca."

With a broken sound, Luca let loose and gave me exactly what I'd asked for. Rough thrusts took me higher as his cock repeatedly brushed over my prostate. The bed banged into the wall so loud that I hoped the hotel had invested in soundproofing.

I couldn't bring myself to care. Not when Luca was making me feel more complete than ever before.

I wanted to tell him. Wanted to share that with him.

But I was so fucking scared. Scared of what might happen if I started to let that emotion pour out. Scared about laying it all out there only to have my heart broken when the tour was over.

"Touch yourself," he rasped, his eyes tinged with desperation. "I can't last."

My hand shot between us. Part of me wanted to savour this feeling of Luca filling me, but I was too close to the edge myself. A few firm tugs had me spilling between us.

My hole clamped around Luca's cock, and his hips shoved forward ruthlessly a few more times as he shot his load into the condom.

Still gasping, he pulled out of me slowly. I winced, the sensation ten times weirder than when I'd removed the plug. There was no pain, thank fuck. Just a strange... ache. I didn't mind that.

It was a reminder of how thoroughly Luca had owned me.

While Luca disposed of the condom, I grabbed tissues from the bedside table to wipe myself. By the time I was done, Luca was crawling back onto the bed. Exhaustion weighed heavy on him. Now that his lust was sated, the toll of the show rode him hard.

He collapsed on top of me before stiffening. “Shit, sorry. I’m probably squashing you.”

I wrapped my arms around him firmly before he could move. “Nope. This is perfect.”

He turned his head so he could smile at me. “Was that okay?”

“Okay?” I gave an incredulous laugh. My earlier fear of sharing with him was nowhere to be seen. With all my guards down, I couldn’t help the raw emotion leaking out. “Luca, you’ve ruined me for anyone else.”

He said one word before catching my mouth with his.

“Good.”

Chapter 17

Luca

If I'd thought I was needy before, giving Ollie his first taste of bottoming had introduced me to a hitherto unknown level of codependency. I had to physically stop myself from reaching for him at every opportunity. When it was just my bandmates or Jack around, I let myself touch him. I trusted them more than anyone. Besides, they'd listened to me drone on endlessly about Ollie during the five months we'd been apart. There was no point hiding my feelings towards Ollie when they already knew how I felt.

It wasn't even the act itself that had me wanting to drape myself over him every hour of the day. No, it had been those whispered words about me ruining him. That night had opened a door between us, cracking the shields Ollie kept around his heart and letting me slide inside.

I knew why he had them, and I completely understood why he needed to keep everyone at arm's length. Even if he hadn't been royally screwed by his ex and former best friend, his turbulent childhood meant he was more guarded than most. He hadn't told me much, but the halted conversations in the dark of night had filled in enough of the picture for me.

Coupled with the way he'd lost his mum...yeah. It made perfect sense that he was encased in armour several inches thick.

But understanding why didn't stop me from getting frustrated. There was always a point during those conversations when Ollie would hit a wall. Where his words would refuse to come out. That was when he'd roll me over, distracting me with his hands or mouth until I no longer remembered what we'd been talking about.

I was trying so hard to take things slow with Ollie. The problem was that the more time I spent with him, the more I wanted to push.

I wanted him to be mine. To know we had a future once this tour was done.

Ollie wasn't ready for that. He held himself so tight that sometimes I was scared he'd make himself crack.

My brain was no better. My anxiety was well controlled, but it made me overthink things. Everything, really. I'd spent hours agonising over every decision with Ollie, considering what the outcome might be with each one.

Things might've moved on between us physically, but thanks to Ollie's bottled emotions and my dickhead brain, we were nowhere near where I wanted us to be emotionally.

Maybe today would help us take another step towards it. We had a rare day off, and I'd arranged a surprise for Ollie. What better place for romantic wooing than Paris? It was so cliché, it would almost be rude not to.

When Kevin asked me what I had planned for

today, I caught myself before I told him. He was my manager. I should be able to trust him as much as my bandmates—more even, given the level of control he had over my life and career.

But I'd been watching him as closely as he'd been watching Ollie. I didn't like it. There was a gleam in his eyes like he was concocting some scheme. Regardless of what it was, I didn't want him anywhere *near* Ollie.

So I lied, the words tripping easily off my tongue. A quick message on our group thread with Arlo, Kai, and Silas had me covered. If anyone asked, they'd vouch for me spending the day with them songwriting.

Only Jack knew what I really had planned. I wasn't stupid enough to stroll around a foreign city without security. I'd learned the hard way that no disguise was infallible. It was one thing if I was spotted by a fan wanting a selfie, but if the paps caught up to me, my cover would be blown.

Oh well. That was future Luca's problem. Current Luca wanted to take Ollie out for a busy day of sightseeing, and nothing would stop that from happening.

"Where are we going? And why exactly are you wearing that?"

Jack drove us away from the hotel while Ollie and I huddled in the backseat. My fingers were entwined with his. Here, with the privacy glass and my disguise, we were free to just be us. "I'm incognito."

Ollie swept his gaze over me, one brow raised. "Who have you been taking disguise tips from—the Avengers?"

I lowered my sunglasses to frown over them. "What?"

He gestured vaguely. "You know, they all chuck on

a baseball hat and a pair of sunnies, and suddenly, no one knows who they are. I'm pretty sure it won't work with your fans."

I pushed my glasses back up and grinned. "You'd be surprised. If people don't expect you to be there, they don't tend to look at you long enough to notice."

"And if they do?"

"Then we smile, I do a selfie, and we move along."

Ollie tapped a finger against his thigh. "And if it's the paps?"

"Then Jack will get us out of there. That's why he's here."

Ollie hesitated. "Won't people think…you know, that we're together?"

A band of iron tightened around my ribs. I hated that Ollie was afraid of being seen with me. "Would it really matter that much?"

His cool gaze met mine. "It would if it means I lose my job."

I squeezed his hand. "You won't lose your job."

"You can't know that."

Jack's eyes met mine in the rearview mirror before sliding away. Like my bandmates, he knew the truth.

"Is that the only reason?"

Ollie shrugged. "Mainly. I wouldn't mind them speculating about me being seen with a *guy* if that's what you're worried about. But wouldn't it cause problems for you?"

"What do you mean?"

"Like if you get all this media coverage speculating about this new guy you've been seen with, and then, once the tour is over and I've…gone home, there will be rumours about what happened."

I was suddenly glad my eyes were hidden by my sunglasses. "What makes you so sure this will end when the tour does?"

Ollie's brows knitted together. "Because that's what we agreed…right?"

That band tightened until it was difficult for me to draw breath. Fuck, he was so hard to read. Did he feel that way because that was what he wanted? Or because he believed it was what *I* wanted?

I was about to ask him, to blurt it all out and admit that I wanted to continue exploring our…dynamic, but just then, Jack stopped the car. "We're here."

Ollie's head snapped around, his mouth falling open. "Holy shit. Have you brought me to the Louvre?"

I forced a smile. Later. There'd be time for the heavy stuff later. Now was about showing Ollie Paris. "Do you like art?"

"Meh," he said, the word at odds with his awed expression. "Could take it or leave it, to be honest. But getting to explore one of the most famous museums in the world? Hell yes."

Jack opened Ollie's door, startling him. He jumped out hastily. "You don't need to open the door for me."

Jack didn't stop surveying the surroundings. "Perks of putting up with Luca's bullshit."

I climbed out after Ollie, choking on a laugh. "Jack! Who knew you had a sense of humour?"

He didn't respond, too focused on searching through the crowds of people for any possible threat. Fortunately, not a single passerby gave us a second glance. It was early in the day, and the pavement was filled with commuters. The museum didn't even open for another hour, but that didn't matter.

Up ahead, a smartly dressed woman with platinum-blonde hair waved briskly. "Ah, there's our tour guide."

"We're joining a tour group?"

"No." I chuckled. "I booked us a private tour."

Ollie's jaw fell open, but I was saved from explaining by the very exuberant tour guide. She ushered us into the silent museum, facts rattling from her at an alarming rate.

Like Ollie, I wasn't particularly interested in art. But I could spend days watching Ollie's face as he took in the architecture and history surrounding us.

I slid my hand into his, ignoring the pang brought on by his widened eyes and panicked glance at the tour guide. I leaned in to reassure him. "It's okay. She's signed an NDA and is being paid to keep anything she sees strictly confidential."

Ollie relaxed, his bright smile returning. I tried to focus on the way my hand felt as he caressed it absentmindedly with his thumb, but I couldn't strike the image of his fear-filled eyes.

Was it just his job Ollie was worried about? Or was it being seen with *me*?

He'd said long ago that he wouldn't like to live in the spotlight, and honestly, I didn't want that for him either.

But I also didn't want to hide how I felt about him.

"And here we have the famous *Mona Lisa*." The tour guide swept to a spot in front of a tiny portrait, clapping her hands together. She gave a reverent sigh. "Isn't she magnifique?"

Ollie crinkled his nose. "I was expecting it to be bigger."

"That's what he said."

Ollie laughed, trying to disguise it as a cough when the tour guide replaced her rosy disposition with a haughty glare. "The *Mona Lisa* is a national treasure. Tourists queue for *hours* just to get a peek at her."

I stepped closer to the guide, flashing her a charming grin. "Apologies, mademoiselle."

She fluffed her hair, giggling like a schoolgirl. "It's madame. I haven't been *mademoiselle* in many years."

I put a hand to my chest in mock surprise. "I would never believe such a thing. Perhaps you could show us some of the other treasures the museum is hiding?"

Mollified, she bowed her head and motioned for us to follow her. Ollie fell into step beside me, his hand slipping into mine like it belonged there. "You really are a charming bastard."

I pulled our joined hands up to press a kiss to his. "I like getting my own way."

Ollie's eyes heated. "Oh, believe me, that's something I'm well aware of."

Suddenly, filling the entire day with various tours felt like a stupid idea when we could've spent it naked in bed.

Those thoughts faded as Ollie's excitement and wonder grew.

We'd started the day so early that it was barely brunch by the time we left the Louvre. After grabbing croissants from a bakery, we were back on our sightseeing mission. We had tours around Saint Chappelle, the Musée d'Orsay, and finally, a boat trip on the river Seine.

My feet were killing me by the time dusk rolled around. But it'd been worth it to hear Ollie wax lyrical about everything we'd seen.

I'd been to Paris countless times before, but seeing the city through Ollie's eyes gave it a whole new colour. It was in the questions he threw at the guides, how he studied every detail in awe, how he grabbed my hand and yanked me over to something he'd spotted.

Ollie relaxed as the day went on without me being recognised. The band around my chest loosened. If it was just my celebrity he was struggling with, then that was a barrier we could overcome.

We'd just come off the riverboat and were meandering along the city streets, killing time before our dinner reservation. Jack hung back several paces, giving us some privacy.

Ollie stopped abruptly before pulling me to his side. "What are they queuing for?"

I eyed the chattering tourists, craning my neck to see what was at the other end. "Some shop, by the looks of it."

"Do we have time to join?"

I raised an eyebrow. "Yeah…but you're telling me you want to queue without even knowing what we're waiting for?"

Ollie gave me a look of mock solemnity, underdone by the humour in his eyes. "Well, it *is* very British to queue. We'd be letting our fellow countrymen down if we bypassed an example as impeccable as this one."

"Heaven forbid. We can't have that. What would our ancestors say?"

"Exactly." Ollie beamed, pulling me to the back of

the queue. "It's an adventure."

I snorted. "I think my years in America must be showing because I can't see how a *queue* is an adventure."

Ollie rolled his eyes, not rising to the bait.

As we drew nearer to the shop front, I was the one to let out a groan. "Oh my god—macarons."

"I take it you're not pissed about the queue now."

"Depends," I said, raising an eyebrow. "Will you let me buy an extra box so I can eat them off your naked body later?"

He blushed before tugging me in front of him.

"What are you doing?"

Draping his arms around my shoulders, he pressed his front against my back. "Thanks to you, I have a little problem. Because it's your fault, you're going to help me hide it until it goes away."

"Hardly little," I muttered, remembering how it'd stretched me the night before. I pushed my rear back against his erection, rubbing against it a couple times.

Ollie growled in my ear. "Tease."

"You know it."

I managed to behave myself for the rest of the queue, and before long, we exited the shop with two boxes of the delicacies.

"Okay, that was definitely worth it." I spoke the words around a mouthful of macaron. "We might need to go back before we leave."

"Aren't we going to dinner?" Ollie asked with barely concealed amusement as I shoved a third biscuit in my mouth.

"Don't care. I'll just live off macarons. Leave me here. I'll be happy so long as that shop is nearby."

Ollie laughed, his eyes soft as he grinned at me.

I swiped a crumb from the corner of my lip as he continued to stare at me. I was starting to get paranoid. "What? Do I have something on my face?"

"No." He stepped closer, his hand coming up to my face. "You're just...I can't even describe it, Luca. I look at you, and it's like I can breathe easily for the first time ever. Everyone looks at you and sees this star, but you're so much more than that. You're witty, caring…free."

I gaped at him, unsure where this sudden burst of emotion had come from. *Don't get me wrong, I loved it.* "Thanks."

He leaned down to peck my lips. "No, thank you, Luca. I'm so glad you chased me. And thank you for today. It's been…amazing."

I swallowed around the sudden lump in my throat. "It's not over yet."

"I don't even want to know how you managed to land a table there," Ollie said as we left Jules Verne. Situated on the second floor of the Eiffel Tower, there was nothing to beat it in terms of views.

"Perks of being a rock star. What did you think of the food?"

Ollie winced. "Okay. I mean, obviously, it was great, but…"

I chuckled. "I get it. It was way too fucking fancy for me too. Give me ham, egg, and chips any day of the week."

He grinned at me in relief as we got into the lift, Jack at our backs. As it began its descent, I couldn't help but remember our first meeting. From the heated sidelong glances Ollie gave me, he was right there with me.

I slipped my hand in his as I considered all the ways I wanted to make him scream once we returned to the hotel room.

All those thoughts shattered when the lift doors opened to reveal hordes of shouting paparazzi.

Ollie dropped my hand like hot coals. Something fractured inside me until I realised what he was doing.

He was standing in front of me. Shielding me from view.

Just as he had all those months ago.

"Damnit," Jack cursed, his arms flying wide to keep the press from entering. I was frozen in place. There was no way we'd be able to get out of this lift. "Back up, everyone!"

"Luca, is this your new boyfriend?"

"Are you on a date?"

"Is it true you're sleeping with a journalist?"

Ollie's back stiffened, his hands curling into fists. I could practically hear his thoughts. His panic about what this would mean for his job.

Someone shoved Jack back a step. Camera flashes filled the small lift.

I tried to breathe in, but someone had capped off my lungs.

They weren't working.

The walls were closing in. The flashes blinding me.

"Luca, over here."

"Luca..."

"Luca..."

"Luca..."

I couldn't breathe. Couldn't move. Couldn't think.

A warm strong chest cradled me, drawing me deeper into the lift. Big arms pulled me close, a hand covering one ear while the other was pushed against cool cotton.

"Jack, get the fucking press out of here. Now."

I closed my eyes. Ollie's cologne mixed with the scent of the wine we'd consumed with dinner. I inhaled, drawing him into me.

Ollie was here. Ollie would make it okay.

The shouts cut off suddenly. Were they gone? Or was it my hearing?

Nausea waged war with dizziness for my attention. "Wanna lie down."

Ollie muttered before shifting me in his arms. "I've got you, baby. Here, sit on my lap."

Numb, I let him move me like a puppet. Somehow we were on the floor, me straddling his lap. "Can't feel my hands. Feet don't work."

"I've got you. It's just us, Luca. You can let go."

Normality returned to me slowly. First, the sensation of Ollie's hands stroking up and down my back. Then the feel of damp cotton under my cheek. Sweat or tears, who the fuck knew.

Finally, the sound of Ollie's voice humming.

"Are you humming 'Something'?"

The notes cut off immediately. "Huh, I guess I am. Must be stuck in my head."

I ducked my head so my face was hidden. I didn't want him to see how deeply this moment was hitting me. There was no way for him to know that I'd written "Something" after going through an anxiety attack alone…wishing desperately to have someone who'd hold me through it.

God, I wanted this. Wanted him.

Always.

"Sorry," I muttered, embarrassment filtering through as the anxiety ebbed away. "Not how I envisaged this date endi—ouch!"

"Quit it," Ollie said firmly, massaging the patch of skin he'd pinched on my side. "I don't want to hear you apologise. You have *nothing* to be sorry about."

"Ollie's right. If anything, I should be the one apologising." Jack's voice had me jumping out of my skin. "We'll be out of here shortly."

I cursed under my breath. "Fuck, didn't know you were still here."

"Wouldn't leave you alone with those piranhas out there," Jack grunted, his fingers flying over his phone screen. "No offence, Ollie."

"None taken," he replied darkly as we got to our feet. "Trust me, that side of journalism has never appealed."

Jack frowned at me, his lips in a thin line. "Someone posted photos of you arriving here for dinner on Twitter. I should've spotted it earlier. I'm so sorry."

I waved Jack's apologies off. "No, I knew this was a strong possibility. As Ollie pointed out, it's not like my disguise is foolproof."

Jack pushed the emergency stop button, and the lift started to move again. In my panicked state, I hadn't even realised it'd stopped. "I've called in the rest of the security team. They've cleared a path, and there's a car waiting."

I sighed, rubbing my hands over my face. "How bad do I look?"

Ollie lifted a hand to stroke over my hair. "You look like perfection. Fuck any of them who say otherwise."

His muscles were tense, small lines framing his thoughtful eyes.

What was wrong? Was it because he was going to be photographed with me again? Was he worried about his job? Or was this too much of a reminder of what the reality of being mine looked like?

My time to ask was up. The doors opened, a million bulbs going off at once.

Jack and Ollie moved into position on either side of me, their faces grim. My heart sank as we pushed our way through the crowd, fans now intermingled with the press.

This was a lot to ask of someone. Especially someone as private as Ollie.

Perhaps it was too much.

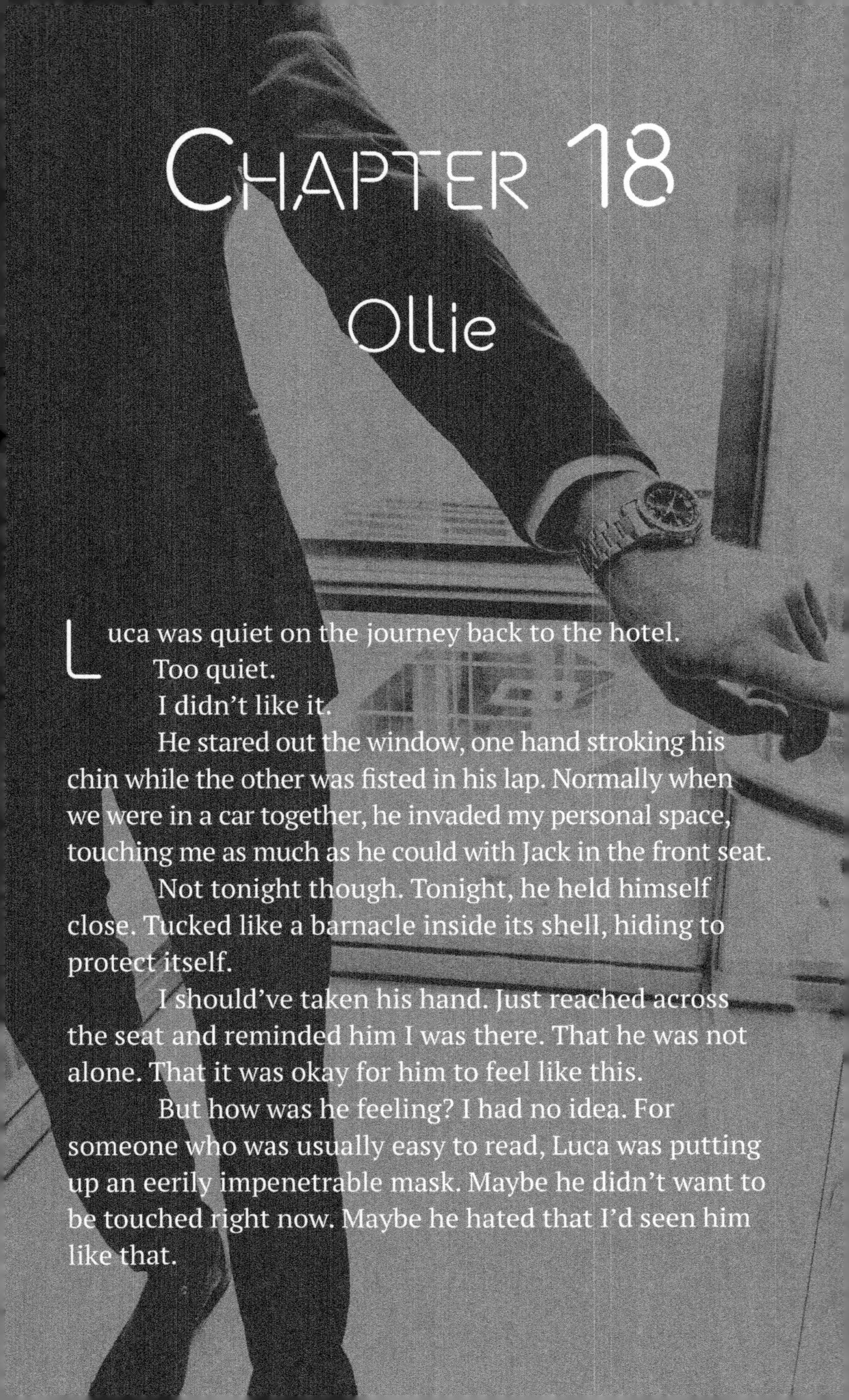

Chapter 18

Ollie

Luca was quiet on the journey back to the hotel.

Too quiet.

I didn't like it.

He stared out the window, one hand stroking his chin while the other was fisted in his lap. Normally when we were in a car together, he invaded my personal space, touching me as much as he could with Jack in the front seat.

Not tonight though. Tonight, he held himself close. Tucked like a barnacle inside its shell, hiding to protect itself.

I should've taken his hand. Just reached across the seat and reminded him I was there. That he was not alone. That it was okay for him to feel like this.

But how was he feeling? I had no idea. For someone who was usually easy to read, Luca was putting up an eerily impenetrable mask. Maybe he didn't want to be touched right now. Maybe he hated that I'd seen him like that.

My own hands fisted on my legs. No. I wasn't going to let Luca push me away. I'd respect anything he asked, but I wouldn't have him punishing himself or hiding from me.

With a trembling hand, I reached across the distance between us, my hand falling on his thigh and squeezing.

Luca jumped, his brows high as he stared down at my hand. After a moment or two, he covered it with his own. His skin was clammy thanks to the panic attack, but it felt like perfection against my own.

But still, he didn't look at me.

I held my tongue for the rest of the journey, as we pushed through the crowds of paparazzi waiting outside the hotel, and during the silent lift ride to Luca's floor.

Jack shot a concerned look at me as he let us into Luca's suite. I shook my head at him.

I'd deal with this. Whatever was breaking him right now, I'd be the one to pick up the pieces and put him back together.

I let Luca stew in silence as he stalked around the hotel room, checking his phone before throwing it to one side with a huff. But when he kicked off his clothes, marching for the bathroom like I wasn't even in the room, I decided enough was enough.

Steam from the shower had already filled the bathroom by the time I'd stripped off and pushed my way inside. Luca's form was blurry through the fogged shower glass. His head hung low, his forearms braced against the back wall as he let the water stream down his back.

I stepped into the stall, reaching around him to grab the body wash he liked to use. Lathering the sponge,

I ran it over Luca's body in soothing circles.

"What are you doing?"

"Taking care of you."

"Why?"

Spinning him around, I lifted his chin with a soapy finger. "Because you deserve to be taken care of, Luca."

He bit his lip. "I come with a lot of baggage."

I dropped a kiss on the end of his nose. "So do I. But I think it'll be easier if we take turns carrying it."

The last of the anxiety left Luca's body. I continued to wash him, only speaking to tell him to lift a foot or turn around. Once he was clean, I shut off the water before wrapping him in one of the many fluffy towels supplied by the hotel.

"I'm not a child."

I grinned. "Really? Your petulant tone would suggest otherwise."

I finished towelling myself off and reached down to grab my pyjama bottoms. Luca stopped me by grabbing my wrist. "Wait, are we not fucking around tonight?"

I raised an eyebrow, noting the exhaustion clinging to Luca like a second skin. "We can, but I figured we'd just take it easy. Maybe watch some trashy TV. Cuddle."

"You'd...you'd be okay with that?"

It hit me then that we'd never spent time alone without having sex. Even the intimate moments we'd shared were proceeded or followed by orgasms.

And as much as I loved that, suddenly, nothing was more important to me than holding Luca close with no expectations. No plans of anything happening aside from me being there for him.

"Of course it's okay," I said gruffly, shoving my

legs into my pyjamas and grabbing my laptop from the table. I jumped onto the bed. "Let's just curl up together and pretend the world doesn't exist for a little while."

Luca hovered at the edge of the bed, his lip between his teeth. I plumped up his pillows, pushing back the thick duvet and patting the sheet next to me. "Come on, get in and get comfy. What do you normally watch to relax?"

His lips twitched, a ghost of his usual self returning. "Promise you won't judge me?"

Something in me relaxed as he slid into the sheets, his legs slipping between mine. "Well, only if it's *Eastenders*."

He gave a mock shudder. "God no. Too fucking depressing for me. Although, I suppose the same could be said about *Air Crash Investigation*."

"You watch *Air Crash Investigation*?"

He groaned, his head flopping back against the pillow. "I know it's weird."

I should've guessed when he said he'd wanted to be an aerospace engineer. With a grin, I nudged him, pointing to the website I had bookmarked on my screen. "Not weird."

Luca's eyes widened in surprise. "Really?"

"Yep." I popped the *P*, clicking on the most recent episode. "This one was uploaded last night, so I'm guessing you haven't seen it."

"Haven't seen any since the tour started. Been too busy."

"We've got a lot to catch up on then."

The familiar voice of the narrator echoed from the laptop's tinny speakers. Luca wriggled around until his head was on my chest, his hand stroking my stomach in idle circles as he lost himself in the programme.

As I wrapped my arms around him and felt him unwind against me, I realised something.

I was happy.

Even with the end we'd had to the day...I was happy. Luca was in my arms. The world was shut away.

And I was *happy*.

I should've known the world couldn't be kept at bay for long.

We were woken early the next morning by Jack shaking Luca.

"Sorry, Luca," he said in hushed tones. "I did knock, but you didn't respond. Kevin wants to see you. He tried to barge in himself, but I convinced him to wait for you in his suite."

I frowned groggily at Luca. "Is it normal for management to be all up in your personal life this much?"

Luca grunted but didn't respond. Maybe I was reading too much into it. Wasn't like this was my area of speciality.

I turned back to Jack. "How bad is it?"

"Bad." Jack's voice was clipped, his gaze averted as Luca and I pushed out of bed and rapidly dressed. "Rumours are flying that the two of you are in a relationship."

"Do they know who I am?"

Jack's pitying look was enough to answer my question.

"Fuck." I slumped down on my bed and rubbed my forehead. What would this mean for my job?

"Hey." Luca was there, his hand firmly lifting my

chin. "Don't worry. You're not going to lose your job over this."

"You can't be sure of that."

He gave me a grim smile. "Do you trust me?"

His question made my breath catch in my throat. Did I? I'd only ever trusted three people: my mum, Callum, and Suzie.

All of them had ended up hurting me in one way or another.

But Luca...I *wanted* to trust him. I wanted to crack open my walls to let him slip inside. "I want to."

He bobbed his head, his lips curving. "Close enough. Leave this with me."

When he left, Jack following a few steps behind, I forced myself to check my phone. Ignoring the alarming number of notifications on my social media apps, I opened my work email.

Dread sank like a stone in my chest when I saw the unread email from Becky. Sent at eleven p.m. the night before, the subject line contained a single word.

Urgent.

Blood roared in my ears as I clicked it.

There was no greeting. No sign-off. Just two simple sentences that cut right to the heart of the matter.

Remember, your behaviour reflects directly on Identity.

I hope you know what you're doing.

I sent the screen to sleep with numb fingers. What *was* I doing? Against all odds, I'd landed my dream job. This opportunity was one even senior writers at the company would *kill* for. Was I going to risk it all for an affair with a rock star?

A sour taste filled my mouth. No. Not for a *rock*

star. For Luca. After the way he'd treated me over the last few weeks, he deserved better than me reducing him to his job.

But still…was being with Luca worth the resulting fallout?

Yes. My heart screamed at me, reminding me of every tender look that had passed between us. Every joke. Every touch. How he'd gone out of his way to make me feel special. Wanted.

But what if a fling on this tour was all Luca wanted? What if, once we were home, he forgot about me?

I hung my head in my hands, trying to sort my chaotic thoughts into some semblance of order.

The only way to know what Luca wanted was to ask him. To be brave and offer up my heart, hoping it wouldn't end up broken.

Again.

But what if I was making this thing out to be more than it was? Sure, Luca had hinted he wanted more, but he hadn't outright said anything. He hadn't labelled us… or even said we were exclusive.

Fuck, I didn't know what to think about anything anymore.

There was only one thing I was sure about.

I was falling for Luca. At some point, without realising, I'd leapt off the tripwire. There was no safety net. No bungee cord.

I just had to hope and pray I'd find Luca falling alongside me.

Chapter 19

Luca

Now that the fog of anxiety had cleared, I was left with two duelling emotions: concern and irritation.

The first was for how the public rumours of our relationship might affect Ollie, and the second was for Kevin sticking his oar in.

I got it about Ollie. I did. His fear for his job was written all over his face. But it wasn't like I could say, '*Hey, unless you straight up told your boss to go fuck herself, your job is safe*'...without confessing what I'd done and how I knew that. I had to hope he trusted me enough to know I wouldn't let anything bad happen to him.

And pray he wouldn't use this as an excuse to push me away. The man had been hurt too many times in the past. I'd *finally* felt like I was getting somewhere with him.

Hopefully, this morning's wake-up call wouldn't set us back on that front.

Irritation bubbled over the concern when I entered Kevin's suite and found him sat at the table. He had a face like thunder, several newspapers spread in front of him, my name screaming from the headlines of each one.

Jack took up a spot by the wall, gazing off into the distance. I didn't acknowledge Kevin, not yet. Instead, I poured myself a much-needed cup of coffee before settling into the chair opposite him. Sipping my caffeine, I waited for him to speak.

"The journalist? *Really*? Could you not keep it in your trousers just this once?"

"It's not about that."

Kevin scoffed, his finger smacking down on a particularly damning photo. Someone must've sneaked a shot in the restaurant. It showed Ollie's hand in mine, our heads bowed together. If our body positioning hadn't given away the intimacy of the moment, the secret smile I wore as I gazed adoringly at Ollie would've. "You're telling me you're not fucking him?"

My temper flared. "I'm telling you that I'm not *just* fucking him. I'm serious about Ollie. And forgive me, Kevin, but the last time I checked, your job is to manage our *band*, not our private lives."

A vein throbbed in Kevin's temple. "I shouldn't need to remind you that when your private life becomes public, it then enters my domain. What kind of image are you trying to present here, Luca? I thought I'd made it clear that the last thing the label wants to see is examples of your fuckboy behaviour."

I took a sip of coffee, using the time to get my anger under control. Either Kevin wasn't listening to me, or he was choosing to ignore what I'd said. "What part of this classifies as *fuckboy* behaviour, exactly? The romantic candlelit dinner? The fact we were holding hands in the lift? The way Ollie tried to shelter me from the press?"

"You can't be telling me you're serious about this boy." Disdain dripped from Kevin's every word. From the corner of my eye, I saw Jack tense.

"That's exactly what I'm telling you. He's not a *boy*, Kevin. He's a grown man capable of making decisions. As am I."

"Jesus, Luca. You can't be this naive. Tell me, what do you think will happen when this inevitably blows up in your face? What's to stop him from writing a tell-all book on you?"

"Ollie wouldn't do that. That's not why he's with me."

Kevin leaned forward, his face solemn. "Luca, I'm looking out for you here. Ollie is a *journalist.* It's his job to sell stories about the rich and famous. And they don't come richer or more famous than you. Hasn't it occurred to you that he's using you?"

I gritted my teeth. "He's not using me."

"You sure about that?" Kevin raised an eyebrow.

I thought about the way I'd pursued Ollie. How he'd fought me every step of the way. How he'd wanted to keep us hidden from everyone. None of those actions suggested he was manipulating me. I'd had many people try and worm their way in with me for one reason or another. I'd bet every penny in my offshore accounts that Ollie wasn't one of them. "Yes. I'm sure."

Kevin grunted, sitting back in his chair. "So this isn't just a fling."

"No."

"You're going to go home and settle down with

him? Get a house? A dog?" He scoffed. "Doesn't really sound like you."

Actually, his description sounded like all my dreams coming true. But I couldn't admit that without Kevin fussing about what it might mean for the future. Not that I had any plans to give up the band...but I was determined to have a normal life too. Jesus, hadn't I earned that?

"Maybe." That was all I'd give Kevin for now. "Are we done here?"

"Not quite." He was tapping on the table now. I could almost see his brain whirring, trying to work out how he was going to spin this. "That's what you and Ollie have agreed to then? To carry this on after the tour?"

I opened my mouth to give him an affirmative answer but stopped with a frown. Had we actually discussed it? Or had I just...assumed?

Kevin patted my hand pityingly. "Maybe you should chat with him before making any grand declarations to the press. I'll go with the 'private interview' line. It won't appease them, but if the two of you aren't photographed together again, hopefully, the rumours will die away."

I wanted to protest. Wanted to shout to the world that they weren't rumours. That Ollie was *mine,* and I didn't give a fuck who knew it.

But that wasn't fair to Ollie. He hadn't asked to be put under the microscope. And he certainly hadn't made his intentions for after the tour clear.

I gave a stiff nod before shoving my chair back to leave. Kevin grabbed my wrist before I could do so. His lips were thin as he cautioned me. "I know you said he isn't using you...but I want you to think about it, Luca. Has he told you he has feelings for you? Made you any promises about the future?"

I glared at Kevin's hand until he released me. "Just...think about it. That's all I'm asking."

As much as I tried to stop them, Kevin's questions wormed their way under my skin. I found myself analysing every interaction with Ollie. Questioning if he'd done or said anything that hinted at a future for us after this tour.

I continued coming up empty.

Remember last night, I told myself, more than once. *A guy who just wanted a fling wouldn't turn down a night of sex to snuggle. He wouldn't wash you in the shower before tucking you up with your favourite TV show. That's the kind of thing a partner does, not a fling.*

Still, the gnawing worry in my stomach wouldn't go away. It didn't help that Ollie seemed to think this would end when the tour did. Was that because we hadn't discussed it? Or was that *actually* what he wanted?

I couldn't seem to get a moment alone with him to talk about my fears either. Kevin kept him busy the whole day, insisting he interview individual members of our vast techie crew to get their perspectives. Meanwhile, I was stuck in sound checks and reviewing possible new song ideas with Kai. The closest I got to Ollie was in the longing glances I couldn't help but throw his way every few minutes.

"Quit it."

"What?"

Kai kicked my leg, forcing me to finally drag my attention back to him. "Watching him. You're making it obvious."

Silas chose that exact moment to stroll past, whistling an unfamiliar tune. Kai tracked him like a predator until he was out of sight. "You're one to talk."

"That's different."

"How?"

"Because it doesn't matter how I look at Silas. He has never noticed, nor will he *ever* notice." He bent and twisted the notepad in his hands. "But Ollie knows, man. You wear your heart on your sleeve around him."

"I've always done that. You guys have known how I feel about him from the start. Why is it suddenly a bad thing?"

He shrugged. "I'm not saying it is...but are you sure he feels the same way? There's no denying you're hung up on him, but..."

Kai's voice drifted off, making my spine stiffen. "Spit it out."

He pursed his lips, leaning closer. "Okay, as clear as it is that you're into him...I don't get the same vibe from Ollie."

"He's a closed book," I said automatically. "Not everyone is as open about their feelings as we are."

Kai nodded slowly. He hadn't revealed his feelings to Silas, but he'd made no effort to hide them from the rest of us. "That's fair. But explain this—you've been mooning over the guy all day, but he's barely *glanced* at you."

That wasn't true...was it? "And?"

He blew out a breath. "And I don't want you to

get your heart broken. Trust me, there's nothing worse than unrequited love. You've not known him long at all. What's the rush? There's no harm in holding back part of your heart until you're sure he's in this with you."

I studied Ollie as he laughed with one of the sound techies, noting how swiftly he turned his back when he felt my eyes on him. Was Kai right? It'd been easy to dismiss Kevin's concerns...but it was harder to ignore Kai. The quiet voices in my mind were getting louder, reminding me how little Ollie had opened up to me. But maybe that was because he was worried about his job. Would he leave me for it? Was his career more important to him than I was?

There was no way he was fooling around with me for a story. I didn't believe that for a second.

But what if I was just some...experiment to him? Some wild oats he wanted to sow before he found someone sensible to settle down with? Someone who didn't spend months at a time travelling the globe. Someone who knew what time zone they'd be in from day to day and whether they could make dinner that night.

Kai wasn't done. "Also...you know his job is secure, but he doesn't. Is it really fair to be so obviously flaunting your relationship, knowing he's worried about it?"

A muscle jumped in my jaw as I turned over his words. "So what are you saying? I need to stop being so obvious about it in public?"

"That or tell him the truth."

I grunted. Yeah, that wasn't happening. I'd prefer to keep my possessive and interfering behaviour quiet as long as possible. That might not make me a good person, but if it kept Ollie within my sphere, I'd deal with it.

One thing was certain, I needed to talk to him. Because Kai was right. I was falling hard and fast, with no idea if Ollie was beside me or not.

Chapter 20

Ollie

"You got a second?"

Arlo caught me as I finished my last interview of the day. Using a drumstick, he pointed at the seat next to him.

I sat, flicking my pad open as I did. Arlo shook his head, the drumstick now twirling between his fingers. "Nah, you can put that away. We've talked about me plenty. I want to talk about you."

Warily, I closed the notebook. "What about me?"

He didn't look at me as he spoke, like he understood I wouldn't like the scrutiny. "You don't open up much."

"That's not my job here. I'm here to write about you all, not make friends."

"What do you call what you're doing with Luca then?"

I sighed. I'd been waiting for one of them to call me out on it all day. They must've seen the photos.

Honestly, I'd been expecting it to be Silas…or maybe even Kai, given how close he was to Luca.

Not the quiet drummer who seemed to be repressing a similar number of emotions as me.

"I call it *private*."

Arlo snorted. "Yeah, that went out the window the second the paps found you."

I rolled my head on my shoulders, the ache of the past twenty-four hours pulsing at the base of my skull. "We're…I don't know what you'd call it."

"Friends? Fuck buddies? Boyfriends?"

"New." I gave Arlo a tight smile. "Look, this whole…opening up to people thing? I'm not used to it."

He inclined his head. "We have that in common. But you like Luca, yes?"

I squeezed my eyes shut. I shouldn't be telling someone before I had the chance to tell Luca, but maybe I could think of this as a warmup. A rehearsal before the big show where I may or may not get my heart broken. "I do. I like him."

Arlo nudged me with his knee. "Good. That's the only thing I care about. You guys will sort the rest out."

My gaze drifted over to where Luca was sat with Kai. All day it'd killed me to keep my distance, but every time I caught him looking at me, the email from Becky would dance in front of my eyes. There was so much more at stake than just my job. If I fucked up *Identity*'s reputation, there was a chance I'd never work in the industry again.

For once, Luca wasn't looking my way. Instead, he scowled at the floor, his back tight as Kai spoke rapidly.

As usual, my path didn't cross with Luca's for

the rest of the day. The closest I got to him was during the show, but even then, it was like I wasn't there. When Luca's performance brought him near me, his attention was fixed on his fans.

You're overthinking things. He's putting on a show for them, not you.

I almost had myself convinced until the opening chords of "Tease" thundered through the stadium. The crowd picked up their now-familiar chant.

Kneel. Kneel. Kneel.

And so he did.

At the opposite end of the stage from me.

I watched from a distance as he made eye contact with a beautiful blonde in the front row. Sucked a finger into his mouth and ran it down his bare chest. Made her squeal as he shot her a flirty wink.

It felt like I was trying to breathe underwater. Blood roared in my ears, blotting out the other sounds in the stadium. Nothing else existed except the sensual promise in Luca's eyes. The heat of his smirk as he played the woman like a fiddle.

I could do nothing but watch as Luca made me question everything that had passed between us.

Next to me, Jack tensed. I could feel his gaze burning into the side of my face, but I didn't look at him. I didn't want to see the questions there.

Not when I didn't have the answers.

It's part of the act, I told myself as I sat in the car on the way back to the hotel. I'd tried to find Luca after the show, but he'd had a queue of fans waiting for autographs. One glimpse of the girl he'd been flirting with had me turning my back and deciding to get out of there. Even if it was all fake, no part of me wanted to see Luca charming anyone else.

I was still stewing on it when Luca finally let himself into the suite several hours later.

His easy grin faded as he took in the glass of whisky in my hand. "Everything okay?"

"You tell me." I sank the final inch of the amber liquid. "Have fun after the show?"

Luca halted a few steps away from me, raising an eyebrow. "Not really. Just the same bullshit as usual."

Don't say it. Just leave it. You're being jealous and irrational.

"What about the girl?"

He tilted his head in puzzlement. "What girl?"

Fuck. I pinched the bridge of my nose. "Nothing. Forget it. I'm being a wanker."

He prowled across the room, his fingers pinching my chin as he forced me to look up at him. "Were you jealous, Ollie?"

"No."

"Really," he drawled. "Then why do you look like you're chewing glass?"

I shoved his hand away. "Just forget about it. I shouldn't have said anything."

"No, I don't think I will. Why were you jealous? You know *full* well you're the one I'm coming back to every night."

"Do I?"

Hurt flickered across Luca's face. "I've made my feelings pretty clear, Ollie. You're the one who keeps everything locked away in a vault more secure than fucking Fort Knox."

I flinched as his comment hit home. "That's not fair."

"Isn't it?" Luca prowled closer, crowding my space. "I'm not the one spoiling for an argument. If you're done with me, just say it. Don't push me away."

"That's not what I'm doing."

"Then why did you avoid me all day?"

"Because we're not supposed to be seen together," I exploded. "Jesus, Luca. It's okay for you. Even if you piss off your management, you've got enough in the bank to get by. Don't you get it? If I lose this job, I lose *everything*."

"I told you to trust me. You don't need to worry about your job, I promise."

I gave a hollow laugh. "That's just it though. You can't promise me that. I'm the one putting it all on the line. Not you."

A muscle jumped in his jaw. "I'm not putting anything on the line?"

"Not like I am."

He turned away, stalking over to the minibar. He didn't bother with a glass, just popped open the stupidly small bottle of vodka and necked it. Chucking it to the side, he braced his arms on the counter, his back to me. "Tell me, Ollie. Once this tour is done, what happens to us?"

A yawning pit opened in my stomach. I knew what I wanted, but did Luca want the same? Maybe I just needed to be brave. Put it all out there and find out where we stood. "We agreed this was just going to last while the tour di—"

"Right." Luca cut me off before I could finish my sentence. "Well, seeing as you're so *worried* about your career, maybe we should end this early."

Or maybe we should talk about it. I'd like to keep

seeing you.

That was what I'd been about to say. But Luca's ready dismissal had the words crawling back down my throat. The walls around my heart slammed up.

See, the traitorous voice inside my head whispered. *See what happens when you open yourself up?*

I couldn't just leave it like this. I opened my mouth to tell him I liked him. That I didn't *want* this to end.

But to my horror, that was not what came out. "Is that what you want?"

He didn't turn. Didn't so much as *look* at me as he shredded my heart to pieces. "Yes. Maybe…maybe that's for the best. I think you should leave."

That pit grew wider, numbing my whole body. I wasn't even here. I was watching this from several feet above my body, totally detached from what was happening.

Fight for him, my heart screamed.

But I'd had enough of listening to my heart.

Without another word, I grabbed my packed suitcase, thanking God I hadn't had a chance to settle into the room yet. I paused at the door one final time, but Luca had his head turned away, his knuckles white as he leaned on the table.

I didn't slam the door. That would be giving in to my emotions. To the desire to scream, rage, and plead.

If I'd opened those floodgates, I would've thrown myself at Luca's feet and made a fool of myself.

No more.

Jack was positioned outside Luca's door alongside Steve, the night guard. Normally Jack was gone by now, returning to his room to catch some kip. The sight of him there threw me off.

"Do you…?" My voice was gruff. I cleared my throat, aiming for normalcy. Pretending I wasn't drowning in the fear that what we'd had was done. "Do you have a room key for me? Or should I go to reception?"

He held up a plain white rectangle, sympathy shining in his eyes. "I thought you might need this, so I grabbed it for you. Room 204."

I swallowed my rising nausea, nodding my thanks. The fact Jack had *known* this was about to happen was beyond humiliating.

Maybe Luca is right, I told myself as I entered my own hotel room for the first time in weeks. *Maybe it's best we stop this before he really breaks my heart.*

But as I lay on my bed, rubbing at the ache in my chest, I realised it was too late for that.

With nothing but the darkness as my witness, I closed my eyes and finally let the tears fall.

I'd fucked it up. I'd had my chance to tell Luca I wanted him. That I wanted *everything.*

And now it was too late.

It took approximately four hours of staring at the ceiling to figure out I was behaving like a pathetic idiot.

I'd replayed every interaction I'd had with Luca. Every word. Every kiss. Every touch.

You know what I realised?

Not a single one hinted that Luca planned to ditch me once the tour was done. To my horror, I realised that *I'd* been the one who'd assumed that. It was me who'd gone into this thinking we were on a time limit, not Luca.

No wonder he'd pushed me away. He ended things to protect himself.

That was something I couldn't hold against him.

Once that realisation hit me, I knew what I had to do. I owed it to Luca…to *myself*, to be honest.

I didn't bother getting dressed. Grabbing Luca's room key, I left my room and jogged up the stairs to his floor.

Steve, the night guard, was positioned outside Luca's room. His head snapped around, a small frown creasing his forehead. He pulled out his phone and tapped something out before sliding it back into his pocket.

That was odd. He didn't normally bother to do more than nod at me if our paths crossed. Like Jack, Steve was well-aware that I was the one Luca spent every night with.

As I approached Luca's door, Steve stepped forward, barring my way with his massive body. "Sorry, Mr Winters. I can't let you go any further."

I halted, my brows knitting together. "What do you mean? I have a key. I always spend the night with Luca."

Sympathy and pity danced on Steve's face. A door opened behind me, snapping Steve's gaze in that direction.

I spun on my heel. Unease began to wend through my veins as Kevin joined us in the hallway. Since when was he roomed next door? He was normally on a different floor from the rest of the band.

"Hi, Ollie," he said quietly, gesturing to his open door. "Why don't you step into my room for a minute."

I stared at him, the unease growing. "No, I think we should talk here."

Kevin sighed, lifting his chin at Steve. I heard him

shuffling back a bit, presumably giving us some space. "What's going on?"

"I'm afraid Luca's instructed us to remove your access to the room and for you to return home early."

Blood thundered in my ears. "He's *what*?"

Kevin winced. "I wish it wasn't down to me to tell you this, but this is how Luca wants it."

"Absolutely fucking not," I seethed. "If Luca wants me to go, he can tell me himself."

I spun on my heel, ready to bang on Luca's door until he grew some balls and faced me. How dare he make Kevin do his dirty work?

Before I could take more than two steps, Steve was there. His face was flushed now, the quiet guy unable to meet my eyes. "Let me pass. Now."

"Ollie, you don't want to go in there." Kevin's tone was calm. Measured. "He's not alone."

Everything in me stilled as my world fell to pieces. "What?"

Kevin turned me to face him with a gentle tug on my shoulder. "I'm sorry, Ollie. I was hoping you wouldn't come up here tonight so we could avoid this. But Luca has another man in there, someone he met backstage tonight. He called him up not long after you left."

Bile rose in my throat. I closed my eyes. "No. Luca wouldn't do that to me."

"Didn't he end it with you tonight?" Kevin asked gently. "Because that's what he told me."

The hallway seemed to tilt beneath my feet. "Yeah, but...it was an argument. I didn't think..."

Didn't think he'd replace me so quickly.

"I'm sorry, Ollie. I really am. This is why I didn't

want you getting too close to him. Every time this happens, Luca always leaves me to pick up the pieces."

The words hit me like bullets. *Every time.*

I couldn't believe I'd fallen for it. Couldn't believe I'd thought what we'd had was *special.*

"Why don't you return to your room and grab your stuff?" Kevin was still talking. "I've arranged for the jet to be on standby to take you home. Steve can drive you to the airport."

I couldn't process what Kevin was saying. Unable to think past what Luca was doing.

Doing with someone who wasn't me.

Fuck, why did this keep happening to me? I rubbed my chest as a painful realisation hit me.

I'd rather have caught Suzie and Callum a thousand times over than just hearing about Luca and someone else once.

"Don't worry about your job. I'll smooth everything over with your boss."

I almost laughed at that. For all the worrying I'd done about my career, suddenly, it didn't seem that important.

Something told me that losing my place at *Identity* wouldn't have been anywhere near as painful as this.

"None of this is your fault." Kevin's hand squeezed my shoulder, and my skin crawled under his touch. "This is what Luca *always* does. He doesn't care about people. He uses them and discards them, never thinking of them again. It's a game to him."

I nodded, stepping sideways so Kevin was forced to release me. "I think I'll take that ride to the airport now."

Relief flashed over Kevin's face. "Good. And I'm

sorry, Ollie. Like I said, this isn't on you."

But as I stared unseeing at the city sights zipping past the car window, I knew Kevin was wrong. This was absolutely on me.

I'd been burned before. I should've known better. I'd known that going in, but I'd still thrown my bleeding heart at Luca's feet.

So yes. This was on me. It was my fault.

I should've known better.

Chapter 21

Luca

I got fuck all sleep that night.

I spent the whole time replaying my argument with Ollie. Kai's and Kevin's words had wormed their way under my skin, making it all too easy to pick up the gauntlet thrown down by Ollie and run with it.

By the time dawn broke, I questioned if I'd done the right thing. Sure, Ollie hadn't admitted to wanting anything more with me…but he hadn't been ending it either.

Fuck, I was such an idiot. Was I really going to let fear push him away?

I thought it over as I numbly went through my morning routine. It felt so odd to do it without Ollie at my side. It might've only been for a few weeks, but I'd got…used to having him here.

Now his absence haunted the room like a ghost.

It was no good. I couldn't leave it like this. I would call him right now and ask him to come up here. No more bullshit. I was going to tell him exactly how I felt. Maybe that was stupid. Maybe he'd break my heart.

But it had to be better than this despair currently hollowing out my chest. At least then, I'd *know* there was no future rather than pushing Ollie away because of an assumption.

To my frustration, my phone was nowhere to be found. I was riffling through my jeans from the night before when there was a knock at my door.

Ollie.

I flew across the room and yanked the door open. My heart sank when I saw Kevin standing there, his mouth set in a grim line.

"Oh. It's you."

"As welcoming as ever," Kevin muttered, pushing past me and striding into the room.

I peered into the hallway, praying I'd see Ollie's familiar blond hair coming out of the lift. But there was only Jack. His eyes connected with mine, and he gave me a small sympathetic smile.

I bit back a groan as I returned his nod before shutting the door. Great. Of course he knew what'd happened last night. He'd probably heard every word through the door.

Kevin was sat at the table, his hands clasped in front of him. Alarm pinged the back of my mind. I warily took the seat opposite him. "Why are you here so early?"

"A lesser man than me might say it's to tell you *I told you so*, but that seems rather mean."

Seems rather mean, yet he'd essentially said it anyway. "What do you mean?"

"Ollie's gone," he said bluntly. "Came to me as soon as you kicked him out of your room last night and requested to be let go from the assignment early."

"No." I shoved back from the table, striding from the door. "No, he can't leave."

"Luca, he already has." Kevin's words had me freezing with my hand on the doorknob. "Steve dropped him at the airport at four a.m. He's due to land in London any minute now."

Numbness began to creep over me. What had I done?

I paced the room, my hands shoving into my hair. *Think. Think. Think.* "Okay, so we have a show tonight, then two days off. I'll take the jet back to London to speak to him, and then I'll be back in time for Warsaw."

"Luca." Kevin stood from his seat. "He doesn't want to see you."

I waved that off impatiently. "That's because I was a dick. I just need to talk to him and then..."

"No, Luca, you don't understand." Kevin grabbed my arm, forcing me still. "Ollie was *grateful* you kicked him out. He told me he was going to end it anyway."

"What?" My chest tightened, pins and needles pricking my fingertips.

Kevin's brows knitted together. "Fucker admitted it was only ever going to be a fling. The second his job was at risk, he knew he needed to call it off. But you got there first."

"No." I shook my head, trying to force away the black spots creeping in at the edge of my vision. "No...it was just a fight. He didn't *want* to leave. I made him."

"He wanted to, Luca. You know what he said? He told me he was *relieved*. That he'd felt you getting too close and didn't know how to break it off without you firing him. But once it hit the press, his office told him to get his arse back to England. He was going to break up with you...but you got there first."

I remembered the way he'd been sitting when I'd entered the room. The baseless accusations he'd dropped at my feet. How he'd been looking for an argument.

"I'm sorry, Luca. I wish I didn't have to say I told you so, but..."

"Get out." I stalked across the room, yanking open the minibar. "Now."

There was a beat of silence before Kevin spoke. "Seriously, don't let yourself get down over this. He's not worth it. He's a piece of shit who was using you to get ahead, just like I told you."

I wanted to put my hands over my ears. Wanted to do something, *anything*, to drown out Kevin's hateful words. Somehow, hearing Ollie was done with me was so much more painful coming from him than it would've been from Ollie himself.

"Get out," I repeated. "Now."

Kevin sighed, and there was a soft thud as something landed on the bed. "Fine. There's your phone, by the way. You left it in the dressing room last night."

I ignored it, not even bothering to turn around until I heard the door close behind Kevin.

There was no point reaching out to Ollie now. There was one call I did need to make, though, one promise to follow through on.

Because no matter how Ollie had let me down, I wouldn't do the same to him. At the end of the day, it wasn't his fault I'd fallen in love with him.

He hadn't promised me anything.

This was all on me.

I grabbed my phone, making the call fast and efficient. When I was certain my orders would be followed, I hung up and let my head hang between my shoulders.

Somehow I knew I should be grateful it'd ended like this. If Ollie never intended for us to last, then I'd been right last night. Better to call it quits now before I ended up getting more hurt.

Judging by the shards currently slicing through my chest, I wasn't sure that was possible.

Walking out on stage that evening was one of the hardest things I'd ever done. Only the thought of letting my fans down had me forcing down my heartbreak and stepping into the spotlight.

I tried my best, but each time I glanced at Jack in the pit, the reminder that Ollie had left would hit me like a sledgehammer. More than once, I stumbled over lyrics, my voice catching on notes and wavering through others.

Fortunately, my bandmates stepped up. I had no idea if they knew what had happened, but they put on a show like no other. Kai and Silas worked the crowd into a frenzy while Arlo played his heart out.

When "Tease" started, I froze. The spotlight was on me, the audience starting their chant.

All I could see was Ollie the first night I'd knelt before him. The heat in his eyes. How his tongue licked over his full pink lips.

Had that all been fake? Had he really played me?

Someone wrapped an arm around my chest and

a guitar bounced against my back. Speaking into his microphone, Kai shouted. "How about we all *tease* tonight?"

Silas came around my front, his back to the crowd. He was shaking his arse, his fingers flying over the chords. It was so at odds with the concern on his face as he studied me. "Okay?"

I shook myself out of my stupor at his mouthed question. What the fuck was I doing? Thank God for the others. By grinding themselves up against me, Kai and Silas had managed to hide my spiral and keep the crowd entertained.

I couldn't let them down.

Winking at Silas, I dropped my head back against Kai's shoulder. I didn't normally play with either of them on stage. That was their usual schtick.

But tonight, it was a good distraction. If it helped me get through the final hour on stage, I'd take it.

When the show finally ended, I stormed off stage before any of them could stop me. As grateful as I was, the last thing I wanted was to go over the whole situation. I needed time to process the fact Ollie had abandoned me without so much as a goodbye before I hashed it out with the others.

I had two days before the next show. I intended on using every minute to get my head screwed on right.

But as I crashed into my bed, a half-empty bottle of vodka clutched between my fingers, I realised the horrible truth.

Forty-eight hours wouldn't be long enough for me to forget Ollie.

Something told me even a year wouldn't be enough.

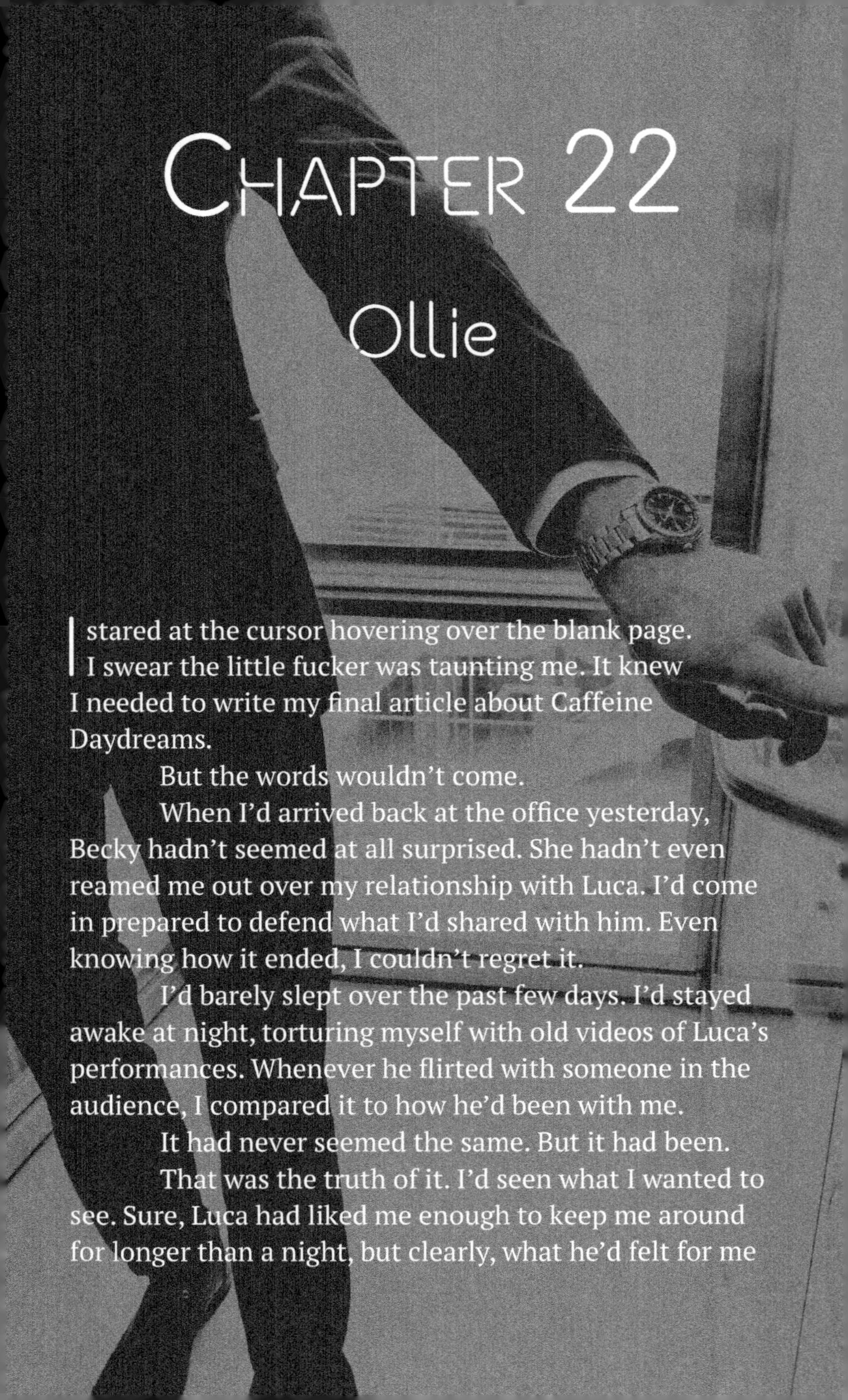

Chapter 22

Ollie

I stared at the cursor hovering over the blank page. I swear the little fucker was taunting me. It knew I needed to write my final article about Caffeine Daydreams.

But the words wouldn't come.

When I'd arrived back at the office yesterday, Becky hadn't seemed at all surprised. She hadn't even reamed me out over my relationship with Luca. I'd come in prepared to defend what I'd shared with him. Even knowing how it ended, I couldn't regret it.

I'd barely slept over the past few days. I'd stayed awake at night, torturing myself with old videos of Luca's performances. Whenever he flirted with someone in the audience, I compared it to how he'd been with me.

It had never seemed the same. But it had been.

That was the truth of it. I'd seen what I wanted to see. Sure, Luca had liked me enough to keep me around for longer than a night, but clearly, what he'd felt for me didn't compare to how hard I'd fallen for him.

I hadn't watched the concert from the night I left. I hadn't even opened social media for fear I might stumble across a clip. It was hard enough watching Luca from before he knew me, wondering if he had invited the person he was flirting with back to the hotel.

But if I watched his last concert or the one he had tonight, there was no way I'd cope. I couldn't watch him seduce another, knowing they'd take my place going back to his suite. Slipping onto my side of the bed.

I just needed to get this final story done so I could move on. One last piece, then I could tuck Luca away into that box I kept deep inside. The one I never dared open. The one I never dared think about.

Once I'd done that, I could throw myself into my career. Never again would I open myself up like this. At least my job couldn't cheat on me. Couldn't break my heart. Couldn't make me cry myself to sleep at night wondering how I could be so *fucking stupid.*

One more story.

But the words conspired against me like they knew the longer they took to come, the longer I could hold on to the memory of Luca.

Because no matter how much I *needed* to forget him…I couldn't.

I didn't want to.

A loud thud on my desk had me jumping out of my skin. "Motherfucker!"

"Sorry," Riley said, not sounding apologetic in the slightest. "I did say your name a few times, but you didn't respond."

I ran my hand over the scruff I'd let get far too long. "Sorry. I'm not very with it."

"Understatement of the century." Riley sat on the edge of my desk, crossing his arms over his wiry chest. "Wanna talk about it?"

This wasn't the first time he'd asked me over the last week. And just like every other time, I shook my head curtly. "Nope."

If I talked about it, I'd have to allow myself to feel. I was having a hard enough time burying my emotions as it was. The box I normally shoved them into was in full revolt. It refused to contain Luca and all my thoughts involving him. Work was my one safe space where I couldn't *let* myself break down.

Home was another story...which was why I'd spent pretty much every waking minute in the office.

Hadn't stopped me from thinking about Luca though. Wondering how the final week of his tour was going. Who he'd chosen to warm his bed. Had he found another steady fling among the crew? Or was he opting for a different partner every night?

I didn't want to know. But not knowing was also killing me slowly.

"Have you done your last article yet?"

I groaned, slumping in my chair. "Nope. Becky has given me a few more days."

I still hadn't hit on a topic for that final article. Caffeine Daydreams had added a few extra tour dates in London at the end of next week. Because of that, Becky had extended my deadline, wanting the article to come out just before their final show.

"Okay, I'm officially intervening." Riley clapped his hands on his knees, his blue eyes thoughtful behind his glasses. "You've spent too long moping around. That's clearly not helping your creativity, so let's try something else."

"What do you have in mind?"

Riley's answering smirk made me shiver.

"I'm not sure how this is going to help."

I'd never been inside the club Riley dragged me to, a place a few streets from our offices called The Closet. The name wasn't much of a surprise, given it was a gay bar.

To my horror, he'd marched us straight up to the front of the line. "Umm, Riley, there's a queue."

"It's fine," he said breezily, blowing a kiss at the hulking bouncer as he let us in. "I know the owners."

I hustled after him, trying to ignore the glares being shot our way by those waiting.

What Riley was wearing tonight was a far cry from his conservative work clothes. He'd poured himself into some bright-blue booty shorts and topped it off with a black crop top.

Sure enough, Riley wasn't short on attention inside the club. He waved off guy after guy, choosing instead to keep me company at the bar as I attempted to drown my sorrows.

"This place is fun, right?"

I sipped my vodka and Coke, glancing around the packed dance floor. "I guess."

That wasn't fair. The club actually had a great vibe. Lots of people dancing, having a great time. No one was getting aggressive or starting fights. In fact, the opposite. Almost everyone around me was paired off, grinding against each other and disappearing into dark corners to take things further.

Even the bartenders were getting in on the action. The massive one who looked like a Viking currently had his tongue down a similarly good-looking bloke's throat while the young lad who'd served me was now surrounded by not one but two gorgeous men.

It was a painful reminder of how pathetically alone I was.

"Hey, there's Tom!" Riley was on tiptoes, waving impatiently at someone I couldn't see.

"Who?"

"New guy. Started while you were away. They sent him to the London office for training the day before you got back. He returned last night, so I texted him to meet us here."

A fresh-faced man with baby-blue eyes and dark-brown hair joined us. After exchanging a hug with Riley, he held out a hand for me to shake. "Hey! You must be Ollie. I've heard so much about you."

"Thanks," I said, shaking his hand, feeling bemused. He was like a puppy, all wide-eyed with an eager smile. It made my cynical heart not quite know how to act with him. "How've you settled in at *Identity*?"

Tom lit up with enthusiasm, positively gushing over all the mundane facets of his job. I took a backseat, letting him and Riley lead the conversation.

"I just need to find somewhere to live," Tom said. "Can't crash on my mate's sofa forever. I swear, rent around here is just getting higher and higher."

"Why don't you ask about the employee accommodation?" I sipped from my glass, hoping the alcohol would numb the ever-present ache in my chest. The first drink hadn't, but I lived in hope.

Riley and Tom stared at me like I'd spoken in a different language. "What?"

I frowned. "You know, the building over on Leigh Road. The one that's owned by the company. That's where I live—you get discounted rent as an employee benefit."

Riley gave a humourless chuckle. "Yeah, because that's what the company owner cares about…his employees. That's why he slashed salaries last year and took away our company cars and private medical. I'm in the accounts department, and we see *everything* that comes through. A building for employees is sure as fuck not on that list."

The blood drained from my face. Now that Riley pointed out how obviously stupid it was, I couldn't believe I'd believed it in the first place. "You sure?"

"Very," Riley said in a clipped tone, draining the last of his drink. "Not sure *what* you've been told about your flat…but it doesn't come from the company. I can assure you of that."

I was about to press him for more information when a very familiar tune came over the speakers. My spine stiffened, my blood running cold.

Riley's head snapped around, but I was already shoving past them. I couldn't listen to this. Couldn't hear

Luca's voice when I was trying so desperately to forget him.

I shoved blindly through the crowd, not stopping until I burst through the club doors. I was in such a hurry that I didn't see the man in front of me until I collided with him.

"Shit, man, are you okay?"

"I'm so sorry," I blurted. The big guy had a kind expression, his blond hair flopping over his forehead. A tiny twink appeared next to him, his face beautifully made up.

The smaller guy bared his teeth at me, an arm winding around the blond's waist. "Watch where you're going."

"Low, be nice. He's upset."

I stepped back, shaking my head at the couple. Fuck, their casual touches were too painful to witness. "I'm sorry. I'll be more careful."

"Wait." The twink stepped forward, his brow furrowed. "Are you okay?"

The door to the club opened behind me, Luca's voice filling the air.

"No." My voice was raw as I answered the stranger. "No. I'm not."

Becky didn't even have time to remove her coat before I barged into her office the next morning.

"Who pays for my flat?"

"Good morning, Ollie," Becky said, her voice loaded with sarcasm. "Please do come in."

I dropped into a chair opposite her desk, waiting

for her to hang her coat on the hook and stow her bag. "I'm serious, Becky. Who pays for it?"

She didn't look at me as she clicked her computer on. "Well, given you pay the rent every month, I'm going to say you."

"Cut the bullshit." I probably shouldn't talk to my boss like that, but I was starting to feel unhinged. Maybe this was the result of suppressing my emotions for so many years. Or maybe it was because I'd gotten used to having Luca in my life, only to have him ripped away. "Who owns the building? Who's giving me a discounted rate?"

She sighed, finally looking at me. "I'm not at liberty to share that information."

My nostrils flared. "My company car? Private medical insurance? Higher salary?"

"All the employees receive those perks."

"Really? Because I have it on very good authority that they don't."

Becky tapped a fingernail on the desk. "I told you, the owner subsidises...perks."

"Not according to accounts."

Her lips curved in a small smirk. "I never said *which* owner. Nor which employees."

I paused. I'd done intensive research into *Identity* before my first botched interview attempt. There was only *one* owner. "What?"

"A large number of shares was purchased by an individual. He's a silent partner...apart from on a few issues."

My fingers tightened on the arms of the chair until my knuckles whitened. "Who?"

She pulled off her glasses, pinching the bridge of my nose. "Why are you asking me when you already know the answer?"

Luca. "Is that why I got the job?"

"Of course not. You got the job on merit. We approached you, after all."

I ground my teeth together. "Would you have phoned me again after I missed the first interview?"

There was a long pause before Becky finally answered me. "Probably not. But I will say I'm glad we did. You've proven yourself to be a valuable asset to the company. I'd happily go to bat for you even if someone didn't have a...vested interest in your success."

"But why?" I asked, utterly confused. "Why would he do that?"

"Now that I can't answer. But you're a good journalist. I'm sure you'll figure it out." She studied me, seeming to come to some decision. "I will tell you two things."

I nodded numbly, gesturing for her to continue.

"First, I had to sign an NDA stating I'd never impart who was behind all this. As did the entire senior management team. That's why I won't confirm who he is...even though you clearly know. He didn't want you to find out. Ever."

My mind was reeling. Why wouldn't he want to take credit for it? Okay, so he might not initially...but why keep it hidden forever?

Becky apparently had the answer. "I think he was trying to protect you. He gave me the impression you hadn't had many people looking out for you in the past, and the last thing he wanted was you thinking this was charity."

I had no idea how I felt about Luca interfering in my life. Logically, I knew I should be mad, but...I wasn't. It suggested he...cared. Cared enough to make my life better.

I couldn't be mad at him about that. Not when he was the first person to do that in...well, ever.

"What was the second thing?" My voice came out hoarse.

"The day you returned to the UK, I received two phone calls. The first was from the manager of Caffeine Daydreams."

"Yeah, Kevin said he'd call. Told me he'd make sure I didn't face any repercussions from leaving the tour early."

Becky blew out a whistle. "That's interesting. Because when he phoned me, he filed an official complaint about your work ethic. He heavily implied you'd set out to seduce Luca to further your career. In fact, he went so far as to suggest that if you weren't fired, we'd be barred from accessing several acts managed by his associates."

It felt like the world was slipping sideways from under me. "Why would he do that?"

"That's not the real question, now is it." Becky studied me hard. "The real question is why did I receive a *second* phone call, barely an hour later, from our new investor. One where he was keen to remind me of the terms of our initial agreement and to ensure your position here at *Identity* was secure and would remain so going forward."

My head sank into my hands as I tried to make sense of the various bombshells Becky was throwing my way. "Why would Luca do that when he told me to leave? Why is he still looking out for me if he doesn't have feelings for me?"

Becky's smile was kind. "As I said, that's the real question."

Oh god. What if Luca *hadn't* had someone in there?

Had Kevin manipulated me into doing what he wanted?

If that was true...fuck. I filed that away to think about later. When I wasn't sitting opposite my boss.

Because if that was what happened...there'd be no shoving that rage away. If my stupid insecurities had cost me Luca, I wasn't sure I'd ever recover.

I thought back over what she'd said about Kevin. "Would you have fired me if Luca hadn't called?"

She sniffed imperiously. "Of course not. I don't take orders from entitled white men high on self-importance and ego."

Despite the tumultuous emotions spinning through me, I couldn't help but smile at that. "Thanks, Becky." My mind continued turning, Kevin's interference ringing alarm bells. Everything I'd always found odd about his behaviour, from his adding additional tour dates to parading the band around his friends, started falling into place. Just how far did his influence over the band's affairs go? And how much of it was working in his favour?

"Becky, I think I know what I want to write my final piece about." If you suspected someone wasn't acting in someone else's best interest, the first place you looked was at the money. That was exactly what I intended to do. I quickly filled Becky in on my suspicions that Kevin might be up to no good, outlining the research I wanted to do to support my theory.

She thought about it for a long time before she nodded. "Okay, but on one condition: whatever you discover, you cannot directly name Kevin. The last thing we need is a libel or defamation lawsuit. Keep it factual, and keep it anonymous."

"Done." I could work with that.

If Kevin was making Luca's life more difficult in any way, I would make sure the world knew about it.

Chapter 23

Luca

"Luca, wake up."

I swatted at the hand shaking me awake, my hangover making itself known before I even had my eyes open. "Fuck off."

Bright light streamed into the room, making me groan loudly. "Jesus, Kai. You're killing me here."

"Nope, you're doing that to yourself." I could hear him rummaging through something. "For fuck's sake, Luca, did you drink for three days straight?"

I pinched my brow, begging the room to stop spinning. "Maybe."

"Idiot."

I pulled myself into a sitting position, wincing at the state the room was in. While I hadn't trashed it, I hadn't tidied up after myself either. I needed to leave a massive tip for housekeeping.

"Here." Kai thrust a mug into my hand. His warm brown eyes were full of pity and understanding. "Drink this."

"Thanks," I muttered. The caffeine hit my tongue and forced my hangover back a few inches. "What day is it?"

"Friday. We've got a show tonight." His gaze drifted to my phone, plugged in on my bedside table. "You heard from him?"

I shook my head sharply. It'd been a week since I'd seen him. A week since I'd heard his voice. Touched his face. Kissed his lips. Pride had kept me from reaching out, but I wouldn't risk missing a message or call from Ollie. Even with everything Kevin had told me, I couldn't help but wish I could hear his voice. Just once more.

I missed him…even though I knew I shouldn't. That was not how heartbreak worked though.

"What happened?"

I sighed. I hadn't told the others what had happened, but I couldn't put it off forever. Really, I was grateful they'd given me this much space. I wouldn't have been so generous if it was the other way around. "What you predicted. He just wanted a fling. He was looking for an excuse to call it off."

"What a fucking cunt."

I winced at Kai's harsh words. "Don't call him that."

Kai raised a brow at me, folding his arms over his chest. "Why not? He's been shitty to you, so why shouldn't I badmouth him?"

"Would you like it if I said the same about Silas?"

Kai scoffed. "That's different. He hasn't hurt me."

Now it was my turn to raise a brow. "Hasn't he?"

A muscle worked in Kai's jaw before he gave a huff. "Fine. I'll keep my thoughts to myself. What did Ollie say before he left?"

"Nothing." I took another sip of coffee, hoping that

would squash the swirling nausea. "Nothing to me anyway."

I filled him in on what Kevin had said, Kai stiffening with every word. "So that's it. It came down to me or his job, and I wasn't the thing he chose. You were right. Ollie doesn't feel the same way I do. I thought it was just him struggling to open up, but..."

Kai shifted on his feet. "I know what I said, but don't you think it's odd that you only heard that from Kevin?"

"What do you mean?"

He shrugged. "Just seems odd he wouldn't tell you that to your face. Ollie doesn't strike me as the kind of guy to take the easy route out. But hey, maybe we didn't really know him."

Kai's words made me pause. Why hadn't Ollie come to me directly? Why had he gone to Kevin, of all people?

I shook myself, offering Kai a thin smile. "I guess you're right. I guess we didn't really know him at all."

Another week passed. The end of the tour should've been in sight, but thanks to Kevin, we now had a handful more UK dates. He'd announced this like it was something we should be grateful for, despite the fact we were all clearly exhausted.

Silas and Kai had gone so far as to argue against the additions, which had pissed Kevin off. I'd watched him carefully as he'd ranted and raved about how ungrateful we were being, noting the smug expression when my bandmates backed down.

How long had we been letting Kevin manipulate us like this?

Knowledge dawned on me as I recalled Ollie questioning the level of involvement Kevin had in our lives. How much of it was normal?

I was still stewing over it several hours later when Arlo dragged me into an empty dressing room. "I need to talk to you. Sit down."

I sat on the sofa, one of my arms stretching over the back of it. "What's up?"

Arlo perched on the table in front of me, his fingers twitching on his legs. "Why did Ollie leave?"

I sighed. "Come on. I know Kai filled you in."

Not wanting to go over the story multiple times, I'd asked Kai to tell the others.

"I know what Kai said happened, but I want to hear it from you. What happened before Ollie left your room that night?"

I quickly outlined the argument, from Ollie's jealousy to his unwillingness to commit to anything once the tour ended.

When I finished, Arlo was flat-out glaring at me. "You, Luca, are a fucking idiot."

"Don't sugarcoat it," I said sarcastically.

He smirked. "That's not how we do it here. You should know that by now. Let's start with the fact he was jealous. Why did that piss you off?"

"Why *wouldn't* it piss me off? Ollie should trust me. I'd never fuck around with someone else. The only reason I was even doing that was to draw attention away from us because he was worried about his job."

"Did you tell him that?"

"About me technically being his boss? Don't be stupid."

Arlo kicked me lightly in the shin. "I'm not the stupid one here. You should've come clean with Ollie *weeks* ago about all that crap. But that's not what I meant. Did you tell him why you behaved that way on stage?"

The *yes* was on the tip of my tongue...but had I? Or had I just jumped straight to the defensive? "Fuck."

"Even if you had, shouldn't Ollie be entitled to his feelings? He was betrayed by his best friend and long-term girlfriend. The guy's bound to have some trust issues."

"How do you know about that?"

"He told me," he said simply. "We talk. Or at least, we did, until he pulled a vanishing act in the middle of the night."

I grunted, a headache beginning to brew behind my eyes. "Still...he should've trusted me. There was no need for him to get jealous."

There was a sharp tug on my ear. I let out a howl, grabbing the lobe and glaring at Arlo. "What the fuck was that for?"

Arlo was unrepentant. "Do you *hear* yourself now? Ollie has no need to get jealous? Remind me—how did you behave whenever the makeup artist cosied up to him? Unless I'm wrong, you physically dragged him from his seat on the plane and to the bedroom. *Twice*. You weren't subtle, Luca. Everyone, including Marta, knew what you'd done and why."

My shoulders slumped. "Shit. You're right. I'm such a hypocrite."

"And as for the rest of it." Arlo was on his feet now, hands on his hips as he glared at me. "Did Ollie actually tell you he didn't want anything after the tour?"

"Yes." That much I was sure about. "I pushed him to tell me, and he reminded me we'd agreed it'd only last as long as the tour did."

"He told you he didn't want anything else?"

"No, but it was pretty obvious... Why are you glaring at me like that? I'm not the one in the wrong here."

Arlo's expression didn't change. "Would love to agree with you, but you definitely are. You get that he has difficulties opening up, right?"

"Of course."

"Yet the first time you pushed him to open up, instead of giving him a chance, you told him to leave? Do you really think that's what he wanted?"

The fracture in my heart grew a little wider. "No... that's not..."

The memory of Ollie's final question echoed through my mind.

"Is that what you want?"

He didn't say he didn't want it.

He asked me if it was what *I* wanted.

"But he didn't fight for me," I said desperately. "He just...left."

"Because you weren't fighting for him." Arlo's voice gentled as he crouched in front of me. "Take it from someone who knows. It's near impossible to fight for someone if you think they don't care for you."

"Ollie knows I care for him."

"Does he? Did you tell him that?"

"No, but...he *had* to have known." He couldn't have mistaken all my behaviour towards him as anything other than me falling for him...right?

Arlo blew out a breath. "I probably shouldn't be breaking his confidence like this, but fuck it. I can't watch you mope around any longer. Before the show, Ollie told me he cared for you but had difficulty opening up to people."

My chest tightened painfully. How could he tell Arlo that but not me? "Maybe I'd believe you if he hadn't vanished like a thief in the night. You didn't hear what he told Kevin. He was…using me. When it got too real for him, he ditched."

"About that…" Arlo stood, striding for the door. Puzzled, I readied myself to follow him. He held up a hand, pity shining in his eyes. "You're going to want to be sitting down for this. Trust me."

Puzzled, I watched as Arlo stuck his head into the hallway, his words too low to be discernible. He stepped back as Steve entered with Jack close behind him.

The two guards came to stand opposite me while Arlo perched on the sofa beside me. His hand rested on my knee like he was offering me support.

Steve's face was a ruddy red, his eyes fixed on the floor. He was trembling slightly, his hands fisted at his sides. Meanwhile, Jack glared at his colleague with undisguised fury and disgust.

"What's going on?"

"Tell him," Jack barked. My eyes widened. I'd never heard that tone on him before.

Steve shifted on his feet. "Ollie came back to your room that night you argued. Kevin told me to text him if he appeared and not to let him in."

Everything in me went still. "What?"

Steve continued, his voice so quiet it was barely above a murmur. That wasn't a problem though. I could hear him loud and clear. "Kevin came out. He told Ollie you'd given instructions for him to leave."

Blood roared in my ears, but Steve wasn't finished. "Ollie tried to argue, to insist he speak to you directly, but…Kevin lied. He told Ollie he couldn't go in there because you weren't alone. That you'd called someone up to keep you company."

"No," I said in disbelief. "Ollie wouldn't have believed that."

Steve hesitated. "He didn't…not at first, anyway. But Kevin was pretty convincing. He made it sound like you do this all the time. That you'd used him and replaced him just as easily."

My hands pulled at my hair as I sank back against the sofa. I turned back to Steve. "What happened then?"

Steve gulped, his eyes darting up to Jack. My usually stoic guard bared his teeth at him. "Tell him. Now."

He paled, his eyes flicking around the room but never landing on me. Like the shame was eating him alive. "I took him to the airport. He was…devastated. He tried to pretend he wasn't, but…"

I let out a roar, leaping to my feet. Steve jumped back in alarm, but my rage wasn't directed at him. Well… not only him.

I got in his face, forcing him to finally meet my gaze. "You've known about this the whole time and didn't think to say anything?"

"Kevin made me promise…told me he'd fire me," Steve said hastily. "I didn't have a choice."

Arlo's clipped voice came over my shoulder. "Like I said earlier, if you'd come to us, we would've protected you from Kevin. It shouldn't have taken both me and Jack to get this information out of you."

I stepped back, looking between the drummer and guard with confusion. They'd worked together to help me?

"You're fired," I said to Steve hoarsely. "I'll give you a reference, but I can't trust you going forward."

Steve nodded. "That's more than I expected. Thank you."

He took a step towards the door, but Jack stopped him. "Remember, not a word to Kevin."

Steve nodded once more before slinking from the room.

"Kevin orchestrated all of this."

"Yes," Arlo said, grabbing my shoulder.

"Why?"

Arlo glanced over at where Jack now leaned against the door. He was staring at Arlo, doing nothing to disguise it.

Arlo turned back to me, his lips set in a grim line. "Because he wants to control us. The last thing he wants is for any of us to be in a stable long-term relationship. Not when we are more marketable if we're single."

"Such a backwards way of thinking. He's so fucking fired." I grabbed my phone out of my pocket. "First, though, I need to phone Ollie. I need to sort this out right now."

"Wait." Arlo pulled his own phone out, his body tense as he brought something up on his screen. "Before you do, there's something else you need to know. I think there's another reason Kevin wanted Ollie gone. I think he knew he was getting close to the truth. Close to fucking everything up for him."

"What do you mean?"

"Here." He thrust his phone into my hands. "Read this."

My breath hitched as I took in the headline.

JUST WHO POCKETED THE PROFITS FROM CAFFEINE DAYDREAMS LAST TOUR?

According to figures released by the band's management, the Dreamers tour grossed profits clearing a billion pounds. The public tax returns for the band don't reflect anything near this figure.

So where has this money gone? Identity's Ollie Winters investigates.

"Is this true?" I barked even as I continued reading. Jesus, Ollie had really gone to town on the evidence. Even without Arlo's confirmation, there was no arguing with the data in front of me. "How the fuck could we not notice?"

Arlo huffed a breath. "Let's be honest, none of us are good at that shit. When was the last time you even checked your bank account? That's why we have Malcolm."

Malcolm was our accountant...and Kevin's brother-in-law. "They've been fucking us over."

"Yep," Arlo said, indicating to Jack. The bodyguard opened the door, and Kai and Silas filed in with matching thunderous expressions. "I know you need to sort shit out with Ollie, but we need to take care of this first. He doesn't name Kevin in the article, but it's pretty fucking obvious who he's alluding to."

"Agreed," I muttered, handing Arlo his phone back. "We need to come up with a plan to deal with Kevin and Malcolm and make sure none of this blows back on Ollie."

Just saying his name made pain lance through my chest. I closed my eyes. This was beyond fucked up.

What if Ollie wouldn't give me another chance? With everything Kevin had told him, I wouldn't blame him.

I opened my eyes to see my bandmates all studying me, varying degrees of fury and determination on their faces. I knew without a shadow of a doubt they'd have my back.

First, we'd deal with Kevin. Then, I was going after Ollie.

"I have a plan."

Chapter 24

Ollie

The ticket sat on my phone, taunting me.

Caffeine Daydreams: Wembley Arena

"Staring at it won't make tonight come around any faster."

I closed the screen, swivelling my chair to face Riley. "Maybe I shouldn't go."

"Don't start this again." Riley had cornered me after my meeting with Becky and forced me to spill the beans. "Have you tried calling him?"

"Yes. Still blocked." My stomach churned. With everything I'd learned from Becky and my research for the article, I no longer believed that night had gone down the way Kevin said it had. "I thought after the article went live, he might contact me, but…"

"Don't read too much into that," Riley said firmly. "You need to go tonight. What's the worst that could happen?"

Given my plan was to push my way to the front

of the pit and jump around, hoping to catch Luca's attention…lots could go wrong.

"He might not see me. Or he might, then he could ignore me. Or have me thrown out."

"And how would that make you feel?"

"Heartbroken." I knew that without a doubt. "It'd gut me."

Riley shrugged. "You're already heartbroken, so don't let that scare you off. But if you go and end up reconciling, what will that mean?"

I blew out a breath. "Everything. I'm not even thinking about that though. At this point, I'd give anything just to have a chance to clear the air with him."

I hated that our final exchange had been full of bitterness and anger. Now that I understood the extent to which Kevin had been fucking them over, I wanted more than anything to just talk to Luca.

The fact I was still blocked spoke volumes. Luca wasn't ready to talk to me. I didn't have any of the other band members' numbers. Why would I? It wasn't like I'd needed them. Like most celebrities, Luca didn't handle his social media accounts himself. I'd racked my brain trying to come up with another way to get a hold of him, and going to tonight's concert was the best I'd been able to come up with. Originally this concert in London hadn't even been on the tour. I could thank Kevin's greediness for that.

"I'm surprised we haven't had any blowback from the article, especially given it went viral."

"Tell me about it." I ran a hand through my hair. I'd thought Kevin was dodgy, but never in a million years had I expected to uncover the level of fraud that I had. It was so easily accessible too. The band's accounts could be found on the Companies House website. It didn't take a genius to work out that they weren't reporting anywhere near as much profit as they should've been. Which meant either they were evading tax...or someone else had been pocketing more than they should.

More research uncovered that their accountant was none other than Kevin's brother-in-law. The pieces had been easy enough to put together.

My bosses had been thrilled with the publicity, but we'd all expected to hear...*something*. Even though I'd been careful not to point the finger at the culprits, it didn't take much brain power to uncover the picture I'd painted. "I keep waiting for the other shoe to drop."

"You know what they say: no news is good news."

I snorted. "Pretty sure absolutely *no one* in this office would agree with that."

He fell quiet for a moment. "You've gotta go tonight. You'll regret it if you don't."

"Yeah." I tapped my phone. Riley was right. But was that enough to put my heart on the line again? "Maybe."

I was still unsure what to do as I got onto the lift a few hours later.

Given the show was in London, I'd taken the afternoon as annual leave. I was going straight from here to the train station. It didn't start until eight p.m., but if my plan was going to work, I needed to get there early. All my time spent on the treadmill probably wouldn't help me outrun thousands of teenagers to get a spot at the front, but I had to try.

As the lift started to move, every doubt I'd had bubbled to the surface. What if I was wrong? What if Luca really had wanted me to leave?

Was I doing the right thing?

Opening my phone, I pulled up the photo app. All the images of Luca on there were ones snapped during those hidden moments just for us.

Luca just waking up, face creased from the pillows.

Luca standing beside the bed, that feral grin I loved on his face.

Both of our faces pressed together, smiling brightly for the selfie.

God, I looked so...*happy*. When had I ever smiled like that?

That was my answer.

I had to try. I had to.

I flicked through them all. When I got to the last one, a selfie of us at the restaurant before everything went to shit, I returned to the start.

I was so focused on the photos that I barely registered the lift doors opening and someone else entering. We weren't at ground level yet, so I didn't bother looking to see who'd joined me. If I knew them, they might expect small talk.

Fuck that. I didn't want to do anything right now but torture myself with Luca. If they thought I was rude, then fine.

The lift started to move before the lights cut out.

I was transported back to that fateful day months ago. My hands flew out, grabbing the rail as the emergency breaks screeched, grinding the lift to a stop.

"No, no, no," I muttered into the darkness. The light from my phone screen did fuck-all to illuminate the space. This couldn't be happening. Not now. I had to get to London. I had to get to Luca.

"Why the panic, Ollie?" The voice was a spotlight in the darkness. "Last time, it was me freaking out, not you."

My mouth dried. My phone slipped from my numb fingers, hitting the floor with a thud. "Luca?"

The emergency lights kicked on, and my throat constricted.

Luca was in front of me, his hands pushed deep into the pockets of his coat. His hair was wind-swept like he'd just come in from outside. He smiled at me bashfully, making my heart stutter.

"I was upset you were so absorbed in your phone that you didn't realise it was me...until I saw what you were looking at."

I couldn't believe he was here. "You've always been nosey."

He gave me that crooked grin. "Only where you're concerned."

"What are you doing here?" I breathed.

"I had to see you." He stepped closer, and I found myself backing up until I hit the railing. Luca frowned at me, his eyes shuttering. "I wanted to...talk. But maybe this isn't a good idea."

He went to step backwards. Both my hands shot up, grabbing the lapels of his coat. "No." I blurted. "I just...wasn't expecting to see you here."

He gave me that familiar easy smile, and something in my heart began to heal. "Were you expecting to see me somewhere else?"

I was still holding on to his coat, terrified that if I let go, he might disappear. "Yes. I was on my way to Wembley."

He sucked in a breath. "You were?"

"I was. I planned to push my way to the front and make a scene until you noticed me."

His lips twitched. "Now I'm regretting this elaborate plan. I'd like to see that."

I gestured at the motionless lift. "I take it you had something to do with this."

"Maybe." He lifted a hand to cup my face. "I wanted to talk to you somewhere that you couldn't run away from me."

"I didn't run the first time. You made me leave."

"I did. And I'm so fucking sorry about that." He leaned his forehead against mine. "There's no reason for you to give me another chance. I just...want you to hear me out. I behaved like a complete prick that night. I was scared. I'd fallen so hard for you, and when you said we would be over when the tour was done..."

"I never said that."

His fingers tightened on my chin. "Yes, you did."

"No," I corrected him. "What actually happened is I was halfway through saying 'We agreed this would end when the tour did, but I don't want it to'...when you cut me off."

"What? Why didn't you tell me that?"

I let go of Luca's coat, suddenly needing a bit of distance. "You weren't the only one who'd fallen hard, Luca. I had no idea how you felt about me. For all I knew, you were done with me. Forgive me for wanting to walk away with a shred of my dignity intact."

Luca crowded me, his arms coming up on either side of my head. "I'll *never* be done with you, Ollie. I'm done dancing around my feelings. I did it before and lost you. I want you in my bed. At my side. In my life. No one else. Just you. I don't care if it's too fast. I don't *care* what the press will say. Literally, the only thing I care about is *you*."

I swallowed. Luca was saying everything I'd dreamt of him saying. Now it was my turn. My turn to be brave. "That's what I want too."

"Really?" Luca's voice cracked as his eyes searched mine. "Don't say it if you don't mean it."

"I do mean it. That's what I came back that night to tell you. That I'm a work in progress. That I might struggle to open up. But I want to…for you. I want to try."

Luca's face darkened. "Yes, let's talk about that night." He dropped his arms, stepping back and lifting his chin. "Steve told me what happened. What Kevin told you."

The memory still stung. "Yes."

Luca crossed his arms. "I'm surprised you haven't asked me if it was true. If I really had someone else with me."

"I don't need to." The realisation hadn't come in suddenly but in pieces. First in Becky's office, then becoming concrete over time. The deeper I'd delved into Kevin's betrayal, the more obvious it had become that I'd been played. "Kevin played on my insecurities. I shouldn't have fallen for it. I should've trusted you. I'm sorry."

Relief poured from Luca as he drew close once more. "No, I'm sorry. You should never have been put in that position. If I'd been honest with you…if I hadn't made you leave…none of this would've happened."

My lips quirked. "Wow, looks like we're both

really sorry."

"How British of us."

We exchanged a secret smile before mine faded. The question I'd been holding back broke from me in a whisper. "If that's how you felt...if you knew why I'd left... why didn't you call me? Why did you block my number?"

"What? I didn't block your number." Frowning, he grabbed his phone from his pocket. "Motherfucker!"

He tilted the screen to my contact info, the little red text at the bottom showing *Unblock Caller.*

"Guessing that wasn't you then."

"Nope." He clicked to unblock me before putting the phone away with a sigh. "And there was me doing the gentlemanly thing and waiting for you to reach out. Makes me want to fire Kevin all over again."

"You fired him?"

"Of course." He looked bemused. "The day your article came out. You can't honestly think we'd let him continue with everything you exposed. Thank you for that, by the way. That was a massive risk for you. I'd already realised I'd fucked up by that point, but seeing you put everything on the line for me really hammered it home. You cared about me...even believing I'd cheated on you. You still *cared* about me."

"Wasn't that much of a risk now, was it?"

Luca's expression turned guarded. "Ah, I'm not sure what you mean by that."

I raised an eyebrow. "You're telling me you're not the mystery investor in *Identity* who's made my job and benefits iron-clad?"

Luca bit his lip. "Maybe...but please don't be mad at me, I just—"

I cut him off by putting my hand over his mouth. "I'm not mad."

His eyes widened in surprise, so I continued. "Well, I was a bit at first. You can't just interfere in my life without telling me about it."

I felt his smirk lift against my palm. "Let me rephrase that. You can't interfere in my life *again.* If we're going to give this a go, we need to be completely honest with each other."

I removed my hand so he could speak. "I won't do anything like that again. And I didn't do it hoping it'd make you fall for me."

"Why did you do it then?"

"Because you saw me," he said honestly. "There you were, your life in tatters, and yet you helped me. You didn't judge me. Didn't treat me differently. For the first time in *years,* someone didn't look at me and wonder how they could play my fame to their advantage. You weren't hoping for a story to tell. You didn't judge me for having an anxiety attack, just talked me through it before offering me a very private part of yourself."

My cheeks flamed, and Luca chuckled. "Get your mind out of the gutter, Ollie. I meant telling me about your mum, not the blowjob."

"Oh." I blushed deeper.

"I knew I'd fucked up asking you for the NDA," he said softly. "I couldn't reach out after that, but...I also couldn't let you go. Especially knowing what you were going through. There aren't many perks to my fame and fortune, but I knew I was in a position to help you achieve at least *some* of the happiness you deserved. So, I interfered. And I don't regret it. If I had to go back in time, I'd do exactly the same thing again."

"You didn't even know me," I whispered.

"I knew enough." His hand cupped my throat, my pulse jumping under his thumb. "People like you, Ollie, deserve all the happiness in the world. I knew that then, and I'm even more certain of it now."

Chapter 25

Luca

I appeared to have stunned Ollie into silence.

"Say something," I pleaded. "Anything. Even if it's to tell me to leave. If that's what you want, I will."

I'd find it near impossible, but I'd do it. If Ollie wanted me out of his life, I'd make it happen.

Even if it broke me in the process.

"I don't want you to leave." Ollie's hands went around the back of my neck, pulling my forehead to lean against his again. "I want you. This. Us. Whatever that might look like."

"There'll be a lot of press speculation. We won't be able to hide this. We don't need to go around doing interviews or anything like that." As much as I begrudgingly accepted the media as part of my life, there were lots of things I'd like to keep private. Ironic that it was now a journalist who held the spot at the top of that list. "But I can't hide how I feel about you, Ollie. I don't want to."

His thumb ghosted over my bottom lip. "I don't want to either. These past few weeks without you have been hell. If being in the media occasionally is the price I need to pay to be by your side, I'm willing to pay it."

"What about the travelling?" I persisted. "I'll try and take you with me as often as we can swing it, but there'll be times when you need to work. Are you sure you can cope with it?"

Ollie leaned back, amusement twisting his lips. "If I didn't know any better, I'd ask if you're trying to push me away again."

I froze. Was that what I was doing? "I'm not…I just want to make sure you know what you're getting yourself into. I might be an easy person to be with, but *Luca Weston* is a totally different kettle of fish. I need to know you can cope with that going in because I'm not sure I can cope with losing you again."

The tiny space spun as Ollie flipped our positions. Now I was the one with my back to the wall, Ollie crowding me in.

"Listen carefully, Luca." His voice was soft, but there was an unmistakable note of steel weaving through it. "There is one single thing I can't cope with. One. And that's not having you in my life. It might be too fast, might sound soppy as fuck, but nothing matters to me except that."

Tears burned at the back of my eyes as I struggled to keep my cool. "Really?"

"Really." He brushed his nose along my jaw. "Fuck, Luca. I'm not used to…this. Admitting this shit. But please don't make me feel like I have over the past few weeks. I'll cope with anything else so long as you don't break my heart again. I'm so fucking in love with you, Luca, and if you—"

His words cut off abruptly, his whole body stiffening as he realised the truth he'd let slip.

I caught his lips with mine, silencing him before he could take back the most beautiful words I'd ever heard. Our kiss was hard, bruising. A brief pause as we reminded ourselves of what we'd almost lost. "I love you too, Ollie."

He pulled back, his eyes shining. "You do? It isn't too soon?"

I laughed gruffly. "Who gets to decide whether it's too soon? Pretty sure I knew how I felt the first day I met you."

Ollie surged forwards, his hands cupping my face. This time his kiss was ferocious. Claiming.

When he eventually pulled back, I was panting. "So, we're doing this?"

"We're doing this." His lips drew together thoughtfully as he eyed the security camera. "That camera definitely off?"

"Yep." Not only was it off, but Jack was guarding the monitors to make sure no nosey fuckers turned it back on.

His hand drifted down my front, stopping at the button on my trousers. "How long did you arrange for us to be trapped?"

My cock throbbed, aching at the thought of feeling Ollie's touch. "An hour."

Ollie's tongue ran up my neck, making me shiver. "Hmm. Did you think we'd need the extra time to mess around?"

"No." I gasped as he palmed my erection. "I figured I'd need that long to persuade you to listen to me."

"Well, lucky for both of us, I was in a listening mood." His deft fingers unbuttoned my jeans, pulling the zip down smoothly. "Because I can definitely think of more fun ways to pass the time."

This man was light years away from the Ollie I'd met in this lift six months ago. This Ollie knew exactly what he wanted, and from the way he was touching me, he had no issue with going after it.

"I seem to have the same dilemma as last time," he drawled. "I remember you mentioned a few different ways to take care of it for me."

I groaned as he nibbled his way along my jaw. "You weren't ready for it back then."

He slid his hand around my hips and toyed with my crease. "Question is, are *you* ready for me right now?"

I knew what he was really asking. Even without the camera working, it was still risky for us to fuck in public. Just the fact he was worried about it, worried about *me*, had me wanting this more than anything. "There's lube in my wallet. Should be a condom too."

He fished it from my coat pocket. "Got the lube, but there's no condom."

I bit back a groan. "Don't suppose you have one."

"Nope…but I haven't been with anyone else. And I was tested after Suzie and I broke up."

"I haven't been with anyone else." I wove my fingers between his. "I swear to you, there's been no one else but you."

"I know that. I trust you."

My heart swelled in my chest. It might be a small

thing, but Ollie being willing to take me bare proved just how much he trusted me.

We didn't bother stripping off. The lift shouldn't move for another thirty minutes, but we didn't want to risk getting literally caught with our trousers down. I pulled mine to my knees while Ollie simply lowered his enough to free his dick.

"Fuck, I've missed this." I couldn't resist bending and swiping my tongue over the slit of his cock. "Missed the taste of you on my tongue."

Ollie hissed and pulled me back gently by my hair. "Enough of that. I don't want to blow until I'm buried deep inside you. I want to watch you on stage tonight, knowing my cum is leaking out of your hole."

I groaned. "God, yes."

Ollie didn't rip the lube open as I'd expected but instead twisted me around until my chest was against the wall.

"Hands on the rail," he said gruffly. "Stick your arse out for me."

I bit my lip. "Where've you been hiding this version of yourself?"

His hands froze on my cheeks. "Do you not like it?"

I grabbed one of his hands and wrapped it around my throbbing shaft. The amount of precum I was leaking was ridiculous. "Does it feel like I don't like it?"

"Good." He sighed, and I felt his breath on my rear. He must've knelt behind me. "Because I've had a lot of time over the past few weeks to think about what I wished I'd done to you. And this was at the very top of the list."

That was the only warning he gave me before his

tongue tentatively probed my hole. A desperate moan broke from somewhere deep in my chest.

Ollie chuckled, his breath hot against my sensitive skin. "I'll take that as a good noise."

I couldn't respond. Not when Ollie spread my cheeks with his hands and buried his face between them. His five o'clock shadow scraped against my skin, contrasting deliciously with the sensation of his tongue spearing deep inside me.

He didn't hold back. There was no way to know this was his first time doing this. He ate me like I was his favourite dessert, his tongue devouring me with abandon.

And the noises he made…small, satisfied grunts… were enough to have me hurtling towards the edge.

"Stop," I gasped when I could take it no more. The thin wooden rail creaked under my grip. "I'll come if you keep going."

Ollie kissed his way up my back, his hands leaving my backside as he rustled with something behind me. "As fun as that would be, I have other plans for you."

"Yes," I hissed as he slipped a lubed finger into me. It slid in with ease, Ollie's talented tongue having softened me.

He prepped me quickly, both of us aware we were on a time crunch. The small space was stiflingly hot, sweat running down me as Ollie notched his cock against my hole.

Impatient to feel him, I surged backwards, wincing at the burn. It wasn't enough to stop me though. I kept moving until I felt his pubic hair brush against my cheeks.

"Oh fuck," Ollie whimpered, his fingers digging into my hips. "Luca, I'm not going to last."

"That's okay," I panted, pulling off him slightly before thrusting backwards again. "We don't have much time. We need to make this fast."

"Good, because I can't hold back." He punctuated his statement with a hard thrust that had me throwing my hands against the wall to keep from crashing into it.

"Yes," I moaned as he dragged his cock across my prostate. My nerves were singing, begging for more. "That's it. Fuck me hard. I want to feel you while I'm up on stage."

He growled, his hips slamming forward as he did as I asked.

He reached around to grab my cock, but I batted him away. "No. I want your hands on my hips. I want you to own me."

Letting out a loud groan, he did as I asked, using his grip to drag me against him with even more force.

Spitting in my hand, I stroked myself furiously. I was so close. It wouldn't take much to send me over the edge.

Ollie went first. His hips stuttered, and he sank his teeth into the tender skin between my shoulder and neck. The sharp sting had my orgasm slamming through me, my vision whiting out. I caught my cum in my hand, careful not to spill any on my jeans or the floor.

Ollie leaned against my back, his breath heavy in my ear. "Missed you."

I twisted my head around so I could snag my lips with his. "Missed you more."

It was only after he'd pulled out and helped me right my clothes that he spotted the mess I'd made in my hand. "Hang on, why didn't we think of that last time?"

I smirked at him, pulling a tissue from my pocket

and using it to clean up. "If I remember rightly, I offered you some tissues. You told me you'd prefer my mouth."

His heated gaze settled on my full lips. Despite the very recent orgasm, I could feel arousal wending through me once more. "I definitely made the right call."

With gentle hands, he took the tissue from me and took over clean-up duty. He'd just finished when the overhead lights flickered on, making us both wince at the sudden brightness.

"That was good timing," he said. "You, ah, might wanna sort your hair."

I squinted at my blurred reflection in the lift door. Running my hands through it a few times, I gave up with a sigh. "Nah. There's no use. I can't hide the fact I've been thoroughly fucked."

Ollie slid his arms around me from behind, nuzzling where he'd bitten. "True. If the hair doesn't tip Jack off, then this bruise will. Sorry."

I rolled my eyes. "No, you're not. I think you like the fact I'll be up on stage later with your marks on display."

He paused. "I hadn't thought of that, but...yeah. I kinda do like that."

The doors opened. As we'd planned, Jack was waiting for me alone. His searching gaze swept over us, taking in our rumpled clothes and the way Ollie was embracing me. He huffed like he was annoyed at the risk we'd taken, but I could see the truth hiding behind it.

He was happy for me.

"You guys good?" he asked gruffly.

"We're good." I stepped forward, taking Ollie's hand in mine. "And just in time too. We've got a show to get to."

The show that night was the best one of the Rude Awakenings tour.

I was a good-enough actor to fake my way through performances without my fans being able to tell the difference. But even so, tonight was leagues above where I'd been over the past couple of weeks.

Maybe people would say it was because we were on home soil. Or maybe because it was the second to last show of the tour.

But I knew the truth.

It had everything to do with the man standing at the front of the stage.

I couldn't believe he'd been planning on coming here tonight. That he'd been willing to chase me down. To fight for us.

There was no jealousy on Ollie's face tonight. Just pure pride as I sauntered across the stage and delivered the show of a lifetime.

Ninety thousand fans were held in the palm of my hand as I teased and flirted with the stadium. All of them believed I was singing to them. That they might be the one to catch my attention and hold it.

But there was only one who knew the truth. The one who'd looked and seen beyond the rock star to the man beneath.

When "Tease" started, I didn't hesitate. I passed my bandmates, Arlo grinning and Kai throwing me a wink as I made my way to where Ollie stood. They'd had my back with Kevin. Once they'd found out the truth about Ollie, they'd helped me come up with the plan to trap him in the lift where we'd first met.

When we'd arrived at the venue that afternoon, my friends had treated Ollie like a returning hero. He'd been fist bumped, clapped on the back, and hugged. At first, Ollie had been bewildered, but as he handed over his phone at Arlo's insistence, his expression turned secretly pleased. By the time the three of them finished adding their contact info, Ollie almost looked like he was blinking back tears.

"I don't have many friends," he'd confided in me quietly after. "Just Riley, really."

My chest had squeezed at that. "Don't worry, babe. You can't escape them now. The three of them are like needy fucking barnacles."

"Hey!" Silas had protested, overhearing my comment. "Rude."

"And accurate," Kai had added, smirking at Ollie. "You're stuck with us now, I'm afraid."

They'd gone out of their way to make Ollie feel like one of us before the show. Now they were watching me, waiting for me to perform my party piece. The song we *all* knew Ollie was waiting for.

The audience was ready. The shouts steadily rose across the stadium.

Kneel. Kneel. Kneel.

I stayed standing, ignoring everything except the amused smirk playing around Ollie's lips.

The chant rose to a roar. My bandmates continued to play the opening chords over and over, Silas riling up the crowd and encouraging them to yell louder.

But my knees were locked. Waiting.

Finally, it dawned on Ollie what I wanted. A flash of heat crossed his face before his full lips parted.

The word was soundless, lost in the clamour surrounding us.

Kneel.

I lowered myself to the ground, grinning at the feral smirk pulling at Ollie's lips.

I might be performing for a sold-out stadium, but there was only one man who got to see the real me.

And from this day on, I'd kneel for no one else.

Epilogue

Ollie

Two years later

"There's too many paps out the front," Ryan said from the driver's seat. "Think we might need to enter via a different route."

"Whatever you think's best," Luca said to his bodyguard, squeezing my hand on the seat between us.

There'd been a lot of changes in the aftermath of Kevin being fired, including a switch around in the protection detail. The band hired a kickass new manager, Betty. She'd taken Caffeine Daydreams under her wing like the mother hen she was, protecting her boys with the ferocity of a rottweiler. When the contract negotiations with the label rolled around, she'd handled it with ease, landing them with better terms than Kevin could've dreamt of. With her at the helm, Caffeine Daydreams were working less yet putting more money in the bank.

Kevin and Malcolm, meanwhile, had been investigated by HMRC and then the police. They were currently serving time for multiple fraud charges. Turned out Caffeine Daydreams weren't the only clients fucked over by the duo.

Ryan had been working with Luca for almost two years now. He was a great bloke. Unlike Jack, it was easy to extract a smile from Ryan. But most importantly, Ryan kept Luca safe. He had the same vigorous attention to detail where Luca's security was concerned. Something we were grateful for, given the uptick in media attention since the Rude Awakenings tour.

The news of my and Luca's relationship had broken sooner than expected. Luca hadn't exactly been subtle with all the attention he'd been laving on me during the show the night we'd reunited. Some fans in the pit had snapped a few photos and videos of him interacting with me during the show. When we'd heard about it, we'd discussed playing it off as just a performance.

Then we'd watched them. Yeah…there was no way anyone would buy it. Not with the way we'd been staring at each like we'd be tearing each other's clothes off the second we went backstage.

Which, in fairness, was precisely what happened.

Rather than let everyone speculate and keep it in the media, we'd decided to get ahead of the news. Luca had shared a selfie of us on Instagram along with a short caption.

The rumours are true. Ollie and I are in a relationship, and I love him with everything I am. Please respect our privacy - L.

While the fans…tried to follow Luca's plea, the press held no such compunctions. They'd been relentless. They'd camped outside our homes, outside my work, making it near impossible for us to live any sort of normal life.

It'd been easier than I'd expected though. Don't get me wrong, there were many times my frustrations got the better of me. Never did I think I'd be furious with the industry I was a part of. But there was a massive difference between what I considered journalism and what the paparazzi had tried to achieve. But somehow, Luca had made it easier to bear. Or perhaps it was because I knew what it was like to live the alternative.

And living without Luca? That just wasn't an option.

If it hadn't been for the antics the rest of the band got up to, we wouldn't have had a moment's peace. But with everything that had happened, the spotlight had been off us and focused on the others.

Honestly, I felt bad for them. Well, for Arlo.

But Kai and Silas? With how they'd behaved during their final show on the Rude Awakenings tour, they'd doused the rumour mill with fuel and set the fucker alight. A lot had happened since then, but all of that guaranteed extra press attention.

"What's so funny?" Luca asked, frowning at me from the other side of the car. We'd moved in together three months after reuniting, and I'd loved every second of it. Yes, he was a messy fucker. Yes, I might one day kill him for putting his washing on the floor *right next to the fucking basket.*

But I loved him. I loved being in his space. Watching him cook us Italian food and then snuggling in front of *Air Crash Investigation*.

I surveyed the long lines of his body, willing my cock to soften. When Luca wasn't on tour, he liked to live in jeans and comfy T-shirts. It was difficult enough to resist him in casual wear.

But Luca in a fucking suit? That was my kryptonite.

"Nothing." I lifted our joined hands, already counting down the minutes until we were back home. "Just thinking about Kai and Silas."

He groaned. "Don't get me started. What were they expecting? You know that's why there's so much press here tonight."

"Either that or to get more juice on Arlo." We exchanged a significant look.

None of us would let them get near him. Not after what he'd been through.

Luca tapped his phone on his knees. "I've already messaged the group chat to make sure their details take them to the rear of the restaurant."

We had a private room booked in an upscale restaurant to celebrate the band's eighteenth anniversary. Since the day I'd turned up at Wembley holding Luca's hand, the others had accepted me as one of their own. I was also close to Riley and Tom, the guy who'd joined the company while I'd been on tour with Luca. We'd become a tight-knit team both inside and outside the office.

Luca constantly pulled strings so I could travel with him as often as possible. Knowing it was pointless to argue with him, I worked twice as hard as anyone else. When I'd been offered the promotion to editor last month, I was able to accept it with a clear conscience, knowing it was my own talent and work ethic that had gotten me there.

Ryan pulled the car into an alley behind the restaurant. I waited in the car until he was at Luca's door. I followed my boyfriend out from his side of the car, automatically protecting the side Ryan wasn't on.

Luca rolled his eyes. "No one is going to jump me in an alley, Ollie."

I raised an eyebrow as a door swung open in front of us. "You realise that's where *most* people get jumped, right?"

"Welcome, gentlemen." A smartly dressed woman gestured for us to enter. "You're the first to arrive. I'm afraid we'll have to cross the main floor of the restaurant from this entrance."

Ryan scowled at the woman who held up her hands hastily. "But don't worry. My staff has temporarily locked the front doors to keep the press out, and we've closed the shutters. You'll be able to pass through without any of them seeing you."

"What about the other patrons?" Ryan growled, his usual sunny demeanour clearly having fucked off over this development. "How will you stop them from taking photos?"

The hostess winced. Poor woman. She probably didn't sign up to deal with the demands of A-list celebs. Wasn't like there were many of them rocking around Southampton. Until Caffeine Daydreams, the city's biggest claim to fame was Craig David. "I'm sorry, sir. It's the only route to the private dining room."

"It's fine." Luca stepped forwards, flashing her his trademark grin. "Not a problem at all."

The hostess's expression cleared. "Excellent. Please, follow me."

Ryan indicated for me to take the lead as he covered our backs. One of his hands rested on the concealed weapon I knew was strapped at his waist.

Before Arlo, I would've said he was being

overcautious.

Now though...we knew better.

A discernible hush fell over the dining room as we entered. Not everyone recognised Luca, but there were enough who did.

I kept my eyes down as we followed the hostess. Whispers followed us, and I'm sure more than one camera was pointed in our direction. That was fine. They wouldn't get anything other than a photo of Luca and his boyfriend being affectionate.

With the way Luca couldn't keep his hands off me in public, the number of those on the internet probably outnumbered his nudes. A fact he was immensely proud of.

We'd almost made it to the other side of the dining room when a feminine voice piped up with a gasp.

"Ollie?"

I stopped so fast that Luca hit my back with a faint *oof*.

No. It couldn't be.

But as I turned in the direction the voice had come from, I saw the odds weren't in my favour.

Suzie gaped at us, her eyes flying between myself and Luca. Opposite her, Callum watched me with a wary expression. They were still together then. That fact made me feel...

Nothing. I literally felt nothing. Maybe a vague sense of nostalgia. But most of that was reserved for the friendship Callum and I had once shared.

Oh, there was also gratitude. Because if I hadn't caught them that day, nothing would've happened with Luca.

I couldn't imagine how different my life would be

now. How much worse. Turned out I needed to hit rock bottom to learn how truly unfulfilling my life with Suzie had been.

"Hello, Suzie. Callum." I inclined my head at them, all too aware of the phones pointed in our direction.

Luca's hand slipped into mine as I greeted them and squeezed. The next thing I knew, he'd extended his other hand to my ex. "Hi, Suzie. I'm Luca."

The shock was replaced with gushing awe. She jumped from her seat and stood before Luca, practically vibrating. "Oh, I know. I'm your *biggest* fan. I couldn't believe it when I saw the post about you and Ollie." She trilled a high-pitched laugh that had me wincing.

"I almost reached out to Ollie so many times to see if he could introduce us." Her voice was breathy and her hand clutched Luca's like a lifeline. "Did Ollie tell you about me? We're *such* good friends."

That was the moment I knew Luca lost it. His charm slipped, and alarm bells rang at the back of my mind. "Oh, Suzie. Ollie has told me *all* about you."

Her smile wavered as if it was just now occurring to her that she was the villain in my story. "I mean, that's all water under the bridge now, right, Ollie?"

"Right," I said smoothly, letting go of Luca's hand to wrap my arm around his waist. I pulled him snugly against me, my fingertips soothing his side under his jacket. "All water under the bridge. After all, if it wasn't for you and Callum, Luca and I would never have met. So I suppose I should probably thank you."

"T-t-thank me?" she stammered, her gaze darting between us as she undoubtedly tried to figure out what part she'd played. "Um...you're welcome?"

I bit back a grin at her bewildered expression. "Anyway, lovely to see you, but we need to get going."

"One second," Luca said, pulling free of my grip. He shot me a wink over his shoulder that had me worrying. What was he up to now?

Ryan moved close to him as Luca clapped Callum on the shoulder. He leaned down and whispered something in my former best friend's ear that had him blanching white and then flushing deep red. Callum's gaze was filled with shame as it cut to me before hitting the floor.

"Like Ollie said, so lovely to meet you all." Luca pulled back from Callum, his lazy grin painted on. To the casual observer, the whole encounter probably looked like old friends catching up. "Do have a nice life."

I didn't say a word until we were seated at the private table in the dining room. "Do I want to know what you said to Callum?"

"Probably not."

"Luca," I said warningly.

He took a sip of his drink before answering. "I just pointed out that, no matter how he felt about Suzie, betraying you was shitty. That he'd been your closest friend, your family, and he'd thrown that all away. And that I hoped it was worth it."

My throat thickened. I brushed a rough kiss over Luca's stubbled cheek. He jumped in surprise. "I thought you'd be mad at me."

"How could I be mad at you?" I asked hoarsely. "You're right. What he did was shitty. But it was worth it. I've got you in my corner now. What you did proves that."

The door slammed open and the rest of the group

poured in. I leaned closer to whisper in Luca's ear. "And when we get home, I'm gonna show you just how damned grateful I am to have you."

Fire lit his eyes, and if it wasn't for Silas grabbing his attention, he'd probably have pulled me off into the nearest bathroom.

But that wasn't what tonight was about. Tonight was about Caffeine Daydreams. About celebrating everything they'd achieved. Everything they'd survived.

Luca was right. Callum *had* been my only friend. My only family.

But the one I had right here was worth a million times more. These men had given me such happiness that some days, I didn't know how to contain it.

Especially Luca. I watched him laugh with his friends and my whole heart swelled.

He was worth *everything*.

THE END

READY FOR KAI AND SILAS?

Preorder here: https://mybook.to/GreenLight

Want to get a head start on their story? Find early chapters on my Patreon here: patreon.com/larktaylor

NEWSLETTER

Want to read about Ollie and Luca taking the stairs instead of the lift? (In a spicy fashion...)

Sign up for my newsletter here to get your hands on this bonus scene and more – https://subscribepage.io/larktaylor

STALK ME

Join my Facebook group for the latest news, exclusive teasers and promos, and to witness me generally screaming into the abyss as I write (it's fun, I promise. Well, fun for you, not necessarily for me) - Romance Larks (Lark Taylor Author group)

Website – www.larktaylorauthor.com

Instagram - @LarkAuthor

Twitter - @larktaylorauthor

TikTok - @larktaylorauthor

ACKNOWLEDGEMENTS

To my alpha and beta readers, Cora, Liz, Willow, Jesse, Nicole, Jax and Mads: thank you for reading this while I was writing and reassuring me I wasn't losing my mind by giving this story a chance. I love you all!

To Abbie Nicole: thank you for helping me whip this story into shape and making my words all shiny!

To Mads (aka Breathless Lit): I am so hecking lucky to have found you. Not only do you take a literal fucktonne of work off my back, but you're already one of my biggest cheerleaders. Plus you send me the BEST smutty recs so you're stuck with me literally forever. Good luck.

To Margaret: thank you for reading a super early arc and helping to locate any pesky lingering errors.

To Willow, Anka and Krystal: thank you for helping me come up with band names for this book! More bands will be appearing in future so I need all the help I can get.

Finally to my readers: thank you reading Ollie and Luca's story. This popped into my head when I was *supposed* to be taking time off over Christmas and refused to leave until I got writing. I'm so glad I did as I enjoyed every moment of their story.

ALSO BY LARK TAYLOR

The Reckless Damned - paranormal

Devil's Mark

Devil May Care

Deal With the Devil

Luck of the Devil

Damned Connections - paranormal

Patience (coming soon!)

Caffeine Daydreams - contemporary

White Noise

Green Light (coming soon!)

Printed in Great Britain
by Amazon

61854534R00167